A Retirement Disturbed

Anthony Coles

For Renate who disturbed my retirement.

This is a work of fiction. Names, characters, places, and incidents either are the product of the author's imagination or are used fictitiously. Any resemblance to actual persons, living or dead, events, or locales is entirely coincidental.

Copyright © 2018 Anthony Coles

All rights reserved. No part of this book may be reproduced or used in any manner without written permission of the copyright owner except for the use of quotations in a book review. For more information, address: avcoles@gmail.com.

First paperback edition June 2020

1. Death and Resurrection

It was much smaller than he remembered when he wasn't there. It always was. Like the old days when he used to go to Lord's in London; the days when he was trying hard to be clubbable. He used to arrive at the famous cricket ground, and it seemed tiny, almost like a traditional village ground in spite of the stands that held twenty-eight thousand people. As the day went on, imperceptibly the ground seemed to expand until by the end of play it seemed enormous, as big as it often appeared to be on television. Twickenham rugby ground too. Originally, he thought the progressive and continuous intake of alcohol through the day had something to do with it. He seldom recollected leaving either place completely sober. But the Amphitheatre disproved that. He had never drunk anything except water during a corrida and the same thing happened here as well.

Bullfighting was always going to be a bit of a problem for Peter Smith's English friends – those few that would bother to come to Arles, that's. But as he didn't seem to have too many of those, it didn't really concern him very much. It is, however, central to Arlesian culture. Of course, there were some – many, perhaps – who in varying degrees disliked it all the way to detesting it, but, in general, in the town itself it is at worst tolerated and at best supported with a passion that's profound and serious. Toleration, primarily with a typical Provençale eye to business. Bullfights bring in tourists and tourists bring in business and fill the restaurants, the street-side bodegas and hotels. But the passionate and vocal enthusiasm of twenty thousand involved and seemingly knowledgeable people at a corrida often changes visiting doubters into believers and opponents into grudging acceptance, usually expressed in some of the usual standard weasel worded: 'it wasn't as bad/bloody/cruel as I thought it would be' or some self-conscious reference to ballet or bottoms.

Now again to him the place looked small and, at half past one on a September afternoon, piercingly hot. You could see the heat. The place was virtually empty of course. Other than the gaudy posters fixed around the outside railings that stopped tourists getting into the building without paying, there was no indication that three weeks later the Feria would start, the place would be heaving with people and eight fights killing some forty eight bulls would occupy the town almost to the exclusion of everything else. The stadium would be filled with noise, passion, art and death. Occitan would be heard almost as much as French or English. Now, however, it just looked slightly down at heel and, it must be admitted, somewhat depressing. The grandeur of the great round arched double colonnade can't be seen from inside.

Desultory tourists wandered about slowly in the heat, while a small group of Japanese clustered closely around their harassed guide, drawn to the raised umbrella as if it was the signum militarum it resembled. Even they were uncharacteristically quiet while they listened to the usual spiel that was mostly the usual rubbish. No, he thought as he listened, it never had three stories like the Coliseum in Rome; no, they never slew Christians here; no, gladiators were not untrained criminals casually slaughtered for the entertainment of the Gallo-roman public; no, they do kill the bulls now. That is what a bull fight is. Anything else would be an insult to the bull. No, it's not smaller than the one up the road in Nîmes. That one is just better preserved, and it sits on flat ground and therefore looks bigger. Arles is actually three metres longer and six metres wider - a small difference but a significant one in Arlesian society, where size really does matter. Perhaps their relative silence was due to the heat or perhaps they just wanted lunch. Whatever; he enjoyed the unusual, if short-lived, experience of a quiet group of Japanese tourists.

The arena proper, the actual sanded oval where the fights take place, was tiny, about seventy metres by forty, give or take. It was, he thought, a small area to share with more than a ton of irate, sharp horned, bull, armed only with a piece of violet and yellow canvas and a ballet dancer's dexterity and balance. Around it stood the terracotta - painted *barrestre*, the wooden barrier that separates the arena from the rest of the amphitheatre with its three narrow escapes for bull fighters when the bull goes for them. A small space, rather like a moat, separates the *barrestre* from the rising ranks of stone and wooden seats - wooden seats built up on metal scaffolding erected over some of the ruined terraces, standing testimony to the fact that recycling had started in Arles centuries before. Bits of the Amphitheatre had been regularly stolen to build houses in the town.

He sat in his usual seat up in the *secondes*, about twenty-five rows up in the *luppé*, the area in the middle of the western side that would be shielded from the sun in the late autumn afternoon. It had been his favourite spot for years, representing as it did, the best compromise that could reasonably be expected. A ticket in this place was affordable – just. The shade made sitting for two and a half hours in the sun bearable. It was the side of the arena where most of the fight was played out and the people around him tended to be locals and knowledgeable - aficionados. It was a part of the arena that was both noisy and respectful, demanding, and appreciative.

But now, empty in the early afternoon sunshine it all looked a bit shabby. The millions of euros that had been spent recently on restoring the outside of the building in that particularly aggressive French manner to a perfection that would delight Hollywood, and which appalled him, had yet to penetrate the inside. There it still showed that wonderfully scruffy magnificence that had drawn him to this town more than fifty years ago. It had been the first of Arles' monuments he visited. It had also been his first Roman amphitheatre and he never entered it without remembering. This time, like so many of these Arlesian places that he'd more recently revisited, was different. He was no longer a visitor. The arena was now his neighbour. He could see it out of his study window, a view on the quarter of the exterior that was, as yet, un-sanitised by the high-pressure water hoses and in the insertion of the machine-cut bits of stone of the restorers. They had mercifully stopped their work before getting to 'his' east side. God willing, they would run out of money before they started again. Yet the anticipation of the Feria was truly exciting for it is people that make the place live; people actually using the place not just assaulting it through their self-sticks. A building only lives when you use it. Looking at it may nor not do something for you but it does nothing for the building that breathes more slowly than you do. The place would be full for the Feria and, two thousand years after its construction, the great building would again come alive. Passive observation is just data collection, meaning little. Use brings the building to life and the old stones will breathe yet again. The bullfight was only part of why he loved Feria.

With a slight surprise he realised that he was now completely alone. The tourists had left for a late lunch and their afternoon replacements were still similarly preoccupied. He also discovered that he was sitting there baking and empty headed. He felt a smile of contentment at the same time though his had no real idea why. He also realised that he was sitting in possibly the hottest spot in Arles that was no place for a modestly overweight sexagenarian with a white skin and a slight heart condition. Even his Lock straw hat wouldn't protect him forever. So he rose gently from his seat on the hot stone terrace as if to avoid disturbing all those from previous centuries who were there in spirit, walked to the end of the row and turned down one of the many passages that led from the seats to the outer layers of the arena. He walked into the shadow and it immediately felt deliciously dark and cold around him. By the time he walked slowly around the north passageways to the exit opposite his house on the Place de la Major, he thought his temperature might have returned sufficiently to normal to enjoy his own late lunch.

'What will it be today?' he wondered as he trod carefully through the darkness, eyes still not adjusted, feeling the stones through the thin soles of his deck shoes. He certainly didn't have the strength to cook the small piece of fish he had left over from the previous evening. No, having gone earlier to Mme Henri to buy his usual gros pain, an oversize baguette, it would almost certainly be pâté and Camembert with a glass of chilled Provençale rosé. That would please Arthur, a large greyhound who shared his solitary retirement and who habitually consumed a significant part of his lunch. Without him, Smith would have made do with a smaller baguette. The glass of wine, at least, would remove all thought of doing anything else until at least 5 o' clock. He still had not learned to like the siesta. He always felt dreadful when he woke up, but an afternoon prone in front of the cricket on his misappropriated UK satellite system would more than suffice. Content with his plan, his perambulation continued until through the gloom he spotted the passage that ran off at right angles out towards the exit. His pace quickened slightly as he turned the corner, then suddenly the back of his head exploded in pain, then light and everything, as they say, went black.

Not that he had ever given the matter much thought but, had he done so, he would have guessed that Heaven was probably coloured white with some gold bits. Hell would have been some sort of dark flaming red. What he didn't expect was either place to be like the midnight sky over Sydney Harbour bridge on Millennium night. He certainly didn't foresee this sort of welcome had it been decided that he was to spend eternity in either place. Complete darkness with an occasional explosion of light was a little unexpected but exciting, nevertheless. This death business was much, much more interesting than he had imagined.

What he had not expected was how difficult breathing was in this new place. Perhaps breathing was not necessary when you were dead. That made sense. But the pain in his chest was not exactly what he expected as the painful punishment for a thoroughly misspent and unsuccessful life.

The darkness cleared slightly. Not immediately, or even quickly; but clear it did. Slowly. Not to light, but to a sort of consciousness that was equally dark but slightly fuller of what some people might have described as sensory perception. The blackness was not tar-coloured but mud; grey not black. He felt something that reminded him of his boarding school matron who sewed empty cotton reels into her boys' pyjama jackets to stop them sleeping on their backs and disturbing the dormitory with their snoring. It was the reason he had slept naked ever since. He had a pain in the middle of his back. His outspread hands gradually sensed the gravel and, in spite of the crushing weight on his chest, he began, not without some initial disappointment, to realise that he was actually alive not dead.

Shit. That meant that all the pain was real, and he was still a part of the real world. With a conscious and painful effort of will he began to list some things that would make survival good, rather than a disappointment and got only as far as being able to see the girls again. Gin would be nice, but he was sure that they have that in the other places. He came more to his senses and realised with some clarity that he was alive, hurting a lot in numerous places and trapped underneath the dead weight of what was obviously a dead body.

'OK,' he thought as he lay there, 'what next? I can't stay here, and, in any case, I haven't had lunch yet and nor has Arthur.'

Reality was returning at speed. Bit by bit he prised himself from underneath the body of man who, when viewed from a slight distance looked, a good deal slimmer than he had imagined when he'd actually been underneath it. Looking down as he steadied himself unsteadily against the stone side of Vespasian's amphitheatre, he saw prone before him the dark shape, dressed in a casual but smart shirt and trousers, prone and lifeless. He bent over to check for a pulse in the wrist as he has been taught in the Boy Scouts fifty years ago, using the three forefingers not the thumb (it has its own pulse, he remembered dimly). The man was very dead. His exploratory hand slipped down the body to the shoes, always the best indicator of a man's personality and status. They were leather, both uppers and soles, smooth and therefore polished, with those little leather tassels that only the best Italian shoemakers can get away with using and only the richest of men can get away with wearing without affectation or pretentiousness.

At that point his recovery faltered. The new reality that he was experiencing, disappointing and intriguing in equal measure, gradually lost focus. The great stones against which he was leaning began to lose their reassuring solidity. The body below him was losing its definition. The world, insofar as he perceived it, began to swirl about him and for the second time in quick succession, life went black.

This time he knew where he was. The last time this sort of thing had happened, he had ended up in the Barnet General Hospital, North London, surrounded with loud, pushy nurses, uninterested, self-important doctors and 'in -your-face' orderlies. Myocardial infarction they'd called it.

'Shit,' he thought, 'I retired to Arles to get away from this sort of thing.'

He was strapped into a narrow bed, chrome railings

separating him from the expanded aluminium floor a metre below in what was clearly a speeding ambulance driven by someone who had somewhere important to get to. Sirens wailed. The world rocked and this time it wasn't him. He closed his eyes for a moment and saw that his progress sounded like Inspector Maigret in pursuit up the Rue St Honoré in his *Traction Avant*. Opposite sat a grim-faced paramedic in full black uniform, black overalls tucked into black boots, looking steadfastly out of the window as Arles swept by. Obviously, he had not been rescued by a civil ambulance crew but by the much vaunted emergency service *Sapeurs - Pompiers* and he was being taken off in one of their bright red vans equipped to deal with every emergency from a road crash to nuclear attack. Smith raised his hand in what he hoped was a pathetic, pain-ridden gesture.

'Hello,' he ventured tentatively, hoping for a sympathetic response but willing to accept anything. Nothing came back. The guy didn't even glance in his direction.

'Hum,' he thought, 'so this is what the much-vaunted French health system is all about. Time to take stock of what's going on.'

He was obviously alive. His hands were painful where they had been grazed on the gravel in the Arena and he now felt the pain in the front as well as the back of his head. It hurt like hell, closely followed by the rest of his body. He was tied into the narrow, hard cot in a perilously speeding ambulance accompanied by a man who looked and acted more like a Gestapo storm trooper than an angel of mercy. The sensation of being tied down brought back the memory of Somalia a few years ago. However unfriendly his current companion seemed, he was not likely to attach electrodes to his testicles and start prodding other bits of him with a dirty bayonet. Running quickly through the possibilities of what to do next as he lay bouncing over the badly made roads of Arles, he settled on the most obvious and only possible. Nothing.

The van swept noisily into the forecourt of the *Centre Hospitalier d'Arles*, the rear doors were opened, and he was unceremoniously and unfeeling wheeled out and whisked though the A & E doors and into the building.

The hospital proved to be much like any other he had recently and regrettably experienced – only much more lethargic. The English hospitals had been slow and smelled. The smell was of a mixture of dust and disinfectant. No, it was just one of those smells that one associates with hospitals the world over but on this occasion, it was seasoned with more than a dash of indifference. Familiarity, this time however, bred a measure of contentment. Over the last few years he seemed to have spent hours lying comfortably but solitarily on trolleys in various hospitals. He caught a glimpse of a clock that much to his surprise said 2:15pm. His adventure had only been going for an hour or so. It felt much longer. The ambulance men pushed him up against side furthest away from the wall-mounted air conditioner and left with the urgency of two men who had been denied lunch at the proper time and were intent on making good the error. He was completely alone apart from the faint click of the clock, the gentle whirr of the air conditioner and the rock drill inside his head. Had he not still been tied to the bed; he would had got up and gone. But he was and therefore he didn't.

He tried closing his eyes but that only made the pain more focussed. However inanimate the scene outside his head, its perception did at least divert some of his attention from the throbbing inside it. The floor was tiled red, the walls and ceiling painted white. Ranged around the walls were the paraphernalia of emergency. Oxygen cylinders and masks on a trolley. He recognised the defibrillation equipment from his close association with it during his last visit to hospital. He shuddered slightly at the memory. Tables with various unidentifiable bits and pieces. A bright red fire extinguisher. Large medical posters showing some of the basic procedures for resuscitation whose advice he thought shouldn't have been necessary in such a place. Illumination was from harsh fluorescent lights and a strip of shallow windows just below the ceiling. It was very obviously lunchtime.

The stock-taking ended with the entry of what he took to be a nurse and a doctor who looked just old enough to be her son. 'Ah, Mr. Smith,' he smiled with the sincerity of someone who has not the least interest in whatever you might say. 'I'm Doctor Dumont and how are you feeling now?'

'Why is it that doctors always seem to ask such daft questions?' Smith mused to himself silently.

While nurse undid the restraints that had prevented his bouncing around in the back of the red van, Dumont reached for Smith's wrist to check a pulse but without actually referring to a watch of any sort nor did he wait for or even seem to expect a reply.

'Nasty bump on the head, I see.'

'God, it gets worse,' Smith thought.

It crossed his mind to ask how the doctor could actually see such a thing when he had made absolutely no effort to look for it, then, given the obvious pointlessness of the observation, Smith just stayed silent.

'You must have been knocked unconscious for a while after you fell over.'

For the first time, the doctor flicked a quick glance at Smith and in that moment, he saw a brief flash of discomfort cross the boy's shiny face. Or perhaps not, as it seemed to vanish as quickly as he had imagined it had come.

'You've probably got a touch of concussion, Monsieur.'

Then, turning to the nurse: 'Make sure you clean the wounds on his head and hands, Sister', he continued, beginning to turn away, his examination seemingly complete. 'And send him home with a week's supply of pain killers.'

Smith saw a momentary look of annoyance in the sister's expression as she bent to her task, carrying out instructions that had almost certainly been second nature to her since before the doctor had been born. Dumont was halfway back to the door before stopping briefly, looking back over his shoulder, with the final admonition that Smith should take it easy for a couple of days. With that, he left.

'He seems to be rather busy, Sister Thier,' Smith said to the nurse, reading the name tag on her starched breast with difficulty.

'Yes,' came a disinterested reply.

'God,' Smith thought, 'is it part of the therapeutic process to be as rude as possible? Oh, sod it, say nothing. The sooner I get out of here and back home the better.'

Treatment was finished, bandages applied, a couple of pills, presumably pain killers, offered with a small clear plastic cup of lukewarm water, and that, it seemed, was that. The nurse, too, started to beat a hasty retreat before also turning back.

'Monsieur Smith, you will be taken home immediately, and you will be given some medication but hopefully you will have nothing worse than a headache for a day or two.'

The perfunctory nature of all this was beginning to annoy him. He thought that at least an X-ray, a proper examination or even a scan might have been in order, especially in the light of his previous medical history to which they were clearly both indifferent and in ignorance. He was on the point of risking the nurse's wrath by making a suggestion or two along these lines when a man in a beautifully cut dark suit entered. He walked quickly up to Smith's trolley with an air of self-confidence, dismissed Sister from the room with a glance, spun a chair off the nearby wall, and sat, crossing his legs with a practiced gesture that was both stylish and minimised the chances of creasing his immaculately trouser leg.

'Monsieur Smith' he said in precise and cultured tone. 'I hope you are feeling better.'

The voice managed to express concern and complete indifference at the same time. Unlike the paramedic, the doctor and the nurse, however, this man's gaze was hard, self-confident and very direct. Smith said nothing. A new and slightly unexpected dimension had just been added to all this and, even in his befuddled state, he felt that this was the point where he felt he should not try to make the running but just sit back and listen.

'I'm Detective Chief Superintendent Blanchard, Monsieur Smith. I hope you're not feeling too bad. You have had something of a shock, I think.'

'Good afternoon, Chief Superintendent' he replied with brevity and with what he hoped was an measure of sang froid appropriate to an Englishman. He was not the only one who could be terse.

Blanchard broke out a smile that under other, more Anglo-Saxon, circumstances could have been termed urbane. However, his voice was faintly acidic.

'You were involved in an incident at the Arena, today, I believe,'

'If you can describe being unconscious as being involved, Monsieur, then, yes, I was.'

'You had an accident, Monsieur. You fell and hit your head.'

It didn't seem to Smith that this was a question. It was more a statement of fact that didn't require an answer. He treated it accordingly.

'You were found lying on top of a body, I believe,' Blanchard continued, still without a trace of a question.

Normally, Smith thought, he would be consulting some sort of record, a notebook, for instance, but no such reference was being made.

'You tripped over the body, Monsieur Smith, hit your head and became unconscious. You were found lying on top of the body of Monsieur Robert DuGresson, one of our most prominent citizens.'

'Monsieur DuGresson?'

'Yes, a local businessman who had obviously died of a heart

attack while taking his lunchtime walk in the shade of the Arena. Monsieur DuGresson was a well know member of the business community and, of course, we are all *desolés* to hear of his death'.

It now became obvious to Smith that he was not even being questioned let alone interrogated. The policeman had a story and gave no sign of wanting it changed or even to have it confirmed. His explanation seemed to Smith to be both inaccurate and lacking in detail, given the experience he dimly remembered. However, the detective was continuing almost conversationally.

'Yes, you were both found by a tourist who telephoned the emergency services. You were lying unconscious on top of Monsieur DuGresson. Clearly you tripped over him and hit your head on the Arena wall. All rather unfortunate.'

'For Monsieur DuGresson, as well, I think,' remarked Smith unwilling to let the elegantly suited Blanchard make all the running. The smile froze momentarily on the detective's face then as quickly returned.

'Certainly, monsieur', he murmured, 'That goes without saying.'

'Perhaps you will give me the details of this tourist who rescued me?' Smith said. 'I'd like to thank him when I get home'.

Blanchard allowed his face to sadden slightly.

'Unfortunately, he is leaving Arles this afternoon, monsieur,' he replied with an archetypal gallic shrug.

Having at least gained a small foothold in the conversation, Smith was reluctant to abandon it so quickly.

'Perhaps you might like me to make a statement?'

Blanchard for the first time started to look a little exasperated.

'But why, Monsieur Smith? You were unconscious. How can you possibly remember anything? I'll ask the ambulance to take you home now and I hope you will try to forget this unfortunate experience. Goodbye Monsieur Smith.'

Without waiting for any reply, he got up and smiled yet again. He automatically extended his hand but then withdrew it when he saw Smith's bandages.

'My apologies, Monsieur,' he mumbled, temporarily taken aback and then walked out leaving Smith yet again alone with the clock and the air conditioner.

The ride home was uneventful. He was walked unsteadily to a private ambulance, helped by a charming white uniformed attendant, who lowered him into the passenger seat and the drove him slowly back home. The attendant insisted on helping him up the four steps to his front door, took his key from him and opened the door for him and led him inside. Arthur was ecstatic to see him, of course. He even got up off his sofa for a while at least. The attendant set down the paper bag that Smith presumed contained his new pills down on the sideboard in the hall.

'Now monsieur, you really ought to go to bed for a few hours.'

Without really waiting for a reply the attendant took another firm grip on his elbow and led him upstairs to the bedroom. To be honest, Smith was quite grateful. He still wasn't feeling too steady on his feet but he did have the presence of mind to decline the attendant's initial attempt to undress him. Some things he could do for himself no matter what his condition.

'Perhaps you could let yourself out?', he said to his helper, 'And thank you for your help.'

The man withdrew with the lubricated grace of a head waiter on first glimpsing a customer's platinum credit card. Not bothering to get undressed, he lay down on his bed and began to think over the events of the last couple of hours or so.

Certainly, the detective's story seemed entirely plausible. He had been found on top of a body and he had a bruised head - but it was bruised both front and back. He also had the vaguest recollection of finding himself under the body not on top of it as well. However, the recollection was getting vaguer as his bedroom started to rotate slowly. He was left with three lingering thoughts as he slipped gradually and gratefully into sleep. If one of the pills he'd been given in hospital was a painkiller, what was the other one? Secondly, why did the name tag on Dr. Dumont's white coat read Dr Alfonse Prieur? Finally, why hadn't he heard the front door close?

The two rode with that natural ease that comes from being introduced to the saddle at birth and from having spent their entire lives never too far from it. The two Camargue horses ambled along side by side under the heat of the afternoon, their unshod hooves making little sound on the gravel track. They were that dirty grey of all such horses, but these were a good deal finer that the usual examples of the breed that can be seen doing cattle shepherding and tourist duties. By many standards, the breed, standing barely above a large pony at a maximum of fourteen hands, may lack the grace and elegance of many thoroughbreds. But these two would be about the best you would ever see of the hardy and reliable breed that laid claim to be one of the oldest of all. These two were perfectly conformed, fit and in extreme good health bearing none of the usual scars that usually adorn the flanks of working Camargue horses.

The woman sat erect, hands relaxed in her lap, controlling the horse instinctively with slight, unconscious shifts of weight and leg pressure; the older man the same. Both wore guardian boots, jeans, white shirts and black fedora hats. The similarity was unintentional but natural between father and daughter. They were in deep conversation.

'So, that's that?' The old man sighed. For all his erect seat on the horse, his shoulders seemed to have slumped.

'Yes.' Her reply was quiet, her beautiful face solemn but

unmarked by tears.

'What's being said about it?'

'The police are now saying it was suicide'
'God. That's ridiculous.'

'Yes. I think that even they are embarrassed by the story. I think they panicked a bit.'

'Are we implicated at all?' The old man looked sharply across at her.

'I don't know. Suzanne doesn't think so.'

He made a sharp, dismissive shake of the head as if the very thought annoyed him. She turned her head.

'Papa, you must learn to forget, or at least ignore it. What's past is past. Suzanne was born twenty years after the war finished. You cannot blame her for what your brother and cousins did.'

'I don't hold her responsible. That's ridiculous. But they had bad blood then and they have it now.'

The woman sighed. It was an old sore and one that, by a silent mutual agreement, they never discussed. That part of the family had been estranged well before the Second World War that has brought them all face to face with that great decision faced by anyone living under occupation. Her father and grandfather had chosen resistance; the others collaboration. She looked across with great tenderness at the man she loved, feeling yet again his pain. It was her father as a teenager who had decided to restore the family honour a day or so after the liberation of Arles in June 1944. It was he as a young man who sought out the others and shot them both.

'Whatever you might feel, Papa, we need to know what is going on and she knows more than most.'

'And Claude?'

It was the woman's turn to sound contemptuous.

'He knows what Suzanne tells him.'

'What about this Englishman?'

'Ah, now that's a little strange. He was probably just in the wrong place at the wrong time, I suppose.'

'And is he likely to let it go at that?'

'One would have thought so but there we might have a problem. Claude had the impression that there is slightly more to this man, Smith, I think his name is, than meets the eye.'

'What has Claude found out about him?'

'He's twice divorced, has bought a house in Arles a few years ago and has retired here. He lives on his own with a dog. Pays his bills on time. He has joined the Arles town library and seems to be writing a book on Roman sarcophagi. He has a small family in England and keeps himself to himself. His doctor has no British medical records and Smith has made no attempt to get him copies. He has not got onto the local flic's radar yet. Suzanne is swatting them away, at the moment, for obvious reasons. Not much, as you see.'

'Have they tried to find out anything more than just the local stuff?'

'Now that's the slightly odd thing.' she replied with a slight frown crossing her face. 'Suzanne said they made a few polite enquiries through Interpol to the UK and this man Smith seems to have dropped off their radar as well. She ran up against the proverbial brick wall. Now it's not unusual to get little information from the UK apparently. They are notoriously lax about keeping records on their citizens, compared to us, at least, but this man Smith seems invisible even by their standards. She got the impression that there was some sort of block on the records. They did find that he doesn't seem to have much money although he does not have any debts.'

'That's a way of saying that we don't know anything about him.'

'Yes.'

'Anything else?'

'No.'

'I'm concerned about this Englishman,' he said. 'If for no other reason than he's a loose end.'

'I'm not sure what we can do about it, even if we wanted to, papa.'

'Perhaps you could go and visit him, my dear.'

'Me?' She sounded slightly shocked. He turned again to look at his daughter.

'Why not? You're the grieving widow, after all, and it was he who found your late husband.'

The elegant lady snorted with a force that cause both horses to flick their ears back.

'Come, my dear. You, the beautiful widow. He, the solitary divorcé. If you can't find out about him, nobody can. We need to know if he can do us harm.'

She sighed. 'All right. I'll telephone him.'

'No. I think it would be better if you just arrived at his front door. An English gentleman is a polite animal. He will invite you in. A telephone call will give him the opportunity either to say 'no' to a meeting or, at least, to prepare for one.'

She frowned but nodded her agreement.

2. Entrez la Femme

When he woke up, he had a wet ear. However, it was an indication of his further recovery that he could immediately explain it. The wet ear came from Arthur's nose. Smith's slumber had finally tried the dog's patience beyond his fear of the slippery stone stairs in the house, and he had come up to the bedroom in search of lunch, dinner and an afternoon walk. Being a dog only to bark in the most extreme circumstances - cats in the garden would do it - he obviously concluded that a wet nose in Smith's ear would do the trick. So it proved.

Much of the pain had gone but he still felt a little unsteady. By the time he made it downstairs, fed the dog who was obviously disappointed in plain dog meat straight from the tin, he certainly didn't feel up to his customary walk around the neighbourhood. The next best thing was to open the doors into the garden and let Arthur do his business there. Smith also went out into his small garden, set himself gingerly down into his *transatlantique* in the shade of the vine that combined with a jasmine plant to make a veranda over his little terrace and set to thinking over recent events armed, very unusually for him with a cold glass of fizzy water. Arthur, slightly perplexed by this change in routine, eased himself off his sofa where he customarily slept off the rigours of his own retirement, and came to lie at Smith's feet, one eye half open, watching further of worrying abnormality.

Even taking into account the fact that he had been in a somewhat befuddled state for the last few hours, his recollection of events and that offered by Inspector Blanchard differed significantly. He had indeed been knocked unconscious, but he remembered the hit as coming from behind not as a result of hitting his head after tripping over the dead body. Secondly his recollection of being trapped beneath the body was completely at variance with the police version. If proof be needed that his memory held up under examination, then the fact that he had two distinct and very tender lumps on his head supported his version. Other oddities surfaced one by one. In spite of the fact that episode seemed to involve a death, he had not actually been questioned by the policeman. His story seemed of no interest to the man. His medical condition similarly seemed not to interest the doctor either. The doctor's name tag could easily be a genuine mistake, one white coat looking much like another but other details filled in the picture; the fact that the policeman was dressed in a seriously expensive suit with shoes to match and had not actually shown him any identification. The fast-disappearing tourist good Samaritan. The totally uncommunicative *sapeur pompier,* the silent departure of the attendant who brought him home. What was in those pills he had been given at the hospital anyway?

'Christ,' he said to Arthur, 'I'm getting paranoid.'

The dog, finally realizing that these new arrangements were here to stay, decided that the effort of keeping one eye open was entirely too much and signified his agreement with his master by closing it.

Having gone through it all a couple of times, there was very little else to do. Perhaps it was one of those odd things that happen from time to time, especially in Arles, but apart from a not entirely vague feeling that something was amiss with it all, there was very little he could do about it whatever he wished. Indeed, it was pretty clear to him that he really shouldn't be interested in doing anything about it at all or even finding out more. If the police were happy, why disturb his purposely quiet and unobtrusive new life as a retired English eccentric by seeking explanations for things that were none of his business – or at least from which he would derive little benefit. He had spent much of his working life trying to do the 'right thing' and had been kicked in the balls for his trouble more times than he cared to remember. The inability to say, 'fuck it' and walk away had been a life-long burden and the part of his still throbbing brain that wanted an explanation would have to be controlled. In any case he had other things to think about. The book on the of Roman sarcophagi in the Arles Museum was always there to be worked on. Numerous small jobs needed doing in the house and garden. Arthur was always up for a good long walk and there were still parts of nearby Tranquetaille and Pont du Crau that he wanted to explore let alone other places accessible by car. A large supermarket shop was looming. Most importantly there was the beef.

'Ah,' he remembered, 'the beef'. Given the investment that

he had made the previous Wednesday, the beef had to be done sometime soon, irrespective of his headache.

As usual it had started, like many things, with Arthur. A near neighbour, a Monsieur Enscreva, walked a large and kindly Basset hound around the Arena at the same sort of time as Arthur took Smith on their daily more ambitious perambulations. The basset, Snoopy, was large of body but excessively short of leg and therefore contented himself with a single circuit of Vespasian's canine pissoir. Arthur's antipathy towards other dogs prevented any close social intercourse, but Monsieur Enscreva, now in his later sixties had been a serious walker before the advent of Snoopy who had been bought as a present for a daughter whose interest in the dog had diminished at approximately the same rate as the dog had grown. Smith had thus fallen into an arrangement whereby he and Monsieur Enscreva would both take the car and walk with Arthur once a week in the Alpilles Mountains some ten miles to the north east of Arles. It was during one of these walks that Monsieur Enscreva recommended a good butcher on the market. Why is it, Smith thought, in one of his numerous idle moments, that everyone seems to know a 'good' butcher. Seldom do people admit regularly to knowing a bad butcher. They usually 'know a good little butcher / fishmonger / seamstress / carpenter' as if it were their own particular secret and they are doing you a favour by letting you in on it. Logically anyone in trade who remained such a secret would have gone bust long before. Odd really, he felt. However, such a recommendation here demanded at least one visit to M. Angelole, keeper of the best butcher stall on the legendary Arles street market. That duly had happened last Wednesday.

Smith was no expert on meat - comes from not knowing a good butcher, he thought - and it all looked very nice - red, fresh, that sort of thing. He decided to take Arthur to the market early and get some beef in order to create that great Provençale dish, a Boeuf en daube, and obviously local custom demanded local bull meat not cow. Fresh bones for Arthur were also a priority. Monsieur Angelole assured him that only a few days before the bull had been cavorting around its Camargue *manade* without a care in the world. Now, of course, it remained without a care but somewhat more stationary.

A decent size lump cost an eye-watering amount but the market stall was neither the time nor the place to whinge. Had he done so or asked for a smaller piece, that might have reflected badly on him, on the English in general, and on Smith's walking companion and his wife who he gathered was a retired tax inspector and a personal friend of the butcher. Apparently, she had many such friends in the town. Whether or not Monsieur Angelole saw his shock at the price he had no idea, but he was at least not charged for three large bones for the much admired Arthur - M. Angelole kept rottweilers back at the farm, and therefore knew a thing or two about dogs. The bones had kept Arthur preoccupied and prone in equal measure ever since.

The recipe that was written down in that universal handwriting that all French seem to have was provided by Madam Enscreva. It called for the meat to be marinaded. This was not only to flavour the meat. Camargue bulls may be small, but their meat can be tough and a day or three in a marinade does no harm. Thus having kept the meat in the fridge since last Wednesday's market he took it out, trimmed it free of the most expensive fat in Provence, cut it into 'cubes' and set it to marinade in olive oil, lemon juice, some vegetables and a bouquet garni culled from his own embryonic herb garden and some other odds and sods - including juniper berries that were called for in the recipe but whose function he failed to understand. Like many people, Smith had possessed a jar of Juniper berries throughout most of his adult life and he had yet to understand what they were for. A bit like cyclists, he felt. Gin, he had heard, was flavoured with it. If this were true then that made the case for Juniper berries.

The meat in its marinade was then covered and placed down in the cellar and left for later with a sense of accomplishment and anticipation. The rest of the afternoon progressed less productively with much of it spent reading, prone in the shade of his garden and in his *transatlantique*.

He was, more or less, unchanged and unmoved when at about 7:00pm he was violently brought back from his supine reverie by his next-door neighbour, Georges, shouting over the fence, reminding him that, it was Friday and the bar was open.

Some time ago, Smith had been persuaded to visit a most peculiar bar located in the headquarters of the very right-wing candidate for the next mayoral election. Arles had been led by a communist mayor for some time, since the end of the Second World War, in fact, but the conservative candidate had all the mindless self confidence that typifies all politicians in advance of an election. Even when he had been engaged directly with the world, Smith had been utterly disinterested in politics and politicians. He had no time for them, and certainly no respect for their so-called profession. He had occasionally tottered off to vote but never out of conviction. In fact, he always felt a bit of a sham. But having always lived in places that had safe Conservative leanings, the sense of pointlessness of voting at all had always been stronger than a desire to 'make his vote count'- because it never did. Thus, to be frank, his periodic attendance at what he called the fascist bodega were motivated less by politics or a desire to see the nice, clean cut young conservative thruster from Nîmes elected Mayor of Arles, but more by the fact that there was an interesting cross section of people to talk to there. They liked Arthur and fed him crisps and Pastis was one Euro a shot. He had few friends in Arles – or elsewhere for that matter – and the easy superficiality of the bar relationships fulfilled a strong need for company without commitment.

'OK, Georges, I'll be there in half an hour.'

A quick shower and change saw Smith walking towards the rather shabby shop at the top of the Boulevard Emile Combes that now functioned temporarily as the centre of the local right wing bid for power. He had showered without remembering the dressings on his head and hands and it was only when they became soggy and dropped off and clogged the shower drain, that he was forced to make a choice as whether or not he was going to renew them. He'd decided against it. Thus, looking and feeling relatively normal he took Arthur on his lead and headed off towards the bar.

Usually his entry into the bar was greeted with restrained acknowledgment by the people he knew and indifference by those he didn't. Arthur invariably got most of the attention but he had at least progressed to the point where, having completed the mandatory circuit of handshakes, a Pastis was usually was waiting for him by the time he got to the short end of the bar habitually occupied by neighbour Georges and Adrien, a large, middle-aged, balding, well-meaning, pony-tailed, bicycle-riding salesman of black market dental requisites. This time however, it was different.

Conversation stopped and every head turned towards him as he walked in through the door. Nobody spoke and the ritual circuit of handshakes was conducted in an eerie silence. No one met his eye and usually firm handshakes were limp and, occasionally, sweaty. This time he had to tap a coin on the bar to encourage the barman to produce his Pastis. Gradually the twenty or so in the bar returned quietly to their conversations. Adrien and Georges resumed talking about the Tour de France that had passed though the town a few weeks earlier and had caused universal, if, to Smith, incomprehensible, hysteria and the bar reverted slowly to normality. Smith decided on a policy of doing nothing – always safe if you don't know what to do - and, as he hoped, it was the affable Adrian took the plunge.

'Well, you've had an exciting time, I hear.'

Unwilling to let the frost of his entry into the bar melt too quickly, Smith countered with a curt: 'Oh yes?'

The silence hung like a butcher's salami, twisting gently in the light air. He became interested and angry equally at their obvious embarrassment. Had there been the usual hearty welcome, he would probably not have thought about recent events, but this was different, and he wasn't prepared to let their insouciance pass without making them feel embarrassed by it. In spite of a rising, if irrational anger, he was determined that someone else would break it for it sure as hell was not going to be him. Just as his ire was going to get the better of him, Georges chirped up.

'It must have been terrible finding Robert like that,' he said.

'Robert?'

'DuGresson. The man you fell over at the Arena.'

'Ah. Is that who he was? A friend of yours?'

Smith was conscious of purposely being mischievous. It was highly unlikely that Georges who was a semi-retired street cleaner who also worked in the building trade 'on the black' and this well-respected, high flying, businessman would have moved in similar circles. But the question did indicate that yesterday's events were common knowledge.

'Not a friend, exactly, but we had a few interests in common,' replied Georges, with a slight flush of self-importance about his face, glancing around at the others who were obviously listening but trying to look as if they weren't.

'He was a supporter of our efforts here,' presumably referring to the election campaign.

'That makes sense,' Smith thought. 'A successful businessman would have felt common cause with a more conservative approach to local politics.'

Given that everyone seems to know what had happened and, however reluctantly wanted to talk about it, he felt his earlier decision that he was going to let the matter drop fading. A couple of Pastis, noticeably stronger that the usual measure offered up, also helped.

'Well actually, I'm not entirely sure that the police have exactly got the right story. My memory of what happened seems to be slightly different to theirs.'

Dropping any pretence of minding its own business, a voice from a group further down the bar ventured: 'What exactly do you mean?'

'Oh, nothing really. Just a few details that I remember differently to the police,' he said lamely, realising instantly that he was actually accusing the police of having a memory of the events at the Arena. There had been no mention of other witnesses.

The voice persisted: 'What details exactly?'

He looked across the line of faces that was turned in his direction and located the source of the question. It was a tall, ugly man in that half and half Camargue fashion that locals sometimes affect. Cowboy boots, jeans, a decorated shirt and open black waistcoat. He wasn't smiling.

Smith walked slowly across to him and stood close; not intimidating close but slightly too close for complete comfort and looked directly into his face.

'Oh, nothing significant, I suppose. Just different.'

The man blinked and swayed very slightly back. His tone turned a touch truculent.

'It may be a mistake to question the police version of what happened.'

Smith moved a few inches closer to the man and affected a broad smile that stopped long before it reached his eyes.

'It is extraordinary how difficult I find it to follow advice like that, Monsieur. You were giving me advice, were you not?'

The man took a pace back and Smith brought the conversation to an end by turning his back on the man and immediately starting a different conversation with Georges about the Tour de France. It was both clumsy and rude, but he didn't take very kindly to the general tenor of tonight's gathering and he found his irritation growing.

The exchange hadn't been particularly enjoyable, and he felt no real interest either in talking about the Tour or in migrating along the bar as he usually did to pick up other conversations. Even Arthur was more than usually restless. Perhaps he also felt something in the air or more likely it was the complete absence of crisps and admiration. So, after a further few minutes, Smith pleaded his headache and left to complete his evening walk, feeling acutely the dozen or so pairs of eyes that followed him out.

The evening walk finished; it was about eight thirty when Smith returned home. He rejected the idea of eating, flipped through some television programmes and finding nothing of interest, poured a weak glass of whisky and soda, took Panofsky's Tomb Sculpture, his current reading, and settled into his chair in the garden to spend the last of the late evening sun. Arthur came out of the house, lay down beside him on the concrete terrace, sighed and went to sleep. Obviously in retrospect, it had been a mistake to go to the bar, but he was not to know that everyone there would be so interested in yesterday's events. He had imagined that a quiet drink in familiar surroundings was the right thing to do under the circumstances. The whole experience however had left him feeling slightly out of sorts.

The warmth of the little garden soon enveloped him, and he felt the tension begin to seep away. It was that marvellous temperature that one experiences from time to time where it seems to be the same outside as inside him. Completely neutral. There was the lightest possible movement of air. Even Arthur's slight snoring failed to spoil the tranquillity as yet again he fell to mulling things over.

It was plain to him now that his recollection of yesterday's adventure was accurate and the police, if that was what they were, had, for whatever reason, decided on another story. In addition to his own memory, now fully restored, there were too may oddities about the business. However, he was equally certain that there was absolutely no reason for doing anything other than forgetting the whole thing. The last thing he wanted was to do was to get involved with the police – he had never had good experience of the police – and in any case there was no future in. He could see no benefit at all in doing so, and, if truth be told, he was not particularly interested.

As if to demonstrate his resolve, he put aside all thoughts of dead Frenchmen, went quickly to replenish his whisky, returned to his seat and settled to read. It didn't take long for Panofsky's scholarship to take him over. He remembered how his early career as a mediocre art historian had been guided by Panofsky's writings.

Tomb Sculpture was a short series of public lectures turned into a sort of festchrift. Smith wondered what sort of a public it could have been for Panofsky to make such extraordinary assumptions about their erudition. There was hardly a paragraph where Smith didn't have to make a mental note to return when he had easier access to his reference books. There was a presupposition of knowledge that went far beyond his own and, he was pretty sure, that of the audience that had been lucky enough to be there originally. It probably was not the right book to read in the garden. But he found himself chuckling regularly. There are few of authors who could do such a comprehensive job of bringing you up against you own inadequacies. There are even fewer that can make you enjoy it. The whisky helped.

New glasses - reading ones that is - had been on Smith's list for some time and it was obviously something he had to attend to soon as reading was becoming increasingly difficult. He realised that darkness was falling rather than his eyesight failing and he closed his book and went indoors, closing the shutters and doors behind him. It was slightly past nine, so he decided to watch the television news and then go to bed. A last whisky, perhaps, he thought with that guilty glee that he usually felt when he knew he was ignoring the good advice of both his daughters and his doctor. Don't drink alcohol when you are taking pills was the mantra. Easily solved. Don't take the pills.

Little had happened in the world – or at least little that interested him. Summer rain and floods in England. Give it a week or two and there would be hosepipe bans he thought. It was the silly season, of course, and England's new prime Minster was struggling to make a good impression when most of his subjects were on holiday. They were between cricket test matches; the first against India having been drawn with the visitors being saved by the intervention of rain on the last day. He flipped over onto French news and equally little caught his ear. He made a mental note to buy a copy of the local newspaper Le Provence tomorrow to see if the death in the arena made it into the public domain. Satisfied that the day had nothing left for him, he decided to go to bed and reached for the remote control. It was then that there was a knock on his front door.

For a moment, it crossed his mind to ignore it. He knew of no-one who would call at this time of night. He had yet to install any sort of security spy hole in the door. But he had always thought that Arles was gratifyingly free of the sort of mindless urban violence that soiled other towns. Other than his wish to go to bed, therefore, there seemed little reason not to see who was there. Indeed, his neighbour on the other side was a certain Madame Drouche who lived alone at the age of eighty-six and with whom he had the usual arrangement in case of emergencies. Perhaps it was she. So, having made sure that the television was off, he went to the door.

His visitor was certainly a lone lady. Equally certainly it was not Madam Drouche for in front of him, dimly lit by the energy saving street light fixed to his wall high above her head was a tall and extremely handsome woman in her mid-fifties wearing a dark brown calf-length camel coloured coat, lightly tied at the waist.

'Monsieur Smith?'

'Yes, Madame. I'm he,' said Smith, sounding embarrassingly like a bad French grammar book. The briefest smile flashed across her face.

'I'm Martine DuGresson, Monsieur Smith, I wonder if I might have a word with you?'

For a second Smith felt like a complete prat. Beautiful women didn't swim into his life very often these days. Actually, they never did, and he was too busy taking in the fact that this one actually wanted to talk to him to connect the name with recent events. Remembering names had always been a huge difficulty throughout his life and for a second he just thought that this was yet another name he had simply forgotten. Fortunately, his memory and his manners returned simultaneously.

'Of course, Madame, please come in.'

As she moved past him into the small sitting room, he caught a slight whiff of lightly applied Nina Ricci L'air du Temps. He fought back the memories of his first wife evoked by that that particular perfume. Arthur slid effortlessly off his sofa and greeted the visitor with huge tail wagging. Clearly, he was as impressed as Smith.

'Oh, what a beautiful greyhound,' she said extending an elegant hand with the sort of confidence that only someone well used to large dogs could show. Arthur immediately stood to be petted and looked up at the woman with the sort of liquid brown eyes that she must have experienced many times before. Without lifting her hand from the now besotted greyhound, she turned back to Smith.

'I'm the wife of the man you found yesterday at the Arena. Perhaps I should say widow now. I'd like to talk to you about what happened.'

'Of course. Let me take your coat. Do sit down.' Smith took the feather light cashmere coat and hung it carefully from a hook by the front door. The dog quickly regained his customary position on his sofa with his head resting on the arm nearest the longer version arranged at right angles. Much to his joy, Madam DuGresson sat at his end and resumed her gentle caress of his head. He was transported.

'May I offer you something to drink, Madam?' She looked down at the low table in front of her and saw the remnant of his nightcap.

'If that's a whisky, I'll have the same.'

'It is whisky and soda.'
'Perfect.'

'Ice?'

'Only if the soda is not cold.'

This seemed to be turning into one of those ridiculous exchanges spies use to identify each other in bad movies. He collected his glass and turned to the drinks tray.

'I have Islay Mist, a rather working-class blended Malt, or basic cooking scotch from Monoprix.'

She smiled directly at him and he felt the affect. 'The simple whisky if you please. I'm surprised that you can find soda water in Arles, Monsieur Smith,' she continued.

'Actually, it's Perrier, Madame. It is one of the few sparking waters on the market that has no pretensions about being good for you or tasting of anything. Most of the Italian sparking waters taste like fizzy sewage'

His small attempt at levity was greeted with a surprisingly full chuckle.

'I have never understood the modern passion for drinking fizzy water,' he continued, 'but it has, at least, revived whisky and soda as an accessible drink.'

His candour elicited another chuckle. He set the drinks down on the table and sat on the only available seat at the other end of the sofa.

'I'm afraid I can't offer you anything to eat, Madame', he remarked, remembering the French tradition of offering nibbles available when taking an aperitif.

'Please don't worry,' she replied with a smile that was accompanied by a candid look straight at him. 'I have no great interest in eating little bits of nothing on rock hard pieces of bread at any time, and certainly not this late in the evening.'

Martine DuGresson was an elegant woman in her late thirties by his guess, dressed simply but expensively in a beige silk blouse with a single brooch at the shoulder and tailored grey cotton trousers. She was strikingly beautiful with carefully coiffured black hair that was obviously not manufactured. The colour wasn't uniform. It was liberally highlighted with grey strands. Her shoes were leather, hand-stitched and low-heeled. It was only when he noticed the little tassels that he was brought back to reality of the present. He looked across to her.

'Madam DuGresson, I'm very sorry for your loss, of course, but how can I help you?'

'Thank you, Monsieur Smith,' she replied, adopting Smith's more formal tone. 'I'll be candid with you. I'm not satisfied with the official explanation of my husband's death and I gather that your memory of what happened is quite different from the official story. I would like to hear from you what happened.'

'May I ask, Madame, how you heard that my experience might differ from the police version of events?'

Her glance that still didn't waver from his face firmed very slightly.

'You may, Monsieur. But at this stage I would prefer not to tell you.'

'Very well, Madame.'

He did as he was asked. He told the whole story in as much detail as he could. He felt she deserved that. Never once did she interrupt or ask a question. She just sat there, perfectly relaxed, looking straight at him, taking it all in. The story finally finished with her appearance at his door.

'And that's as much as I can remember, Madame.'

For a moment there was silence then she sighed. 'Thank you, Monsieur Smith. I thought it might have been something like that.'

'Madame, I can only say again how sorry I am.' She silenced him with a slight lift of her right hand.

'Monsieur Smith. As you see, I'm not exactly a grieving widow. My husband was a pig and I'm as unconcerned about him now he is dead as I was when he was alive.'

This was a new Martine DuGresson. Nothing had obviously changed in her appearance or manner, but the timbre of her voice hardened. She continued: 'In case you are wondering, for reasons that you don't need to know, I'm more interested in the way my husband died than in the fact that it happened, and you have been most helpful. Thank you.'

She smiled and quickly reverted to the woman who had knocked on his door a short time ago. Smith saw that her glass was empty although he had never noticed her drinking. Arthur was sound asleep. With a fluid, elegant motion she stood to go. Smith helped her with her coat, and she stepped out into the warm evening. She extended an unsurprisingly firm handshake.

'I'm very grateful for your help, Monsieur Smith. In case you remember anything else, you can always contact me on this number. Goodbye.'

She handed him a business card. It was white and very stiff, slightly small by present day standards, and bore only a single mobile telephone number. Nothing else. Not even a name. Madam DuGresson was obviously used to being remembered. Automatically he ran his finger over the surface. The number felt raised. Equally automatically he did the same to the back and felt the number in recess. 'Engraved, not thermographed,' he thought, impressed yet again.

She walked down the four steps that led down from his front door and without a backward glance disappeared around the corner. He paused before going back inside to look yet again at the floodlit Arena and only because of that did he notice two casually, but smartly dressed men emerge from between the parked cars in the Place de la Major and follow Madame DuGresson out of sight. He dialled the mobile number on her card.

'Madam, I think you should know that two men followed you from my house.'

'Thank you, Monsieur. I know. They are friends of mine. I'm interested that you spotted them. They will be embarrassed. But I'm touched by your concern. Thank you.'

Sitting down quietly next to Arthur, Smith laid a hand on the dog's head and began to stroke it gently while mulling over the recent visit. The dog, unable to distinguish between dedicated, focussed, petting and an absent-minded fondle, closed his eyes with pleasure. Smith looked down with a smile. If you believe that nothing needs analysing, then everything means something - usually contentment. Food and drink, sleep, affection and sex. That's all you really need. Unlike Arthur, he might still be 'entire' but a fat lot of good that did. Personally, he'd be happy with an absent-minded fondle.

OK. He had got hit over the head, woken up in the middle of a murder, had been grilled by the police and now the corpse's beautiful widow had just been in his sitting room drinking his whisky and caressing his dog. This, he felt, was not precisely what he had in mind when he'd chosen to run from the accumulated horrors of an oddly spent life and retire to the South of France. However beautiful, the woman was worried. That much was obvious. He had been under inspection and he hoped that his air of indifference had been convincing. Madam, on the other hand, had been a bag of nerves - elegant but nervous. But not at all like a grieving widow.

His reverie was broken by the unwelcome - very unwelcome - sound of his mobile phone. Glancing at his watch, it did cross his mind to ignore it. Telephones and he didn't get on. The machine, however, said 'David'. Smith had only eleven numbers stored on his mobile and six of those were restaurants. One of the sobering but cathartic things he had done at the first opportunity after diving south though the Channel Tunnel on his way to freedom and his new life, was to purge his electronic address book of all the accumulated crap of twenty odd years of business networking. A strict cull of all those, bar the people he actually relished hearing from cut the number of entries from over four hundred to five. The six restaurants had been added since.

David Gentry was a friend. If truth be told he was probably Smith's only friend. They had worked together for many years. Gentry had been the planner, the organiser, the strategist; sitting in his windowless basement under one of those huge but anonymous government buildings in Whitehall in the heart of London. It was from this tiny subterranean space that Smith went about his somewhat unorthodox business in the name of her Majesty's Government; a name that was, of course, never mentioned. It was to that same little space that Smith had always returned usually but not invariably under his own steam. When help had been required it was Gentry who provided it. That, Smith knew, was the basis of their friendship because he knew what many wiser people know; that true friendship is not based on affection or shared interests or anything emotional. It is based on need; the permanence of mutual need. He and Gentry needed each other. Their lives had been intertwined for years and after their retirement to Arles it continued. He had worked with David for a number of years in that dimly lit and hopefully forgotten time in his life when, for both of them, they had to rely totally on each other or die. They had and they hadn't.

'Christ, Gentry, what sort of time is this to telephone anybody?'

'I'm coming round. Four minutes.'

Gentry had a tiny shop and much larger house buried deep enough in the narrow streets that wind off the Rue de la Calade for no one to find it. He sold old books. Serious books, not the crap that most antiquarian booksellers pretend are worth selling. His books were art, old, rare, often unique. The last thing he actually wanted to do was to sell any of them. That accounted for his commercial invisibility. Occasionally by mistake someone with a big enough chequebook not to be shocked by the utterly ridiculous prices Gentry put on his books, chanced in through the door. Then the book in question mysteriously got lost, was just sold to a museum in Mesopotamia, was recently discovered as a fake, or, on one famous occasion, was buried with someone who literally could not live without it.

Smith delved into the recesses of his sideboard and brought

out a bottle of Islay Mist. It was the only malt either of them ever drank. Typical, he thought, that they should both develop a passion for a blended rather than a single malt. Typical also that it managed to avoid having that foul taste of bog that the eight Islay distilleries have turned into a fetish in the name of marketing. He brought out two cherished deeply cut-glass tumblers, poured three fingers or thereabouts into each. He chucked a palm full of ice into his and set the other untouched on the low table in front of the sofas, the bottle next to it. He sat and waited.

David Gentry walked straight in. He had a key. Arthur, recognising an old and good friend, sprung from his slumber and made an indecent fuss. Then suddenly he stopped, turned, and leaped over the table back onto his sofa, narrowly beating Gentry to the cherished corner spot. It was an old game and one they both enjoyed. David had come with Smith to the kennel on the dark side of the moon just off the east London bit of the M25 where Arthur languished waiting to be rescued after an injury cut short a mediocre racing career. Unlike all the other pairs of dogs waiting hopefully for a new life, Arthur was in a kennel on his own due to his predilection for trying to kill other dogs. The three of them had fallen in love immediately.

Smith looked across at his friend and saw a man who had remained unchanged throughout the years. He was completely average and unremarkable. He was neither fat nor thin, neither tall nor short. No obvious facial features. All completely unmemorable; something that was, of course, useful for someone of Gentry's profession. His appearance was always the same. For briefings and de-briefings alike Gentry always wore the same thing; dark green corduroy trousers supported by black braces over a Tattersall shirt from Turnbull and Asser of Jermyn Street. Polished brown brogues from John Lobb and an I Zingari club tie. When required, a basic and slightly seedy green tweed jacket would complete the ensemble. Smith could never recall his wearing a coat. The fact that he was now living in Arles where the average temperature was considerably higher than in London made absolutely no difference to him. The man had that indifference to temperature that tends to characterise the British abroad. Gentry lifted his glass and without any of the silly extended preliminaries that accompany starting to drink in France, downed it in one. He refilled the glass from the waiting bottle and sat back.

'What the fuck have you got into this time, Peter?' and then as an afterthought, 'You OK, by the way?'

'Not really sure, David,' replied Smith answering both questions with economy. 'What have you heard?'

Gentry had made the break for freedom from serving in one of Her Britannic Majesties more obscure departments at the same time as Smith. A particularly nasty episode in Somalia a dozen or so years back had left them both damaged. Smith had headed back towards the tranquil waters of art history and occasionally selling computer stuff to unsuspecting foreigners around the world when he needed money while Gentry had headed for Arles and instant anonymity.

'As usual, you've ended up to your vitals in someone else's problem.'

'Hardly my fault, this time, to be fair.'

'Fair or not, the word is that you were involved.' Smith didn't ask whose word.
'Coincidence, nothing more, dear chap.'

'Bugger, coincidence. In the space of the last twelve hours, you have been discovered with a dead local luminary, interviewed by a bigwig cop from Den Haag and been visited by the widow who just happens to be a member of the most powerful family in the area.'

Smith knew better than to ask the obvious questions. Gentry just knew. Nothing new there. He had always watched Smith's back, even when it was not necessary, and this time was no exception.

'I honestly don't know. But I'm sufficiently pissed off to want to find out.'

'I don't suppose the fact that Madam DuGresson is rich, beautiful and recently available, has much to do with it?'

Smith didn't reply and the silence extended.

'I wonder if you could do a little quiet digging for me?' Smith asked. 'I'd like to know a little more about this Robert DuGresson.'

He knew that Gentry had a few years head start on him in Arles and by now, if the past was anything to go by, he had sources of information around the area that even the police would envy. Keeping a low profile seemed to come naturally to him and it was precisely that quality that made him such a good foil for Smith's somewhat more extrovert approach. Although they saw each other regularly, they were by no means constant companions since Smith had arrived. Their shared past somehow prevented it. He wondered why Gentry had made such a late-night visit at all. Then it came to him. Gentry had had years to build up his network here and if he thought something was going on, it probably was. Then he remembered again with genuine pleasure that this man actually liked him.

'Do I need you to watch my back, old friend?'

'I rather think you might.' He shrugged with a tired smile. 'Nothing new there then.'

Silently, Smith topped up both their glasses. It was going to be a long night.

3. Meeting and Acquaintances

Leading, as he did, a purposely solitary life, he was unused to people knocking at his front door. Having it happen twice in twenty-four hours was most unusual. This time, however, the knock was more peremptory than that of the previous night. He purposely took his time opening it. A uniformed member of the *Gendarmerie nationale* stood on the top step outside his door. A second was below in the road outside standing by a modest police car. The first made a motion to step into the house. Smith also took a step forward blocking the door. The movement brought him very close to the disconcerted policeman.

'Yes? What do you want?'

The gendarme was struggling slightly with this unexpected invasion of his personal space but was reluctant to step back out of the doorway. It also helped that Smith was a head taller. The matter was resolved by Arthur, whose curiosity got the better of his indolence, came to the door to see what the fuss was about. On seeing the head of a very large dog, and to Smith's great satisfaction, the gendarme did indeed take a pace back.

'You will please come to the police station with us, Monsieur Smith. We wish to clarify some aspects of your statement concerning the death of Monsieur DuGresson.'

It crossed his mind to enquire precisely what statement they had in mind as he personally could not recollect making one. However, these were messengers only.

'Am I being arrested?'

'Of course not, Monsieur Smith. We would merely like your assistance in some matters.'

'Well, of course. In that case I would be delighted to help. Perhaps you would just give me a moment to shut my garden doors and to get my hat.'

With that, Smith turned back into the house, and, much to the surprise of the gendarme, shut the door behind him. He reappeared a few moments later, suitably protected from the summer sun, and motioned a clearly angry policeman ahead of him down the five narrow steps to the pavement. This was obviously not correct police procedure, which presumably called for a suspect to be followed rather than led. However, when the gendarme tried to squash himself into the corner of the narrow-railed step outside Smith's door to let

Smith pass in front, he was defeated by Smith's refusal to squeeze past and by his courteously extended hand.

'After you, monsieur.'

Reluctantly the policeman went down first. Smith stood by one of the rear doors of the car and waited for it to be opened for him. Ignoring the black looks of both men he got in with a broad smile and a most courteous 'Thank you monsieur.' As the car drove slowly away from the Arena, Smith took stock. He was being brought in by the *Gendarmerie nationale* rather than the local civil Police Municipale who more usually dealt with matters within the towns. The gendarmerie was army not civil and usually charged with the administration of law in rural areas and on highways. Being a section of the army, they are effectively, if not in law, the senior force and certainly wielded more authority. In this case they were polite if simmering. A more difficult question was why he was being called in. Apart from a few comments in the bar and his conversations with Madam DuGresson and Gentry he had said nothing to anyone. He was pretty sure that Madame wouldn't have complained. She seemed to distrust the police more than he did. In all probability he had been ratted on by someone in the bar.

Although no great hero nor given to excessive bouts of manly courage, Smith had never taken kindly to being pushed around by anyone, let alone policemen. He had that peculiarly British tendency to respect the law but had little time for those who interpret or enforce it. Thus, in the short time available to him before they got to the police station, he decided that whatever was going on, he wouldn't be particularly supine. He had done nothing wrong and, if for some reason, the police wish to propagate a lie then that was not his problem. He wouldn't, however, connive with the conspirators. He couldn't see that they could do anything if he didn't. In all probability he was going to be warned off, nothing more. So, it proved.

The car stopped outside the right hand end of the two story concrete monstrosity on the Boulevard des Lices that had been built over the beautiful old Jardin d'Hiver in the great burst of tasteless urban redevelopment in 1976 that had engulfed a great garden and the then accessible roman necropolis beneath it, giving the town instead a multi-story car park, a large police station, an equally oversized tax office and an office of social security, all designed with that extraordinary insensitivity to beauty that often afflicts modern French architects. For a country that is so obsessed with its own sense of culture, it occasionally makes mistakes of epic proportions and this group of buildings at the top of Arles' main street was one of their worst. He was led into the police building that houses both the Gendarmerie and the Police at opposite ends like a pair of Siamese twins to what was obviously an interview room complete with table, three chairs and an already seated plain clothes policeman, notebook open in front of him.

'Please sit down, Monsieur Smith.'

Doing as he was asked, Smith replied: 'Good morning. I wonder if you would give me a notebook and pencil?'

The policeman looked up startled.

'I beg your pardon?'

'Which bit did you neither not hear or understand?' replied Smith aggressively, looking the man straight in the eye.

'Why do you want a notebook and pen, Monsieur?'

'Why are you asking questions to which you already know the answer? You may have time to waste but I don't. You can either give me what I want, or we can both sit here until a solicitor is called and he can take notes on my behalf.'

This was clearly not the direction that the policeman anticipated for the interview. He had not expected to talk with someone who was not in the least bothered by being picked up and brought to a police station for an interview. Nor did he expect the subject to be self-confident to the point of aggression. Smith saw that he had gained an advantage, however temporarily, and decided to press on.

'And while you are at it, you can get me a closed bottle of water, a glass and please identify yourself. Additionally, if you are intending to record this interview, please say so and start the recording immediately. Unless you intend to arrest and charge me with something, I shall require a copy of the recording of this interview for the British Consulate in Marseilles.'

Now this was pushing his luck somewhat but as he spoke, he found himself getting angrier. He knew perfectly well what this was all about but and there was no harm in gaining a foothold before the policeman could recover his poise. The man got up and left the room without a word leaving Smith to try to figure out whether he had achieved some sort of victory or had just dropped himself thoroughly in it. Moments later his question was answered for the door opened and a uniformed policeman came in and thumped a plastic glass and a small bottle of Evian on the table in front of him. Having done so, he spun away more balletically than Smith imagined possible for such a big man and left.

Smith left the water untouched in front of him. It had served its purpose, and, in any case, he seldom drank drink water on its own. He casually glanced around. The room was plain with no decoration and no great mirror on the wall as in all the best American crime dramas. A small side table held the recording equipment that had elicited his original question. It had not been switched on. He sat back, closed his eyes, relaxed and awaited developments.

It was not long before the door opened again, this time to reveal the immaculately presented Chief Inspector Blanchard. Smith rose, walked around the table and extended his hand. With a certain surprise, the policeman reciprocated, and Smith was able to give the man a handshake that was slightly firmer than courtesy demanded.

'Ah. Blanchard, how nice to see you again, so soon.'

The Frenchman may or may not have been familiar with the British public-school habit of calling people by their surnames, but he managed to raise a wintry smile – a considerable achievement from a professional working in a country where titles are important.

'Monsieur Smith. I'm glad to see that you are so well recovered from your recent experience.'

Feeling that there was little to be gained by further comment, Smith made none.

'I felt that it was necessary for us to have a little chat ……'

He was halted in mid-sentence by Smith's interruption.

'My notebook?'

'Ah yes, the notebook.'

A more genuine smile crossed Blanchard's lips as he slid an immaculately manicured hand into the inside breast pocket of his beige Armani and withdraw what was obviously by its slimness and its dark crocodile skin cover, his own notebook. He put it on the table in front of Smith and, without taking his eyes off Smith's face, laid a slim gold Cross ball point pen beside it.

'Please,' he said, 'use mine.'

'Thank you,' returned Smith.
Smith picked up the notebook and opened it. Embossed in gold letters on the inside of the front flap were the words Cellarini, Firenze.

'Ah,' said Smith, 'I'm pleased that Alberto's son is carrying on the fine work of his late father.'

'You know Cellarini?'

'Oh yes,' he replied with exaggerated casualness, 'many years ago Alberto made a cover for a miniature pocket calculator for me. I still have it somewhere. He said it was so difficult he would never make another one.'

'Ah, there is nothing to beat true Florentine leatherwork.'

Unable to resist the opportunity Smith replied: 'Yes, rather like Monsieur DuGresson's shoes and yours.'

There was a pause. Blanchard sighed, as if reluctant to be brought back to why they were sitting in that bare room together.

'Yes indeed, Monsieur Smith. I have heard some things that I felt we ought to discuss.'

He paused, waiting for Smith to say something but Smith felt that he had made enough of the running and was prepared to be passive if not downright uncooperative.

'I gather that you have been saying that there is something wrong with our agreed account of what happened at the arena yesterday.'

He paused, expecting Smith to say something. He thought of questioning the 'agreement' but not detecting a question, Smith saw no reason to oblige and contented himself with writing today's date into Blanchard's notebook and beginning to make a shopping list for later. The detective continued with a touch more asperity than before.

'So?'

'So what?'

'Are you?'

'Am I what?'

'Saying that the police are mistaken in what they believe happened to Monsieur DuGresson,' in a tone of voice that was becoming more ragged with each exchange.

'Whatever, I might think, I believe that I'm perfectly at liberty to say what I like about that. I would remind you that I was there, and you were not. Or were you?' Smith added mischievously.

'No, no, of course not,' came the swift reply accompanied by a deprecatory swat of the thin air around his left hand.

'Then why do you wish to talk to me?'

Glancing at the recording equipment and seeing that it was still not working, he continued: 'I gather this interview is not being recorded and therefore you have not arrested me for something and I'm not to be charged with anything?'

'Of course not. I just felt that it would be useful to try to clear up what seems to be a misunderstanding, Monsieur Smith.'

'Nonsense,' said Smith, purposely choosing the least scatological of the replies that came to mind.

The conversation was obviously getting nowhere slowly, and Blanchard leaned towards his subject with a more confidential air.

'I just wanted to talk with you and to say that there is little to be gained by, shall we say, stirring up ideas that will be unhelpful under the circumstances.'

He did, at least, have the grace to look embarrassed and Smith felt a momentary pang of sympathy. He sensed exactly what was Blanchard's dilemma, for here clearly was a man acting under orders and was pretty embarrassed by it. He had brought Smith into the Gendarmerie to tell him to keep quiet about what actually happened at the Arena and to threaten him with dire but un-named consequences if he didn't. Smith, unfortunately, had turned out to be a somewhat more resistant a subject for intimidation than he had anticipated, and he'd prepared no 'plan B.' However, this, Smith felt, was not the time to be accommodating.

'Perhaps, Chief Inspector, in future, if you wish to have a conversation with me, you might not treat me like a common criminal and send a pair of unpleasant-looking flics to drag me from my house and, for instance, invite me to lunch at one of the many decent restaurants in town. You might then find me to be slightly more accommodating company. I assume the police budget can stand that. If it cannot, I'm perfectly happy to offer you're an aperitif in my garden.'

Blanchard was obviously not used to receiving social invitations from suspects.

'Ah yes, Monsieur Smith, perhaps that would be a better way to proceed. Please accept my apologies. I can assure you that I don't regard you as a criminal. I suggest merely that you might be mistaken in your recollection.'

Smith could not help but like the man. He had assumed that his belligerence would have been met with equal firmness. Indeed, he had hoped that it would have been. That way he might have found out something about a situation that was growing increasingly intriguing as time went on. But Blanchard had not risen to the bait and, as a result, had got his warning across without threats and with a measure of decorum. Perhaps, Smith felt, the policeman wasn't just a clothes horse.

'Please let me not detain you any further.'

He stood and opened the door. As he passed the policeman, Smith tore a page from the notebook, and then rather deliberately, the next two bank pages. He had purposely not pressed hard. He handed the notebook and pen back. The two walked to the front entrance of the police station together past the curious gaze of the two gendarmes who had picked him up and were now loitering by the reception desk. The two shook hands and Smith turned to walk home. After a couple of steps, he turned to see that Blanchard hadn't moved.

'Perhaps, when we meet again, Chief Inspector Blanchard, you might like to tell me why, when I telephoned the gendarmerie, this morning, no one here had ever heard of you?'

It was simultaneously a guess and a lie, but he was rewarded with a look of shock of the elegant detective's face.

'Honourable draw,' he felt as he walked back up the Redoute

in the bright morning sunshine. Then the thought: 'asshole,' followed without much delay.

It was mid-morning when he set off towards home, Arthur was pleased to see him. He always was. There are well-established clichés about the faithfulness of dogs dating back more than three thousand years to the Egyptians. In his more cynical moments Smith thought that it was more to do with who fed them and took them for walks than some sort mysterious man and dog bonding. However, he hoped that it was more than that. Arthur's regular greetings when he came home or got up in the morning were a constant pleasure eliciting less than complimentary comparisons with people he had known during his life. With them he seemed to have succeeded in only in disappointing or pissing them off – or so they regularly said. Dogs are different.

'Self-indulgent bollocks,' he thought, without sincerity.

No lift back home was offered so he walked across the Boulevade des Lices, mounted the flight of stone steps up to the Place de la Redoute and was home within five minutes. As he opened the door, he saw a small piece of card lying on the floor. It proved to be one of Madam's elegant business cards with a short message written on the back: 'Please can you call me?'

Now usually, Smith's reaction to receiving a request to contact a beautiful, unattached, intelligent woman would have been akin that of the proverbial rat up a drainpipe. Every bachelor's best fantasy. However, on this occasion, he was annoyed. He was pissed off because this bloody business seemed to be taking over his life. It was only slightly less than 24 hours since he'd been hit on the head and the whole ridiculous thing had completely destroyed what had been a carefully constructed, placid, daily retirement routine. Even meeting one of the most beautiful women he'd ever seen was struggling to make up for that. He took out his mobile.

'Madam, this is Peter Smith.'

'On Monsieur Smith, thank you for calling me.' Her voice sounded warm and genuine.

'Madame, how nice to hear from you again.' he capitulated.

There was a familiar deep chuckle from the other end of the connection.

'Monsieur Smith, you are truly an English gentleman. I suspect that you're quite annoyed with me for asking you to call me. I'm sorry, but I don't seem to have your telephone number.'

Smith let that hang for a moment if, for no other reason, than to attempt a demonstration that he was still free of any great infatuation. She continued: 'I feel that I owe you both an apology and an explanation of what has been going on. I would be delighted if you would have dinner with me tonight.'

Smith's brief resistance evaporated instantly. The prospect of a dinner à deux with Madam DuGresson was entirely too beguiling.

'Madame, I would be honoured.'

'Do you know the restaurant 'Les Dix Anges' in the Roquette?'

'I believe so,' Smith replied, recalling walking Arthur past a small shop front buried in the old Arab quarter of Arles. 'Nine o'clock, then?'

'Until nine, Madame.'

'Now what the hell is that all about?' he mused. He would have loved to think that he had suddenly become irresistible. The discovery of a well-to-do, attractive, unencumbered *compañera* for his retirement on those occasions when he felt the need for companionship, to share visits to the opera, to the theatre or walks with Arthur was a well-established fantasy. None had yet appeared although he did still hope. But this, he felt, was not that. He didn't believe that Madam DuGresson really felt she owed him any explanation and he was intrigued to hear her say that she did. She had received a pretty full account of events from him last evening and she had no reason to assume that Smith had left anything out, as indeed he hadn't. Perhaps she had not yet heard of his second meeting with Blanchard, but he wouldn't bet on it. No, the invitation struck him as intriguing as it was attractive. He certainly felt that whatever he was 'in,' this dinner would almost certainly get him 'in it' further. But, on the other hand, his search for a *compañera* remained firmly anchored to the ground and the most attractive women he had taken to supper since he arrived in Arles eight years ago were his two daughters. Enjoyable evenings each, of course, but hardly…. No, what the hell.

The heat had really got up and Smith and Arthur retired to the terrace with his book, and a very cold bottle of rosé. It was plonk but at a very few degrees above freezing it tasted delicious and was entirely too potable. Within half an hour he had made a considerable dent into its contents and was just beginning to plan lunch. His headache gone, a pleasant and slightly alcoholic lethargy enveloped him and that was perhaps why a modest knock at the door raised neither his concerns nor Arthur from a deep slumber. Having opened the door, he was thus not really prepared for the immediate entry of three large men who forced him back into the sitting room. Normally he would have taken some form of retaliatory action for although both older and outnumbered there were bits of his past that remained sufficiently current for him to have at least a decent chance of dealing with such a situation. The doorway into his house was a narrow one and consisted of a pair of doors less that a metre apart. The chances of thwarting a forced entry were really quite high. However, having seen that one of the three was his unpleasant conversation partner of the previous evening, he was more intrigued than concerned. He was perfectly confident in his ability to extricate himself from the situation if desired. Arthur, finally risen from his prone position of the bakingly hot concrete terrace to greet the three intruders as long-lost friends, added a healthy dose of farce to the whole scene.

Other than the tall thin man, the other two were small, one laughingly so, each dressed in variations of scruffy Camargue dress. Smith decided to defuse what was obviously intended to be a confrontation by offering effusive hospitality. The three just stood there as is if reaching the limits of their rehearsal.

Smith sparkled brightly: 'Gentlemen, please come in. Oh, I see you have already have. I have just begun to open another bottle of rosé. Perhaps you might like to join me on the terrace? Please get a few more glasses from that cupboard over there.'

He pointed at the cupboard beside the door into the garden, took another bottle from the fridge and went into the garden, sat at one of the seats around the garden table and set to work with the corkscrew. With varying degrees of confusion, the three intruders emerged from the house and settled into vacant chairs around the table while Smith poured generous measures.

'Santé,' he proposed as he raised his glass with a cheerfulness that he certainly was not feeling. Actually, he was bloody mad that these people had barged in but he had every intention of finding out more than what was going on before he kicked them out. 'Now, how can I help you, Monsieur...?'

The tall man scowled although the resulting expression was so near his natural expression that Smith felt that he needn't have bothered.

'My name is Mistraux, Monsieur and we have come to ask you about yesterday.'

Smith decided to keep the whole thing conversational.

'I see. May I ask you why I should talk to you at all? Are you policemen?'

The thin Arlesian tried his best to look even more menacing.

'No, we are not. However, it would be as well for you if you talked to us willingly.'

Smith decided not to pursue the obvious question: 'Or what?' but offered a more reasonable question.

'May I ask what business it is of yours?' Monsieur

DuGresson was a friend of ours,' the gaunt man replied.

With some difficulty Smith avoided laughing out loud. The thought of the rather elegantly dressed corpse with which he had recently been so intimate having anything at all to do with these three was risible. But the possibility of getting anything interesting out of the three men under present circumstances was also remote. Smith therefore continued in polite mode and simply retold the story exactly as he had just told it to Blanchard.

'And that's all?' Mistraux asked after he had finished.

'Yup. That's it.'

Insofar as the trio might have actually planned what they intended to do they seemed to run out of inspiration. Smith also realised that he was going to learn very little from them by just chatting. So, having taken control of the meeting, he decided to bring it to an end. He stood up.

'Well gentlemen, if that's all I can help you with, I must ask you to leave. I have some shopping to do.'

With that he got to his feet and went back through the house, held the door open and waited for them to file past him out into the street. It was a measure of their surprise that that was, in fact, precisely what they did. Smith watched them walk across the Place de la Major and disappear down the steps that descended to the Rue Portagnel then stepped out himself and followed.

Following someone without being seen is never particularly difficult. When the person does not expect to be followed and there is a reasonably large number of people around, it is very simple indeed. Smith had learned the craft many years ago and although he had not used it recently, the technique came back easily enough. Having got to the bottom of the steps, the three men went into one of the numerous small bars that were dotted around and took up an animated debate over the first of a series of late lunchtime Pastis. From experience Smith knew that this was going to last at least another hour so, having bought a couple of newspapers, he settled to wait in the rear of an adjoining cafe that gave him the correct view.

It was slightly more than an hour before the trio emerged still in animated conversation and crossed the Boulevard Emile Combes. Still within Smith's view, Mistraux entered one of the tiny terraced houses on the Rue van Ens while the others headed off over the railway bridge in the direction of the suburb of Montplaisir. Smith ordered another *bière pression* and waited for the Pastis to have its inevitable effect.

Another life skill from the past, the ability to get easily through most conventionally locked doors, proved unnecessary as the door to the shuttered number 14 Rue van Ens was unlocked. The snoring could be heard from outside. The little house was dark and cool, and it took less than half a minute for Smith to confirm that it was also empty. As he passed silently through the house, he thought how easily it all came back to him. He picked up a dirty dish cloth from the kitchen and returned to the front room where Mistraux was noisily asleep in an armchair.

Just as following people is not difficult, getting answers from them isn't either. A very few have been trained to withstand interrogation of any sort. It is not usually a subject in most people's education. The secret when dealing with amateurs is not to be clever or subtle but to be very violent. With one fluent movement Smith pulled the man from his chair, threw him face down on the carpet and knelt with one knee in the middle of his back while putting his other heel none to gently on the back of the man's outstretched hand. He took a good hold of the man's hair and pulled his head back. He bent near the astonished man's ear.

'Right, you fucking piece of shit, you are about to give me some answers. You will whisper. If you try to shout, I'll break your hand. Do you understand?'

Mistraux's attempt at shouting for help was cut short by Smith tying the dish cloth around his mouth and putting much more weight on the man's hand. The sound of cracking bones was surprisingly loud, seeming almost to fill small room. Smith waited for the convulsions below him to lessen then pulled the man's head back hard again. He could feel the sweat rising from the man's scalp.

'Now let's try again. I'll untie the gag and you will answer my questions in a normal whisper - or as normal a whisper as you can. If you don't, I'll find another piece of you to break. Now, do you understand?'

The man's eyes were bulging with pain as he nodded. Smith kept the pressure on the hand and loosened the tea towel slightly.

'Good. At least we begin to understand each other. Now who are you working for?'

'Nobody,' came the horse whisper.

Smith said nothing but slightly increased the weight on his right foot. When it came the answer was barely audible.

'Les Frères.'

'And who are Les Frères when they are at home.'

Once someone has started to talk under interrogation and an initial resistance is broken it is usual for them to continue and Mistraux was no exception.

'We are a brotherhood of Camargue farmers.'

Smith also knew that there was very little point is expecting too much information to come from someone like this.

'Why are you so interested in DuGresson's death? What was he to you? He was no farmer. Neither for that matter, are you?'

Smith kept the pressure on the hand.

'We did some business together.'

Smith took the precaution of re-applying the gag as the sound of a few more cracking bones could be heard over the sounds of whimpering. The man was dangerously close to permanently losing the use of his hand. Smith was also getting a little uncomfortable. Although the last time he had done this sort of thing was not too many years ago he was certainly a good deal fitter then. He reached across to the nearby fireplace and took a grip of a heavy iron poker. He bent close again and brought the poker into the man's view and tapped him none too gently on the side of the head.

'Now listen. I'm going to allow you get up and sit in the chair. You will not make attempt to get up or to make any noise other than to answer my questions. If you do, I'll do very much more damage to you that what has already happened. Do you understand?'

The sweating man nodded, and Smith got up and stood back. Insofar as the man ever had any fight in him it had clearly left him, driven out by the pain of his right hand. He settled awkwardly into the chair and looked fearfully at Smith holding his right wrist in his left hand. Smith drew up a straight dining chair close in front of his companion and looked him straight in the eye letting the tip of the iron poker rest gently on the man's knee.

'Now. I think by now you have learned, perhaps, that I'm not the sort of person who takes kindly to interference in his life by scum like you. Threatening me was a very big mistake. How big a mistake you might discover unless you tell me absolutely everything you know about Monsieur DuGresson and what all this has to do with your little society Les Frères. If I'm not completely sure that you are telling me the truth, I'll completely destroy both your knees and you will spend the rest of your life in a wheelchair.'

To emphasise the point, he tapped the man's knee with the poker. The sweating victim jumped convulsively and started to answer Smith's quick-fire questions each punctuated by a further tap.

'I was asked to find out what you know about Monsieur DuGresson.'

'Who by?'

'My fellow members of the society,'

'Which one?'

The man hesitated only to receive another reminder on his knee as Smith said:
'You or him. Your choice.'

'By Claude Chadriol,'

'Why is Monsieur Chariol interested.'

'He is our contact with the men from Marseilles.'

'Who?'

'The men from Marseilles who pay us.'

'Pay you? What for.'

The man shrugged helplessly.

'For, er, um, services. From time to time.'

'Give me a name.' Smith let the poker fall a little more heavily.

'Monsieur, for the love of God, I cannot. They would kill me.'

'So will I, my friend, believe me and with me it will happen a lot sooner. A name.'

The poker tapped again, this time a good deal harder. The voice was barely audible.

'Giacomo Seffradi.'

'And who the hell is Giacomo Seffradi.'

Mistraux's voice remained at a whisper. 'He is head of a crime syndicate in Marseilles.'

Suddenly a few things began to slot into place in Smith's mind. He had obviously stepped into a piece of local crime shit - or rather fallen into it. There was also little more to be gained from prolonging the conversation. The man probably knew nothing more. He was clearly just a low-level grunt. He needed much more information but at least he now knew where to look. Gentry would do the rest for him. Time, the thought, to conclude the interview. Again, he drew closer to the man in the chair.

'Now listen to me very carefully. Very carefully indeed. I don't care what story you invent to explain your broken hand to others but if you ever tell anyone about this little conversation, I'll make sure that your Signor Seffradi knows you gave me his name. I have no idea what he will do to you, but I'm sure that it will not be pleasant. If I ever see you again or find that I have any strange visitors, either from your Frères or from Mr Seffradi, I or one of my friends, will come and damage you, probably terminally. You now remain alive only as far as I want you to. Is all this understood?'

The man nodded. He was still nodding after Smith left the room, let himself out of the house and went towards home. The whole episode left Smith feeling remarkably unmoved. He did find it slightly depressing how easy it was to slide back into old ways when it was necessary. However, it was almost time to prepare for an altogether more pleasant few hours in the company of the mysterious but beautiful Madam Aubanet. First, though, a call to Gentry.

'Yes?' Gentry's mobile was answered before its second ring.

'Gentry, I need a little information please.'

'Oh yes,' came the reply from a voice knowing from experience that things had progressed since their last conversation the previous night and his old friend was making some waves.

'I received a visit a couple of hours ago from that man I told you about in the bar last night. Mistraux is his name, by the way. He and two colleagues decided to visit and interrogate me.'

'Oh God. What sort of shape did you leave him in?' Gentry knew Smith from the past. His old friend, he knew, didn't take kindly to being threatened.

'Slightly damaged but nothing that time can't heal. Actually, I didn't learn very much but I wouldn't mind finding out a little about a sort of secret Camargue society called Les Frères and a Marseilles crime boss called Seffradi.'

The two had worked together many times in the past and Gentry knew better that to ask for an explanation.

'OK. I have heard of Seffradi a little. I seem to think he is fairly middle rank in the criminal hierarchy, but I'll find out more. When do you want the information? Before you see the beautiful widow or after?'

Smith also knew better than to ask. Gentry, as usual, just knew.

'Late tonight would be fine thanks.'

He rang off.

Six o'clock dog feeding led, after an hour's sleep – Arthur's, not his - to dog walking. Then, what to wear was the problem; beige slacks, blue Crew shirt and a light summer jacket? Too hot to wear the jacket but it could always be carried over a shoulder. He didn't think that dining with Madam DuGresson was something one did in shirt sleeves. Somewhere in the bottom of his clothes cupboard, he too had a pair of dark brown Gucci loafers. Yes, he too once had had a small tasselled past. He dug them out to find them covered in dust. 'Christ,' he thought, 'where on earth is the shoe cleaning stuff?'

By the time he'd showered and changed it was 8:30pm. He left Arthur contentedly on the sofa watching television and he set off for a leisurely walk to the restaurant no more than ten minutes away.

It was still light and warm, so he decided on a leisurely route down to the Roquette along the river. The low sun lit the southerly riverbank and bathed the sluggish river and the buildings that bordered it in a golden glow. He never tired of looking at this view. Indeed, it was a regular walk with Arthur. The Musée Réattu, the Great Priory of the Knights Hospitaller, looked stunning, its façade reflecting the late evening sun in a gaunt sort of way. In spite of the fact he was dawdling he was still going to be early, so he stopped and sat on the riverside wall that ran along the walkway set about ten feet above the narrow street. He looked back to his left to see the usual straggle of dog walkers and tourists wandering along. Some like him, were sitting on the long wall taking in the scene. One, a man in jeans and white tee shirt, looked slightly out of place. 'God, Smith, you are getting paranoid.' He suddenly had an image of himself, respectably dressed, sitting on the wall, looking equally out of place.

He got up and, still with a little time still in hand, decided to wander up through the town rather continue on the shorter route along the riverbank. He cut up past the Hotel Arlatan, through the Place du Forum, filled, as usual, with people at table eating one of those utterly unmemorable and expensive meals for which France has become regrettably famous over the last ten or fifteen years. At that time of the evening there were still a good number of tourists wandering aimlessly in search of an evening meal or window shopping along the Rue de la République, although the best shops including that of Arles' famous son Christian Lacroix were all thoroughly shuttered and bolted. He stopped at Optic 2000 to see if there was any indication in a window full of designer glasses frames of exactly what a much-needed eye test and new glasses would cost. There was not. Glancing back, he noted that Tee Shirt was about fifty yards behind. He walked on and after another minute checked again. Still there. Normally, he thought, he should be slightly worried by this. It was not usual for him to be followed. In fact, he could not remember it happening before in Arles. But these, he reminded himself, were not usual times and he surprised himself by being rather blasé about it.

By now he had reached the Rue Gambetta, the street that connects the main Boulevard Clemenceau to the old road bridge to

Tranquetaille; the road that also separates the Roquette from the rest of Arles. Smith knew the Roquette well from hours of wandering over the last fifty years. It is an area of tiny streets, passageways, arches, cuts through and blind alleys. Two- and three-story narrow houses some built so close together that the sun hardly ever penetrated to street level, helping them remain relatively cool even in the height of summer. Originally it was the part of Arles that serviced the extensive boat building and fitting business that had lined the Rhone from Roman times onwards. Now it was populated by a great mixture of people, houses gradually being refurbished by the locals, the town whose policy of pre-empting sales to others and refurbishing houses to rent to locals ensured that the cultural mix in the Roquette remained unchanged and some by foreigners looking for holiday homes.

It didn't take long to lose Mr Tee shirt. A couple of quick back doubles and he was pretty sure that he arrived at the restaurant promptly and unobserved. Feeling pleased with himself, he went in. It was small, dimly lit, containing no more than a dozen tables with a few booths down the right-hand side. The décor was French bistro non-descript and the waiter who came up to him was both badly dressed and similarly mannered.

'Yes?'

'Madam DuGresson?'

The transformation was instant.

'Ah yes, Er, of course, Er, please come this way.'

He led Smith to the back of the room, where his host was standing talking to the chef.

Not that she had any real distance to go but Madam DuGresson had, as they say, scrubbed up nicely – very nicely indeed. She immediately saw him and took a few steps towards him. He purposely stopped a little early to take a good look. She was dressed in a steel grey silk shirt, open enough to show a significant décolletage, a black knee-length, slightly flared, pleated skirt, cinched together with a belt to emphasize an extraordinarily narrow waist. Bare brown legs and high - heeled strappy sandals completed the picture. Her welcoming smile was genuine and devastating. 'My God,' he thought as he extended his hand. On an impulse he bowed his head slightly, took her proffered hand and raised it to towards his lips, stopping just short, of course, of actual contact.

'Monsieur Smith,' she exclaimed quietly, 'and they say that the English are not romantic.'

'Perhaps, Madame, that's because they seldom seem to have cause to be.'

He was rewarded with the slightest hint of a flush on the face of his host. 'Let's sit,' she said and turned back to lead him to the rearmost booth at the back of the restaurant. The reverse aspect was equally satisfying. The tiny waist, shapely brown calves and heels high enough to be sexy yet low enough to remain tasteful.

Reaching the booth, she slid effortlessly into the seat with its back to the restaurant entrance. He took the opposite side. She wore a little jewellery. A couple of thin silver bangles on one wrist, the Cartier Tank on the other. A single strand of pearls around her neck with matching stud earrings. No rings on either hand, he noticed. The only extravagance was a very small diamond brooch near her left shoulder. Only an inch or so high, it was in the form of the trident, heart and anchor Croix des Saintes a symbol of the Arletate. All very restrained and very expensive. She had quickly regained her composure. In fact, he doubted she had actually lost it, however temporarily.

'I suggest that we allow them to choose what we eat. The cooking here will be much better that you might imagine. The chef is my cousin.' The two statements were obviously connected.

Two glasses of champagne were already on the table, poured by the now perfectly mannered waiter. The wine, however, was not champagne.

'It is a Crémant from Limoux just south of Carcasson. Do

you think that we can make an acceptable sparkling wine here, Monsieur Smith?'

'This is better than almost every Champagne I can remember tasting, Madame.'

'Yes, there is a lot of prejudice in favour of Reims.'

'Perhaps that's because Pierre Perignon was as much a marketeer as a monk and turned a region into a brand.'

'Ah, you know your wine, Monsieur Smith.'

'A little of its history, only, Madam DuGresson.'

Her tone suddenly became business-like.

'Monsieur Smith. Firstly, I believe you are owed both an apology and an explanation. You have been involved in a matter that's none of your business through absolutely no fault of your own. You have been attacked and have seen no attempt on the part of the authorities to find and punish your attacker. You have been injured and have received no compensation. We too have received similar treatment from the police who have failed to give us an adequate explanation of the death of my husband. We believe that my husband was murdered by the same people who attacked you.'

Smith replied, if only to get into the conversation. 'Before we start, Madame, I think I should tell you that I believe that I was followed here. I have no idea who he was, and I think I lost him.'

'Do mean that man?' she said smiling, turning around and indicate the tee shirted young man now seated at the small bar at the front of the restaurant.

'Please don't concern yourself for that is another cousin. His job was to make sure you got here safely and that no one was following you. He will be embarrassed that you were able to lose him so easily. You seem to know more of the Roquette than he does.'

Returning to the subject of their conversation, he continued 'Surely you can find some clue as to what happened from your husband's body, Madame?'

Madame DuGresson smiled bleakly, reached for her handbag, withdrew a letter from it and passed it over to him without comment. It was a letter from the Arles coroner's office, informing her that there had been an administrative error. The body of her late husband had apparently been wrongly identified in the morgue and had been cremated late on the day of his death. The ashes had been retrieved, however, and were available for her to collect at her convenience. The letter concluded with formal apologies but little more.

'Pah!' he said, with some contempt. The contents of the letter were at the same time unsurprising and shocking. They did, however, confirm, if confirmation were needed, that there was a conspiracy of sorts at work.

The waiter brought a first course. A plate of white asparagus with a light sauce. The unmistakable smell of a vinaigrette made from balsamic vinegar and truffles rose. A glass of chilled white wine appeared as if from nowhere.

'The truffles are from Carpentras and the wine from the Côte,'

Madam's expression became serious. 'Monsieur Smith, I'll try to explain to you what, I believe, has happened and then I wish to ask you for your assistance in finding out whether or not we are right. There are reasons why I believe that you are able to make enquiries that we cannot. I can assure you that your help wouldn't go unrewarded.'

He tasted the asparagus. It was delicious. He was certainly looking for a small amount of work that might top up his meagre pension. He had begun to put a gentle word around in the bar a week or two before, although, it should be admitted, that this was not the kind of thing he had had in mind. A number of questions arose immediately in Smith's mind, but he sensed this was not the time. He contented himself with smiling his thanks to the waiter who melted again into the background. He looked across at his companion who was looking intently back at him. He noticed for the first time that the high seat back of the booth was higher than her head, thus making her completely invisible to the rest of the room and the street outside. She has chosen her position with care. He settled back to listen.

'My maiden name was Martine Aubanet and I'm a member of a family that has worked as *gardians* and *manardiers* in the Camargue for nearly six hundred years. My family not only raises bulls but also has interests in a number of businesses throughout the region. We are vignerons, we grow corn and vegetables and rice. Amongst other interests we also have an import-export business and we own residential accommodation and hotels here in Arles, in Stes Maries de la Mer, Nîmes and Avignon. The business turns over in excess of forty million Euros a year. My father, Emile, is chairman of the group. I'm his only child and the Managing Director. Together, we own the business between us. There are no other shareholders. I tell you this, Monsieur Smith, not to impress you but to explain that the murder of my husband, for that's certainly what it was, is not an insignificant matter for our business. Robert was our Financial Director.'

Half of his mind listened to her. The other half watched; as he listened, he looked. Like most people in Arles he had heard of the tradition of La belle Arlesienne; that the women of Arles are somewhat more beautiful that average. But, having arrived there, he had soon realised that, as is often the case, a traditional costume often adds an enchantment that's sometimes less than permanent. However, the woman who sat opposite him was indeed a beauty. High cheek bones, flawless pale tan skin, dark eyes, black hair piled onto the top of her head with casual brevity in a dressed - down but still elegant version of the full Provençale style.

Smith thought he should say something, if only to allow her to finish her entrée.

'I'm nevertheless impressed, Madame. I had no idea that

there were any businesses of that size in this area. However, I suppose a family that has been here for half a millennium would have had time to grow.'

'You could say that. I met Robert when we were studying at the École nationale d'administration in Paris. I read law; he finance.'

The entrée was replaced by two plates each carrying two small filets of red mullet and their glasses were replenished. Smith bent and smelled and olive and marjoram cream sauce. The arrangement was balanced by a few slices of tomato.

'I hope you don't mind but I asked for both fish and meat. I much prefer two small main courses to one large one.'

'I'm in your hands Madame.' Fact and fantasy, he thought.

She continued, not without a slight smile: 'Robert turned out to be an excellent financial director but a dreadful husband. We were married for twelve years and have lived separately for the last eleven. We are, or rather were, both catholic,' she added anticipating his unspoken question. 'During his work, Robert not only, of course, came to know every aspect of our business but much about our competitors as well. This is normal and we have never had cause to question Robert's loyalty or honesty. We had a good working relationship over a long time. Robert was well paid – very well paid.'

Smith intervened: 'But not with a share of the business.'

She shook her head.

'No, my father would never allow that.'

'So if he got on with you and your family, did his job well and you didn't seem to think that he was doing anything dishonest, it is a little difficult why anyone would want to kill him – at least from his professional life.'

'Quite.'

'Have you any reason why the police are so interested in making the death seem to be a suicide.'

'Robert was a prominent member of the local business community in Arles. He was also from good family in Lille. I gather that his family are satisfied with the story. Everyone seems to want a quiet and simple result to the enquiry. However, I've a feeling that we are not actually dealing with the police. You have met Chief Inspector Blanchard. So have I and he doesn't strike me as a typical policeman. More a politician. You seem to have struck up something of a relationship with him, I gather.'

Smith let that one pass. 'What do you know of your late husband's private life, Madame?'

'A good deal, I think. He lived in Arles and led a very social life with numerous friends. He was a prominent member of many groups, the Friends of the Theatre and so on, and was active in the Patrimony of the town, co-ordinating the distribution of much of the funding of the preservation on behalf of the town council, the government and the European Community.'

'Did he have a girlfriend?'

Madame looked levelly across the table. 'I don't believe so, nor, to anticipate your next question, do believe he was gay. How was your fish?'

'Quite delicious, thank you.'

A glance over to the waiter standing just out of earshot saw the plates cleared.

'Madame. I can see how this must all be something of a mystery to you. I'm also a little annoyed that I was hit on the head, presumably by the same people who killed your husband. However, personally I'm not terribly interested in who did what to whom and why, even when the whom is me. And, although I cannot remember enjoying an evening as much as this for many months, I'm unable to see how I can help you. If you wish to pay for a private investigation, then presumably there are people who do that sort of thing. A family such as yours would have no difficulty in finding one.'

'You are right, of course. We could employ the best investigators in France but depending on what the answer is, we might have more to lose than you might imagine by doing so. I'll try to explain.'

She took a sip of her wine and continued: 'We are an old family, much respected and, I believe, loved in the Camargue. We are proud of our traditions and of many generations of work and service in the Arelate. My father is still involved in the business but truly his great passion is now his bulls and we raise some of the very best. I sometimes think that my father loves his bulls more than he loves me.'

'Madam. I'm the father of daughters, as well, and you are bound to be completely wrong.'

Perhaps it was the clear recollection of a lifetime of a loving relationship between father and daughter based on the daughter manipulating her father and the father loving it, but her face was suffused by a look of tenderness that made him feel momentarily nostalgic, and irrationally, jealous. She continued:

'Yes, perhaps you are right. I hope so. However, for us to be seen to investigate would mean that we would investigate our friends. Neither my father nor I would like that. Arles is a small place as I think you realise and for it to be known that we are asking questions that could mean that we are suspicious of people whose families we have known for generations, would hurt many people; people who are our friends. We even have good relationships with our competitors that, while not making business easier, certainly makes it more civilised. The only other independent third party who could investigate would be the police but, for reasons that are not yet clear, they either don't wish to get involved or they are party, in some way, to the conspiracy. Robert was a valuable employee, but we have not an emotional bond nor sufficient of a vested interested in him that would cause us seriously to jeopardize all this. In any case, my father wouldn't allow it.'

The meat arrived, again in a small portion, exquisitely presented. Beef, of course. A few noisettes of fillet, browned lightly on the outside and almost raw inside. The sauce was a simple Provençale tomato and tarragon one, unstrained so that it still contained fragments of the herbs and the shallots. A few lightly fried potatoes were perched on the side of the plate. Two glasses of red appeared. Smith bent over the glass and savoured a scent that he had never experienced before. It was as subtle as the best Bordeaux he knew but completely different. It was obviously a Rhone wine but not like those he had learned to like since coming here. Given that the whole meal had been a celebration of local produce and cuisine, he assumed that it must be from the Costière de Nîmes but again he had never smelt anything like it. He pushed his nose closer to the liquid to try to find further clues and failed. Raising his head slightly he gave it a twirl. The deep raspberry red liquid clung to the sides as if reluctant to let gravity take over too quickly.

He set the glass on the table completely experienced but untasted. Occasionally he had come across a wine like this where actually drinking it is unnecessary but not very often. It was unlike anything he had ever drunk. Looking across the table, he could see that she was amused. She was also not interested in letting him off the hook too quickly.

'Well?'

'I admit defeat, Madame. From time to time in my life, I have had the chance to taste a wine such as this, but not very often and never in Provence. I'm glad that I'm not an expert, otherwise I would be embarrassed.'

'It comes from our vineyard to the west of St Gilles. The vigneron is my father. Every year he makes about thousand bottles for the family. This was made in 1952.'

'The year I was born,' Smith mused.

'Yes, I know. We believe that these are the true wines of France, Monsieur. The vines in the Camargue were some of the few in France to escape the attack of Phylloxera in the nineteenth century. Unlike most of the rest of France whose vineyards were replaced with foreign rootstocks, these are the original. We say that both our vines and our society remain alive because we have our feet in the salt water of the Camargue.'

Smith smiled at the thought and went on.

'So why do you think that I can help? I'm a relative newcomer to Arles. I know very few people here and certainly none who move in the circles you describe. I'm also not an investigator of any kind.'

'Most importantly I believe you could do it precisely because you are, first of all, unknown and are not connected with my late husband. Moreover, you were injured and found at the place my husband was killed. It would be perfectly natural for you to ask questions. Thirdly, it may be that this is a business-related matter. You are an experienced businessman. I gather that one of the ideas you discussed with Daniel Hugnet at the bar a few weeks ago was to offer advice to local businesses on doing business with English-speaking countries. This would give you an immediate reason for contacting the business community. Lastly, if you don't mind my being direct, you would receive excellent payment from us for your time.'

He had given up being curious about the things she seemed to know about him. However, becoming some sort of investigator for her seemed an unlikely prospect. She had obviously stopped talking and he could not think of anything to say. A comfortable silence drifted across the table as he finished his beef. Taking some bread, he collected the last of the sauce. It must have been the meat juice that gave the such an extraordinary flavour. He took the last mouthful of wine and wiped his mouth on his napkin and settled back in his seat. Time to take a little control, he thought.

'Madame. From time to time, I have spent acted as an interim manager in business being paid to find solutions, often unorthodox ones, to people's problems. Often, I found that the people who hired me, usually bosses, were prepared to accept much more radical suggestions from me that they were from their full-time staff. Possibly the fact they were paying me more money than they wanted to made even outrageously risky strategies acceptable. One strategy, often the best one, was, however, never acceptable. Do nothing. No one paying a consultant's fees wanted to be told leave well alone. On this occasion, I apologise, but I intend to do nothing for the moment at least. I'll not give you an answer to your proposition now. If I may I would like to sleep on it.'

He looked across and saw, if not actually a pout, then a look of slight impatience. This was a lady who was obviously used to setting both agendas and timetables. But perhaps because she felt that Smith was of very slightly sterner stuff her manner quickly became accommodating.

'Of course, there are many things to consider,' she smiled. Their plates had been removed in the meantime 'I have not asked for cheese. Cheese is not something that Provence does very well.'

It was a statement of fact rather than an opinion, one that Smith tended to agree with. However, he felt that he had done quite enough agreeing with Madam DuGresson this evening, so again he said nothing.

'I did think, however,' she continued gracefully, 'that you might enjoy this.'

The waiter again placed two small plates on the table. On each were three small sized apricot halves each filled with a pale beige paste from which came the unmistakable smell of almonds. A little apricot syrup surrounded the fruit. Almond paste was one of his greatest passions. She nodded approval at the chef hovering nervously in the background.

'Great chefs who should know better usually drown this dish with kirsch or some such. It is a pity. There is absolutely no need to add anything to beat the Provençale almond. It needs no support other than the fruit.'

Again, a fact, not an opinion and one with which he could not disagree. It tasted delicious. A perfect amuse bouche to end such a meal. The final surprise was a tiny glass of a sweet white. Smith, not wanting to spoil the air of fresh almond paste in his nostrils, went straight to tasting it. In this evening of culinary delights, this was yet another, and possibly the best. He was not greatly enamoured of sweet wines. Those he could afford were too suffused with Muscat to be memorable. Their sweetness hit him as soon as they entered his mouth. He had discovered a good and reasonably priced Monbazillac once while travelling with his ex-wife in the Dordogne that stood in his memory but that was only because the others were so unmemorable. Only twice in his life had he tasted Chateau Yquem and the memory remained vivid. He remembered that it was like a silk scarf gliding down his throat. The sweetness – and that was entirely the wrong word to describe it - seemed to come after he had swallowed it. And continued to come. His glass was the same. It was a taste unlike anything else. He found himself closing his eyes to exclude anything that was not the wine. Saying nothing this time was not an option. He could think of nothing to say. He opened his eyes to be greeted by his companion returning a look of genuine pleasure and a slight nod of the head.

'My father will be complimented,' she said before changing the subject.

'We have spent this whole evening talking about my troubles, Monsieur. That could be thought of as rather rude, but under the circumstances I hope you understand. But I would like to hear a little about you and why you have decided to come to Arles to live.'

'Of course, Madame,' Smith was under no illusions about the motives for this meeting. 'However, if there is nothing more that this extraordinary restaurant can offer. Coffee would be an insult. Might I suggest a short digestive stroll along the Rhône. Then perhaps I can tell you a little of the very boring story.'

It crossed his mind that he had no idea of where she lived or if she had a car nearby. But he wanted to move things onto slightly more neutral territory. A genuinely open smile lit up her face.

'What a wonderful idea,' she said without a hint of artificiality, 'I'm embarrassed to say that it has been years since I did that. I would love to. Come let's go.'

With that, she got up immediately causing a certain confusion amongst the restaurant staff who began to rush around in an uncoordinated and very French sort of way. Smith also had not really expected his suggestion to be taken up quite so enthusiastically. The waiter hastily produced Madam's jacket and found with some annoyance that Smith took it from him and offered it up to his hostess. She turned gracefully, keeping her arms to her sides and Smith, taking the hint, gently dropped the cashmere blazer over her shoulders.

Smiling her thanks to the waiter, she almost strode down the restaurant and out of the door. Smith missed the opportunity to thank the chef for one for one of the most memorable meals of his life. He managed to catch up with her outside. Again, reading his mind, she said: 'I'll thank Philip later, don't worry.'

Without delay they walked briskly down the narrow street that led from the restaurant to the riverside. The high heels that would normally have presented most women of Smith's acquaintance with innumerable excuses for not walking five yards seemed to present no impediment to his companion and Smith had to exert himself slightly to keep up. Within a minute or so they reached the river. The Rhône looked stunning. They were looking from the opposite direction to that from which van Gogh painted his famous Starry Night over the Rhone, and the scene was almost the mirror image. Looking up the river to the great right angle bend whose narrowing of the river was the main reason for the Romans to settle here, the lights spaced regularly along the bank and the boat quay ahead shimmered on the slack black water. The main difference was that the reflections were electrically white as opposed to the yellow gas of van Gogh's day. But there also were stars in the sky – not the Plough as in the painting - but equally bright. The medieval town to the right was suffused in a pale orange glow from the floodlit monuments. The river and its south bank were almost deserted.

Madam's pace slowed when they reached the river wall and they turned east away from the motorway bridge.

'Now tell me a little about why you are here.' She slipped a hand through his arm in that distinctive gesture of companionship that continental Europeans find so natural and easy and the British so embarrassing.

'Well, quite simply, I have always loved Arles and when my wife decided that it would be better for me to spend the rest of my life without her, it seems the obvious place to come.' Again, that chuckle. 'I first came here more than sixty years ago with my father when I was a child, certainly before you were born.'

This purposely gently provocative comment was greeted only with a slight harrumph and the slightest squeeze of the arm to acknowledge the unspoken compliment but nothing more.

He continued: 'I started to come regularly from my teens and have been coming back almost every year since. I used to hitchhike here almost every year with no money. I got odd jobs, working in petrol stations, washing up in cafes, sleeping sometimes under the trees in the Jardin d'Été. One owner of a petrol station just at this end of the route d'Avignon let me sleep in the storeroom above his workshop. I spent the time just wandering around the town looking at things. After a while, when I stopped being a student, I could afford to take a bed and breakfast or later even a hotel. Even much later when I was travelling around the world teaching or on business, I always wanted to come back here. My divorce provided me with just enough money to buy a little house here and God gave me a slight heart attack that made me retire. That, Madame, in a nutshell, is why I'm here.'

Their stroll had reached the Tranquetaille Bridge, the site of yet another famous van Gogh painting whose heritage so burdens the city. She withdrew her arm as they descended the few narrow steps that would enable them to go under the bridge, as opposed to ascending more steps that would have taken them over the top. Glancing behind him he noticed that there was the dark outline of a Range Rover matching their pace lit only by sidelights.

'I have a feeling we are being followed, Madame.'

'Yes, that's my cousin. Please don't lose him again. He will die of embarrassment,'

'Ah.'

Having regained the walkway on the other side, he was pleased to feel the arm again in his.

'But why Arles? What is about this town that has brought you back throughout your life so often?'

'People often ask me, and I should prepare a stock answer. But the truth it is a mixture of things. I love the art and the archaeology. The Roman and Romanesque monuments here are magnificent, of course. I look every day out of my windows on the Arena and it has never ceases to give me pleasure. Arles has an extraordinary mixture of cultures, Provençale, French, Arab, Spanish, Gipsy, Camarguaise. I love the bullfights, as did my father. But it is also a working town and often a poor one at that. It has a hard and brutal side. There are rich families and very poor ones too. There are slums as well and great houses. There are slum dwellers as well as owners of great hotels partculières. There are businesses, small industries and much unemployment. The town is surrounded by great *manades* and small farms for whom the twice weekly market is not just a famous tourist attraction to be photographed and fawned over but an essential source of a basic income. The climate is almost perfect, like the town, cold and hard in winter, hot and passionate in summer. Moderate in spring and autumn. The food is satisfying and, as tonight has amply demonstrated, occasionally spectacular. It is a real town not a postcard. The hospital also has a good cardiac unit.'

Possibly carried away slightly with his own enthusiasm in a moment of unguarded honesty he added: 'It is also the only place I know where I have never been unhappy.' The remark was acknowledged by a gentle squeeze on his arm.

They walked on for a few moments in silence, savouring the

night and the company. They had walked past the point where the river turns its corner and had drawn level with the boat dock. Two huge German river tourist boats were tied up and as he looked down Smith saw that they were clearing up the tables in the floating restaurants. These monstrosities regularly brought hundreds of tourists to visit the river towns. The passengers spend the day walking around the town, but returned to their floating gin palaces to eat, drink and sleep.

'I often think,' he said, 'that if all the people who use these awful things actually took their meals in the town and drank in the town cafes, turnover would be doubled. Perhaps they don't feel the need to return something to the town they plunder with their digital cameras.'

'Ah, Monsieur Smith, you are thinking like an Arlesian,'

'I'm not sure, Madame, that you could have said anything nicer to me.'

She laughed. The Place Lamartine loomed. Their walk along the river back had nowhere else to go. Further up was the permanent gipsy encampment and then the industrial sector started.

She turned to him and said, inappropriately, under the circumstances: 'Monsieur, I would like to thank you for a most enjoyable evening.'

'It is I who must thank you Madame. I have had one of the best meals I have ever had, and I thank you for that.'

'One of the best?'

'Perhaps one day I can tell you of a certain old lady here in Arles who, again before you were born, used to have a restaurant on the Rue de la Porte de Laure forty five years ago, who used to feed me when I was fifteen. The food was also not the cuisine we have eaten tonight but as a boy without money it certainly tasted as good.'

'I hope you will.' She smiled.

She continued: 'I'm glad you have enjoyed our meal together. Everything we ate, of course, came from our farms and my father and I are very proud of what we do. I hope that you can decide to help us. It's important that we find out why Robert was killed and whether our family or its businesses are in any way threatened. I believe that you can help up and I hope that you decide that you can. If you agree, then I would propose that you should come to meet my father, possibly for lunch? Our home is near Le Sambuc. Perhaps you could telephone me?'

'Madame, I'll certainly think about your suggestion. I'll telephone you tomorrow with my decision. In the meantime, thank you again for this evening. An evening eating superbly in the company of a beautiful woman is as close to a perfect experience as I can imagine.'

She might have had the grace to blush but in the darkness, it was hard to be sure. The Range Rover appeared at the kerbside and he took her across to it and opened the door. Her parting handshake was firm and business-like. He watched as the car went around the roundabout and went out of sight up the Boulevard Emil Combes. Thoughtfully he set course for the short walk home.

It was nearly eleven by the time he got home and suddenly he felt tired. He took Arthur on one of the shortest of his repertoire of walks. It still included the Place de la Redoute, the highest point in Arles where the old greyhound had to content with just staring balefully at the numerous cats that sat on the cooling car bonnets that were parked there. Smith thought as he walked. It was the episode with Mistraux that interested him most. Although the man was harmless enough, his friends might not be. He had no doubt that his treatment of the man would somehow get back to his bosses and he might well find himself involved whether he wished to or not. The protection and influence of the Aubanet family might come in useful.

Additionally, as Madam had so elegantly hinted, he could do

with a little money. Retiring early had left him solvent but only just. The divorce settlement was enough to buy the house and fit it out but little more than that. At the moment he was living a slight monthly deficit and although that was not an imminent problem, it could be in a year or two.

The answer, no, started to loom, primarily because he could not really think of a good reason to say yes. Then it came to him. How easily had a few months in the tranquillity of retirement blunted his ability to smell a business opportunity when one swam into view. This whole business could easily be business related although, on the balance of probabilities, it wasn't. He somehow couldn't imagine Madam being in any sort of league with scum from Marseilles. However, he had spent part of his public life analysing – investigating, if you like – businesses, how they worked and what they needed. He really had been quite good at it. If there was a business reason why Robert DuGresson had to be killed then he could find it, although finding who did it might be beyond him. It might also be undesirable. He had no great confidence that he could find any other reasons, but it was a start. What he could do was treat Madam DuGresson and her businesses like any other potential client.

By the time they got home, he had made up his mind. He looked at his watch and calculated that if Madam had got home in the time since she left him, then she had little opportunity to do much more. He looked for Madam DuGresson's business card.

'Madame, good evening. This is Peter Smith. I hope it is not too late to call.'

'Of course, not, Monsieur. I have just got home and I'm having a nightcap with my father.'

'Ah,' Smith thought, 'A debrief.' He continued out loud:

'Firstly, I would like to thank you for such an enjoyable evening. The food was excellent, and I much enjoyed your company.'

'And I yours, Monsieur.'

'Madam, I think that I might have found a way to accept your proposal. However rather than just say yes, I would like, in turn, to make a proposal to you. Although I don't wish to impose again on your hospitality, I would like to make my proposal to you and to your father in person.'

The silence was not long enough to be embarrassing but certainly he knew it was not quite the answer she had been expecting. Not for the first time, Smith sensed that this was a lady who was not particularly used to things failing to go in the way she wished.

'Of course. That would be perfectly acceptable. Earlier I suggested that you came to meet my father tomorrow for lunch. You could make your proposition to us both then. Would that be convenient?'

It may have been his imagination, but he thought he detected a hint of steel behind the courtesies. Perhaps having made his point and slight acquiescence would be in order.

'On course, Madame. It would be something that I would look forward to, irrespective of the reason for coming.'

The small game was obviously completely transparent to them both and she acknowledged the fact with that chuckle.

'I look forward to seeing if your chivalry survives if we ever disagree about something important, Monsieur Smith.'

'Madam,' he replied with exaggerated formality, 'In the unlikely event of that happening, I shall endeavour to ensure that it does.'

'I'll send Jean-Marie to pick you up at 11:30am.'

Ah, so that's what Tee Shirt is called. She continued:

'I wouldn't want your enjoyment of lunch to be spoiled by having to drive back to town. Also, please bring Arthur. I'm sure that he would enjoy a day in the country.'

'That's extremely kind of you, Madame. I accept on his behalf. I should warn you that in addition to spending his working life chasing mechanical hares his repertoire has expanded in retirement to cats and other dogs, irrespective of size. I'm afraid.'

'That's fine. I'll try to make sure that we don't put temptation in his way. Until tomorrow. I shall look forward to it.'

'And I, Madame.' The line went dead.

4. Lunch and a Proposition

The next day dawned predictably clear and warm. Early morning tasks were completed. They passed a few early tourists during their walk, looking baffled at why the few cafés that were open at seven in the morning were populated by Pastis-drinking street cleaners who knew no requirement for pains aux chocolat or orange juice or any of the other things that visitors thought were parts of a traditional French breakfast and would be unobtainable before nine. Otherwise the town was taking its usual time waking up. A batch of laundry was put on to wash and he spent an hour or so doing some desultory house cleaning. A shower and a change of clothes and he was ready for the black Range Rover when it drew up outside the house promptly at 11:30. He opened the front door quickly to prevent Jean Marie needlessly climbing the steps, and he and Arthur closed the door behind him. By the time they reached the rear of the car, the rear doors had been opened and after only the slightest encouragement Arthur hopped neatly up the yard or so into the back compartment as if born to this type of vehicle rather than his normal old VW Polo. A lifetime of being transported to and from East London dog tracks in a wide variety of vans made the manoeuvre easy. Smith took off his lead, let himself into the front passenger seat and settled into an expensive smell of leather.

'Thank you for coming to collect me. Not having to drive myself does make the prospect of more of your fine wines more inviting.'

His chauffeur smiled and nodded to head in a gesture that indicted both agreement and a hint of annoyance that he was probably not going to be allowed the same luxury. It crossed his mind to make some sort of apology about losing him in the Roquette, but he wasn't confident that Mr Tee Shirt would see the joke. A closer inspection made it plain that Jean Marie might not be one to be crossed. The handsome, dark, weather-beaten face of a Camargue farmer was crossed by a number of deep scars. The car was driven expertly and very fast.

They crossed the Tranquetaille bridge and took the road

south towards Salin de Giraud. It was the main and most direct road into the heart of the Camargue. The reeds were at their highest at this time of year standing some five or six metres high and the green walls seemed to sway in sympathy with their high-speed passage. It was a typically hot day and the car's air conditioning was working overtime. For most of the local inhabitants, midday heat is to be avoided by any means possible. Just past Le Sambuc they turned right on the little road that goes past the Camargue research centre at Tour de Valat. But before arriving there they swung off to the right up a narrow but well metalled road that had not been signed. Glancing down into the nearside mirror, he caught a glimpse of the heavy electric gate closing the road just before a bend in the road cut the view. The reed beds really closed in now although their speed remained undiminished. God knows what would happen if they met someone around any of these blind bends.

They had been travelling for at least five minutes when they rounded yet another bend and drove through a stone arch and came to a sudden if dusty halt in the middle of a quadrangle of low Provençale buildings. Arthur immediately got to his feet and looked out through the windows for something to kill. Smith put the lead back on, got him out of the car and began to look around him.

However, his examination was cut short by the arrival of Madame DuGresson. She walked briskly towards him from under one of the shaded colonnades that ringed the courtyard. This time she was dressed simply in a white cotton shirt, embroidered with the traditional Provençale patterns, belted blue jeans and gardian boots. Her hair was tied up and as far as he could see was completely without makeup, jewellery or watch until he caught a flash of the diamond brooch hidden in the decoration on her shirt. He hand was outstretched, and her smile was genuine.

'How nice to see you again. Welcome to the Mas des Saintes. Thank you for coming.'

Smith returned the firm handshake.

'I'm delighted to be here, Madame.'

He was slightly miffed to see that her attention was immediately diverted to Arthur who was making an embarrassing amount of delighted fuss. She crouched down, offering a hand to be sniffed in that gesture that knowledgeable dog people use and then proceeded to make a fuss back. Arthur was instantly in heaven. Obviously, Madame DuGresson merited something more than his customary polite greeting on meeting new people. She then stood, took the lead from him and turned both her guests towards one of the buildings and led them in out of the sun.

They passed through a large, low farmhouse sitting room, large fireplace at one end with equally large sofas and easy chairs scattered around. Along the walls were a selection of bookcases cabinets, dressers and side tables. The flag stone floor was dressed with a few expensive oriental rugs. The room was naturally cool without a hint of air conditioning. On the far side of the room was a wide set of doors that led in turn into a large informal shaded garden. Red, white and pink Oleanders, orange and lemon trees, olive trees, of course and a large fig tree, a wide variety of flowering shrubs that he could not identify. The ground was covered with well-tended gravel. Some twenty yards away next to a table set for three stood an erect figure dressed similarly to his daughter. He took a few steps towards them as they approached.

'Monsieur Smith. I'm Emile Aubanet.'

'I'm delighted to meet you, Monsieur.'

He received another very firm handshake from a tall, grey haired man standing very erect. He was well-built and his hands had the sort of calluses that people who had actually used them had. His face was bronzed and relatively unlined for all his seventy-odd years. He then turned to Arthur standing patiently on a loose lead next to Madame looking on with interest.

'And this is Arthur. I have heard tell of his activities amongst the cat population of the Hauteur. You have a find hound, Monsieur. The Camargue is not the natural habitat of a sighthound and we have very few here. Does he still run?'

'Only after the local cats as you say, Monsieur. His racing career was ended by a back injury and I don't keep him fit enough to run him without risk.'

'Ah I see you know your dogs, Monsieur. An unfit greyhound will easily injure himself if allowed to run freely. However, please let him off the lead here. This garden is completely enclosed, and our own dogs are shut away. If one of the farm cats happens to come in, then that's their problem. There are too many of them anyway.'

Monsieur Aubanet didn't give the impression that he was a great cat lover. Without consulting Smith, Madame undid the combined collar and lead and let the dog go. Only after assuring himself that he was no longer to be the centre of attention did he wander off to go exploring.

'You are both lucky to have each other. Please sit down', gesturing to one of the three wicker garden armchairs arranged around a circular wooden table.

Within a few seconds of all three sitting down, a young woman, casually dressed but with the unmistakable demeanour of staff rather than family, placed a chilled glass of sparkling wine in front of each of them accompanied by a small plate to olives, slices of sausage and a hard cheese that he could not identify. The wine was the same as they had had in the restaurant two evenings ago. It remained delicious. It crossed his mind to make a number of complementary comments about the meal, but this was business, at least to start with. However, he felt that it should be the old man who should make the running. When he did none of the old-fashioned courtesies were forgotten.

'Before we start, I must add my apologies to those of my daughter. You have become involved in a difficult business and have done nothing to deserve it. I hope that you have fully recovered from your injury?'

The man was obviously genuine, and Smith was happy to accept. 'Thank you both for your concern and for your apology.'

'Monsieur Smith, as you know we are anxious to find out about the death of my son-in-law and my daughter has suggested that you might be able to help. She has explained why it would be difficult for us to be seen to do that ourselves, especially as the police have decided that there is nothing to investigate. I agree with her. You have told her that there might be a way in which you could help. Perhaps we can have this discussion before we eat. I don't wish to spoil the food with a business discussion.'

Arthur had returned from his preliminary investigation of the garden, hoping for food, to the table and now stood to the side of the old man, gently resting his chin on the old man's knee, looking up at him. A hand was lowered gently to rest on his head and his eyes half closed.

'Rest assured, Monsieur Smith, that even if we decide that there is nothing you can do to help up, you - and your dog - are still welcome guests at my table.'

'Thank you, Monsieur Aubanet. I do have a proposal for you but I'm not sure whether it will meet with your agreement. If I may, I'll describe it.'

The older man lifted his hand in a gesture that signalled both his acquiescence and for a refill of drinks. While this was going on, Smith helped himself to a piece of the hard cheese from the plate on the table. Unsurprisingly it was delicious.

'Disagreeing with your potential clients is not usually the best way to start the presentation of a business proposal but I must disagree with you, Madame. It is obviously possible to make excellent cheese in Provence.'

As he thought it might, he put his finger on what was obviously a running debate between father and a daughter because he was rewarded with loud guffaws from both.

'As you know, I have spent some of the last twenty five years of my life as business consultant, specialising in creating commercial strategies for businesses that, while they are not in any current difficulties, have the foresight to see the need to invest in future planning. I have worked for a wide variety of clients throughout the world and have had some success - at least I have always managed to find business. Much of this work depended on my ability to understand a client's business completely and quickly. Thus, while I'm certainly not an investigator in the criminal sense, I'm very good indeed in investigating businesses, how they work and how the people who work for them operate. My proposals were thus made on the basis of a complete understanding of my client's business, an understanding that I always insisted on finding for myself and not just being given by my clients. I often found that clients often knew surprisingly little about how their business operated.'

The glance that flashed between father and daughter gave him the opportunity to draw breath and take a sip of his newly replenished Crémant. He continued:

'You say you are interested in whether Monsieur DuGresson's death had anything to do with your business. But given that he seems to have separated himself from the family, I suspect that what you really mean is that you want to know, in the first instance at least, whether your business will be harmed by his death.'

Madam drew breath but Smith affected not to notice and went on.

'My initial reluctance to your suggestion that I investigate the death was due to the fact that I could not see any credible reason why I should go around asking questions. I have no authority here nor any particular contacts that would help. However, my proposal is that your Company hires me, in the same way as all my previous clients have done. What would be more normal than for you to appoint a consultant to look at your business - all your businesses - with a view to advising on future strategy. To do this properly I would have to look in great detail at all aspects of your business, even those that you would prefer to keep from me.'

That look was exchanged again.

'This would give me the perfect excuse for asking a lot of people a lot of questions and for your employees to understand why they are being asked. There is no reason why you should not tell them precisely what I'll be doing. I can assure you, if Monsieur DuGresson's death was business-related, I'll find the reason. Given that I would have to look at his business activities in detail, I might even get some clue to his death even it were not.'

Again, he sensed questions but pretended not to notice.

'I would need substantial access to all your companies and their records, especially financial. I would wish to sign the usual confidentiality agreement with you - indeed I wouldn't do this work without one for it protects me as well as you. As long as I was granted the correct level of cooperation and access to information, I would expect to be able to offer you a report relatively quickly. My fee will be 500 Euros per day payable, gross of taxes and other costs, payable when I submit my report. I'll expect all my expenses to be reimbursed by you and I'll submit itemised accounts. Finally, if I discover nothing, then I'll have earned some money and you will have an excellent business plan that you can either use or not, whatever you choose.'

Smith's abrupt finish was followed by a silence during which he sat back in his chair and took another slightly larger sip of Crémant. Arthur, obviously despairing of getting anything to eat came back to his feet and flopped, slightly petulantly, onto the ground and feigned sleep. Smith looked directly at his hosts and waited. Interestingly and slightly surprisingly it was Madam who spoke first.

'That's an excellent suggestion and we accept your proposal. Perhaps, for the purposes of our records and the tax authorities, you could put it in writing. Also, I think it would be a good idea if your proposal and our acceptance were dated well before Robert's death.'

Monsieur Aubanet indicated his agreement by a slight raise of the hand and that, it seemed, was that.

'Good,' he said with a tired smile that, for this first time, betrayed his age, and looked around him: 'This seems settled and perhaps now we can eat?'

Business temporarily put to one side; lunch was served. Salad Nicoise, veal paupiettes in a tomato and herb sauce with little boiled potatoes, an apple flan and that hard cheese again. The conversation was about the Camargue. Smith was a willing listener and the old man was an enthusiastic instructor. Madame looked on with an amused detachment. Arthur discovered that, once the food was on the table, Monsieur Aubanet was as easy as touch as was Smith himself. His happiness was completed when host untied a complete paupiette, and, having raised an eyebrow across the table and received a silent nod of agreement from Smith, saw the entire plate put in the ground at his disposal. Smith wondered briefly whether this whole thing was not giving them both him and his dog unsustainable expectations.

Smith declined coffee. He always did. He could never understand how a drink designed to wake one up in the morning could ever be considered a suitable beverage to complete a meal. Perhaps people were playing some sort of lip service to sobriety. All it did was wash away a succession of intellectually stimulating smells and tastes in a tide of bitterness and caffeine. In any case it was not for him, nor for his hosts, he noted.

'Now, Monsieur Smith, what can we offer you this afternoon, before we have to become business associates?' He thought he detected a note of regret in his host's voice.

He addressed his host directly and, he hoped, formally: 'Monsieur Aubanet. I would be honoured to view your bulls on the farm.'

Clearly it would have been difficult to suggest anything that would have given either of them more pleasure. Both smiled broadly. 'Of course, of course' he said, 'that would be an excellent way to work off lunch.'

As if by magic, Jean Marie appeared at his uncle's elbow and took some instructions in Provençale and left equally subtly.

'Perhaps we can leave our digestive until our return.'

Smith realised from where the daughter got her ability to make a suggestion sound like a decision.

'Do you wish to take Arthur with us?'

'Perhaps he would be happier left here in the shade, Monsieur.'

After a few minutes they rose from the table and went back through the house into the courtyard. Arthur, by that time, lying in the shade of a large oleander, raised his head but was quite happy to follow Smith's instruction to stay and continue to digest his lunch from a prone position. Three grey Camargue horses awaited them in the courtyard with Jean Marie in attendance. Smith felt complemented by the assumption that he could ride. In fact, he was a perfectly adequate horseman - a fact successfully kept secret from his horse-mad family for many years. Monsieur Aubanet turned to his guest.

'Jean Marie had put out some more suitable clothing for you, Monsieur Smith.'

Martine DuGresson led Smith across the quadrangle of buildings to the far side.

'The house occupies two sides of this square, there are stables and associated rooms on the third side and our corporate offices are housed along the fourth. We only keep a small staff here. Robert had his own office in the centre of Arles.'

She led him into the offices and indicated a small room at the end of the large open plan room. It proved to be a cloakroom. In it, Smith found that a selection of belted jeans and guardian leather boots had been laid out on the table. As he changed, he saw through the window father and daughter in conversation. They were both smiling and unaccountably Smith felt a sense of relief. If they were happy, he thought, there was a much better chance of their cooperation making his job easier. Although he was under no illusions that he was now well and truly into the middle of the closed world of Camargue, he was still an outsider and it was that position that made him valuable to the Aubanet family.

'Think of the money,' he said to himself as he pulled on a pair of calf-length leather *gardian* boots and walked with as much unselfconsciousness as he could muster back out into the sunlight. Jeans - no matter how generously cut - had never really been his thing. He had actually never owned a pair in his life. His hosts climbed into the comfortable *guardian* saddles with the natural ease of people who had been doing it all their lives. Smith's mounting was slightly less elegant but not embarrassingly so, helped by the naturally long stirrup length used in the Camargue as well as the relative lack of height of the horse. He was pleased that he mounted without the assistance of Jean Marie who had ostentatiously stationed himself at the horse's nearside rump. It was a small victory that seemed not go unnoticed by Madame if her slight smile was anything to go by.

The next two hours were spent in a gentle meander around the menade, and for Smith at least, it was the greatest of pleasures. The farm was a typical Camargue mixture of grass pastures and barren mud flats with water never far away. A few trees dotted the flat landscape while long reed beds formed the divisions between the pastures. Much of the ride was spent walking though belly-deep water. Occasional white, thatched cabanes, protected from both summer and winter winds by groups of cypress, willow and pine trees, appeared from time to time. The small black bulls ran virtually wild and Smith was treated to a detailed introduction to the history of the herd, its breed characteristics and its current commercial success. At times the old man's enthusiasm ran on to the extent that he lapsed into rodanenc and thus became incomprehensible to Smith whose knowledge of the langue d'Oc was minimal and of this local variation, non-existent. Madam let her father have his stage, but it was evident that, however serious a businessman she was, her shared her family's pride in these prized animals.

For Smith, the tour was over all too soon. Before long they were back at the table in the cool of the garden. Waiting on the table beside a thoroughly restored Arthur, now sitting in the shade being fussed over by the girl who had waited on table, was a glass jug of cold lemon juice and three glasses.

'I offered you a digestive, Monsieur, but I suspect you would prefer something cold?'

'Thank you Monsieur Aubanet. That would be perfect. Thank you also for showing me your bulls. I know little or nothing about them, but it was a marvellous experience to see them and some of the rest of your menade.'

'Monsieur I was delighted to show it to you. But I fear it is time for me to take my afternoon siesta. Perhaps you will learn more about our lives here during your investigations.'

With that he rose, took Smith's hand in a firm grip and looked directly into his face.

'You will have gathered from Martine that Robert had long ceased being a family member. He had, however, become a valued employee on whose judgement we relied almost implicitly. My concern is that his death indicates something that will harm my family. Of equal concern is the fact that the police have made up this ridiculous suicide story. You will probably have already concluded that the police are not to be trusted - or rather this Parisian policeman should be treated with caution. The locals are, more or less, honest. I'm, of course, delighted that our business will have the benefit of your professional expertise, but the protection of my family is my only real interest. Thank you for agreeing to help us.'

The old man's eyes never waived from Smith's and his grip had tightened painfully.

'I'll do my best, Monsieur Aubanet,' he replied.

He turned and walked towards the house, stopping halfway to give a following Arthur a farewell pat on the head.

Smith turned to his new employer. 'Madam, I think I should also return home. I have had a delightful lunch and very much enjoyed my visit to the menade, but I have a great deal of work to a relatively short time.'

The reply came with another genuine smile. 'Of course. I'll drive you back and we can discuss the arrangements on the way.'

Smith changed back into his own clothes and before long they were returning to Arles with Madam at the wheel, Arthur in the back and Jean Marie in the back seat looking as uncomfortable as any red blooded Camargue man would look being driven expertly but very quickly by a woman.

'Now, what do you need first from me, Monsieur Smith?'

'Well, with a business as large and as diverse as yours, I presume that you keep an extensive computer network, Madame.'

She nodded. 'Yes. All our businesses report each week this way. Records are kept on the servers at our offices and are also backed up nightly remotely through a commercial service.'

'In that case, Madame, I shall need remote access to the system. I can get much of the preliminary the information I need from that. Your network manager can arrange for a complete record of everything I access or try to access to be maintained so you can keep track of what I'm doing. I'll not usually print hard copies of any information and will obtain your permission if I need to. Any such material and all my notes will be kept in my safe at home. All will be handed back to you at the end of my investigation. I'll need your personal email address and will keep you informed daily of what I'm doing and who I'll wish to see. I already have your mobile number. In the first instance I'll need full monthly management accounts of all your businesses for the last twelve months as well as the last five year's consolidated accounts. I shall also need sight of all your banking records. I can learn most of what I need to know about the business from these. However, at this stage, I think a visit to your late husband's office would be in order. As soon as possible. Finally, I have a draft form of confidentiality agreement at home and I'll complete it and email it to you this evening. I hope this is all right?'

'Perfectly, Monsieur Smith. I'll contact you with the necessary access codes later today. Robert kept a small office in his apartment behind the Place de la République. His personal assistant, Madamoiselle Claudine Brique, was the only member of staff to work there and I can tell her to expect you. Would ten o'clock tomorrow be convenient?'

'Yes, that would be fine. Thank you.'

'Claudine has worked for Robert for ten years. She is - was - utterly devoted to him and is very fierce. I also have to warn you that she has no sense of humour.'

The rest of the journey back into Arles took very little time and they drew up outside the house. Smith got out and collected Arthur from the back of the Range Rover. By the time he got to the driver's window he noticed that Jean Marie had replaced him in the front.

'Thank you, Madame, for a most enjoyable lunch. Please relay my thanks also to your father and I'm glad that we have found a way to work together. I assure you that I'll try my best to solve your mystery. I'm confident that I'll produce some useful suggestions for the future of your business.'

'I'm delighted you enjoyed your visit and I'm also pleased that you will help us. I can tell that my father shares my confidence and he is usually accurate in his assessment of people. I look forward to the results of your enquiries.'

With that, and a farewell handshake and smile, she drove away leaving Smith and Arthur at the kerb.

It was about five o'clock and, in spite of his paupiettes, Arthur demanded his supper. Having done the necessary, Smith poured himself a long, weak whisky and soda and sat in garden to things through. OK. He was employed, which was good, and at the very worst, he had guaranteed himself few weeks work. The four or five thousand pounds would certainly come in handy. He had done enough of these projects during his life for it to be relatively easy. Irrespective of the actual makeup of the Aubanet family business, many of the recommendations that he would make would be common to most of the projects he had done over the years. Most businesses make the same mistakes and their solutions are often very similar. Slotting a new set of data into an existing format had never been difficult.

He was interested in the fact that Robert DuGresson had seemed to have led a very separate life away from the centre of the business whose finances he directed. His wife didn't strike Smith as being someone who naturally delegated and then let the person set up a separate office some twenty miles away. Perhaps it was an arrangement that developed from the separation. Even had Monsieur DuGresson not been dead, and his client expecting some sort of explanation, the Finance Director would in any case have been a major source of interest for Smith. He was also concerned whether, in the few days since the murder, anyone had taken control of the material that must have been left in DuGresson's office and of the activities of Mademoiselle Brique. He also felt that it would be a good idea for him to have some time in that office before the faithful PA actually knew of his existence.

He pondered on for another half hour or so and, with a sudden decisiveness telephoned his new client.

'Madame. I apologise for bothering you again so soon.'

'Not at all. How can I help?'

'Have you contacted Mademoiselle Brique yet to make arrangements for tomorrow morning?

'No, she usually visits her grandmother in Tranquetaille on Sundays. After what happened, I think she went there yesterday. I was intending to wait until this evening.'

'Good. Has she been working in the office since your

husband's death?'

'No, I felt that as she was very upset, I should give her some time off. I said that we would discuss the future one-day next week, and before you ask, I had the locks changed on the apartment and I changed the code for the burglar alarm. As of this morning it didn't look as if it has been entered. Jean Marie checked it yesterday and this morning.'

'Are the computers still running?'

'No. All Robert's financial information is backed up to our servers here each evening. This last happened last Thursday evening, the day before his death. When I was informed of the so-called suicide during Friday afternoon, I personally went to tell Mademoiselle Brique and I stayed with her until she left the office. I arranged for the change of locks before I came home.'

'Excellent. I think that I would like to have some time in that office before Mademoiselle Brique returns to work. Until we are sure that she has nothing to do with all this, it would probably be unwise to let her have unsupervised access. Perhaps your telephone call this evening could extend her leave for a few days? I would be happy to visit alone if you would give me the keys and alarm codes or for you or someone you trust to be present if you prefer.'

'I'm sure you will work better without someone looking over your shoulder, Monsieur. If we didn't trust you, we wouldn't be talking with you. I'll have the keys delivered to you within the hour and I'll email the numbers for the alarm together with other access codes you wish to you immediately. Our network manager is arranging an account for you at the moment.'

'I'm sorry to be the cause of a disturbed weekend for him.'

A noise that sounded suspiciously like a harrumph came over the telephone. His new boss clearly had little concern for her IT manager's days of rest.

'Robert had a laptop and one of those tablet computers. You

might have to look through the apartment for them. Neither was on him when he was killed apparently.'

'Was his mobile phone found.'

'No. Or at least the police said not.'

Smith thought: 'It is slightly strange that someone who it an enthusiast for mobiles and tablets didn't have at least one of than on him. My experience of people who use those dreadful things tend to be slightly obsessive about them.'

'Yes, Robert seldom went anywhere without it. Perhaps you can telephone me if you find anything significant, Monsieur?'

'Yes, of course. At this early stage I might well need your help in explaining some of the things I find. I'll make a secure set of folders on your server and put anything I might find there. That way you can see what I'm doing and give me advice. I shall surely need it.'

'That will be fine, Monsieur Smith. I'll be interested to hear what you think my daily fee should be for my contribution to your work.'

This time the harrumph came from him. Having finished the call, he went straight to his study and found the draft confidentiality agreement. He made the necessary adjustments to it and settled back to wait for Madame's email. He looked out of the window at the wall of the great Arena where all this had started. The great curved oval of double arches had survived extraordinarily well for two thousand years considering the local population's rapacious appetite for stone over the centuries that had rendered the Antique Theatre down to much less than a third of its original size, the Forum to a set of almost completely subterranean foundations and the twenty five thousand seat Circus Maximus to a vestige in the ground. He had intended that his retirement years were to be spent in quiet contemplation of this view while making a small but, he hoped, significant contribution to the art historical literature of Roman Antiquity.

He drifted into a silent reverie and into the recollection of the long-remembered pleasures of the life of a post-graduate student at Berkeley during the late sixties. The three years he spent there were almost certainly the happiest on his life and not just in retrospect either. Declining the offer of a tenured position in the department there was the only decision he had made in his life that he really regretted. The memory of it was something that seemed to get more painful as time when on rather than less.

He had never understood why Microsoft operating systems make a number of annoying noises from time to time. That opening bar of non-music that he heard each time someone switched their computer on always got on his nerves. The ping of an incoming email similarly although the annoyance was probably more to do with the fact that he had yet again forgotten to disable these wretched noises. So, it was with a slight frown that he opened the expected email.

It was as complete as he hoped. Network URL, username and password and a contact name and number in case of difficulty. It also contained Madam's email address. He sent over the confidentiality agreement and a message to the affect that he would visit Robert's office as soon as she could get the keys to him. The predated written proposal and its acceptance could wait for the next day. The email back confirming that all was in order came by return as well as a series of attachments that proved to be the accounts he requested. Madame was obviously at her computer. He printed off the accounts, replenished his whisky and returned with his wireless laptop to the garden.

The business seemed to be a loose grouping of a very wide range of different companies ranging from a number of different farming enterprises, an import export business, a descriptions that Smith recognised as potentially concealing a multitude of oddities, a property company that owned and rented holiday and residential apartments, and a number of small hotels. All this had a declared turnover of about fifty million Euros - somewhat more than Madam's original description. Additionally, there was a separate investment portfolio that held minority holdings in more than sixty relatively small business all in the local area. All the businesses seemed to be run more or less separately from each other. The last consolidated balance sheet showed no borrowings, a substantial cash balance and a net asset value of more than one hundred and fifty million Euros. All in all, Smith saw, this was a very considerable business. Taking another sip from his whisky, he reached for a pad of paper and calculator and settled into some detailed ratio analysis.

As so often, the punctuation marks in his daily routine were supplied by Arthur. His regular post prandial nap, caused, Smith thought, when the very small amount of blood circulating in a very small greyhound brain was called to the aid digestive system, was over and the next thing on Arthur's list was his evening amble around Arles. Smith was surprised to see that it was past eight o'clock. He never resented the necessity of walking with Arthur in the morning and the evening. Apart from the obvious exercise, he had no intention of letting his enforced but welcome bachelorhood turn him into the self-obsessed personality that some of his bachelor acquaintances exhibited. If walking Arthur or doing some shopping for his eighty-year-old neighbour was not, on occasions, entirely convenient the fact that neither neighbour nor dog ever failed to show their appreciation, made the minor disruption more than supportable. On this occasion having gone through the pleasurable ritual of Arthur's energetic enthusiasm for the fact that his lead had been taken off the peg just inside the front door, putting a couple of the little black polythene bags thoughtfully supplied by the city to collect and dispose of the dog's 'doings', he started the walk and a general mental review of what he had learned about his new client.

He took his 'river' route, one of many choices to prevent over-repetition. This one took him past Notre Dame de la Major, the patron church of the Gardians of the Camargue, through the top of the Hauteur and through the Couvent St Blaise, whose excavations were rapidly exposing the foundations of what could be one of the earliest Christian churches in Europe, down the Montée Vauban and back along the Roman wall, past the city cemetery where he himself would one day reside and down to the river. The walk could take a number of variations from this point and the choice was usually made on the basis of how many gypsies were encamped to the north on the river side of the bus station. These were not Camargue gipsies. These were travellers with huge unlicensed 4 x 4s, caravans the size of articulated lorries, motor driven satellite dishes and unrestrained violent dogs. If this way was barred, as it often was in the Summer, he would turn towards the city along the high river path and choose various different moments to cut up into the town and loop back to his house next to the Arena. These walks were usually uneventful, although a certain vigilance was always necessary to ensure that Arthur didn't revert to his naturally aggressive ways. He seemed gradually to be learning not to attack every dog he met and chase to a kill every cat spotted, but the conversion was still not reliable. Secretly, Smith hoped it never would be.

As they walked, Smith ran over what he had learned. The Aubanet Group was a very solid if diverse group of companies. All the businesses were in varying degrees profitable and many had been set up in quite a sophisticated way. The hotels provided a good example. There were seven hotels in the group, all medium sized, all located in and around Arles. The potential damage that could be done by seasonal downturns in business – lack of tourists due to bad weather, for instance – had been eliminated by retaining the ownership of the buildings but establishing what was virtually a franchise giving the management and staff of each establishment almost complete independence. The result of this arrangement was that the Group's balance sheet saw a continuously increasing fixed asset value as the properties increased in value and an income that, to an extent, was predictable. The hotel management and staff felt they were running their own businesses and were rewarded accordingly. The Group management was not directly involved with the day-to-day running of the businesses and therefore avoided having to maintain a specialist staff.

Smith got the impression that many of their businesses were run as much for the benefit of people employed as the owners. This was born out by the investment portfolio whose details has also been sent. This again consisted in minority shareholding in a large number of businesses, some large, most medium sized or small. Dividend income wasn't high judged by usual standards, but it was more than adequate for an investor who seemed to value participation in and support for local businesses as much as financial return. He actually found the whole thing rather paternal but unlike most of the businesspeople he had met he had never equated paternal with patronising. What Monsieur Aubanet had created was a Group designed both to make money and to support and encourage a wide range of local businesses and to judge by the accounts he had seen, he had made a good job of it.

'All well and good, but what of Monsieur Robert?' Smith thought as they came up to the wall that bounded the south bank curve of the Rhone.

The Group he saw hardly needed a high-powered director of finance. It didn't have a huge investment programme. The commercial reporting procedures between the individual businesses and the centre seemed efficient and uncomplicated. There was no borrowing of any sort that might have needed management or at least the accounts showed no interest being paid. Cash flow was certainly not a problem. There were only two main shareholders. The actual direct payroll was small as well. Smith wondered what the Finance Director actually did with his time. Perhaps the job was a sinecure after the separation. He was certainly the highest paid individual in the company.

'Perhaps,' though Smith, 'It was a case of the devil making work for idle hands.' However, the office might possibly yield something more.

By the time they had got back home, it was beginning to get dark. Groups of tourists still wandered about, possibly wondering why all the street bars had closed and why the idea of drinking the hot Provençale night away turned out to be impossible. Actually, this must be a perennial disappointment to visitors who come to Arles thinking that bars and restaurants kept Riviera hours. The Arlesian bar owner has a stricter sense of priorities than that. Opening hours were not market driven.

As he pushed open his front door, he heard rather than felt a small package that had been put through his letter box while they were out. It contained bunch of keys, some very new – presumably the to the front door of Robert's office – and interior door keys as well as some that obviously opened desks and filing cabinets. A note asked him to check his emails. Sure enough, one was waiting for him with alarm codes and what was obviously the combination to a safe.

'No time like the present,' Smith thought, and he let himself back out of the house and headed towards the centre of town.

Robert DuGresson's apartment and office was tucked away into the space in the Impasse Balze behind the western side of the Place de la Republique and the Musée Arlatan. The ground floor of a well-maintained, three-story façade consisted of a stout double door flanked by two pairs of shuttered windows. The first floor showed a line of five floor to ceiling windows with an elegant narrow wrought iron balcony running the width of the façade. This pattern was repeated on the floor above with a row of smaller windows. As with the ground floor, all the windows were tightly shuttered. This was no mere apartment but a full and extremely elegant eighteenth-century hotel particulière – a town house of the sort that can still be found dotted regularly throughout the ancient town centre. Three new lock faces stood out brightly from the dark varnish of the heavy door. The call button of an intercom complete with camera glowed dimly on the right door jamb. The name next to the button said simply 'Robert DuGresson' and made no mention of any business. A polished brass letterbox, wide enough to take business – sized envelopes was set directly into the wall. Idle curiosity made Smith push the flap of the box. It didn't move.

After a certain amount of trial and error with keys, Smith found himself in a generously proportioned hall, a graceful curved staircase wound up from the far end and there were four doors, grouped in two pairs on either side at the centre of the space. He silenced the bleeping burglar alarm, flicked on the light and looked around. All four high-ceilinged rooms showed that all were used for business. One front room giving out onto the street was an office containing two desks and the usual paraphernalia of business, filing cabinets, shelves with box and lever files. The room opposite across the hall was a small conference room with a fireplace flanked with easy chairs and a central table and chairs for a maximum of eight people. The rooms at the back of the house were obviously Robert DuGresson's own office balanced on the other side by a large cloakroom. The two front rooms were furnished in a contemporary and obviously expensive office style. DuGresson's office was startlingly modern with glass and chrome predominating. From it large double French windows gave access to a small but elegantly set out walled garden containing a few shade trees and planted with formal rose beds and shrubs.

Before settling into his work, Smith climbed the stairs to the first floor. Two rooms overlooking the garden at the back contained a large kitchen and a cloakroom. The whole front consisted of one long sitting room. The roadside was almost entirely made up of the five full length windows and the room was long enough to accommodate a dining table at one end and a fireplace ringed by sofas and chairs at the other. The wall opposite the windows was almost completely covered with filled bookshelves arranged to leave regular gaps for pictures. The top floor above consisted of a large master bedroom with bathroom attached at the back of the house, again overlooking the garden and two other bedrooms and another bathroom. The entire house exuded modernity and money.

It was all at the extreme edge of italo-french designer chic. Brushed chrome, glass abounded. Fabrics were all muted pastels. The only real colour was supplied by the paintings hung throughout. All very modern and all very costly. A quick mental inventory gave Smith a list that included Lichtenstein, Warhol, Hamilton, Rothko, and Barnett Neumann. Others were contemporary and therefore anonymous to Smith but seemed to him of equal quality. A smaller, but similarly classy collection of small sculptures was also displayed. Here at least was evidence of what Robert had spent some of his considerable income on, although Smith did wonder whether, given the market prices for some of these artists, even the handsome remuneration of a Financial Director was enough completely to cover it. It was a serious and knowledgeable collection and could explain, Smith pondered, why the accountant was prepared to do what seemed on the surface to be such a mundane job. Certainly, the whole house showed that Robert DuGression had been reluctant to leave his Parisian roots behind. It must have irked Monsieur Aubanet and his daughter but could go a little way to explaining the separation.

After a while spent browsing, Smith, whose personal taste led him to like the pictures but dislike the décor equally, remembered that viewing a private art collection was not what he was here for and thus he returned to the ground floor office to start his proper investigation. Realising how time-consuming trawling through a computer system can be, he decided to leave that until last. The physical records, files and folders, desks and cupboards could be looked through quite quickly. If there was any evidence of peculiarities to be found it was unlikely that it would be lying around as bits of paper in filing systems. Sure, enough the paper revealed a mundane, if immaculately maintained, record of the business's finances. Mademoiselle Brique obviously didn't completely trust computer records. Her computer was next but again there was little unusual on it. One thing that Smith had avoided telling his new employer was that amongst a very modest collection of life skills that he had accumulated throughout his life rather in the manner that a navel collects lint was a considerable ability with information technology. He was well able to understand most aspects of computing if not actually practice them and a one-year consultancy with a major clearing bank helping to plan marketing behind the launch of their internet banking services have given him a number of useful talents. He also came away with some bits of thoroughly pirated but nevertheless very useful bit of coding and decoding software. He didn't regard himself as any great expert, but anything based on a Windows NT platform was unlikely to remain secret from him for too long. He had been given the passwords to Mademoiselle Brique's computer and he could find no encrypted or hidden files, nor any recent deletions either using the dreadfully insecure Microsoft 'waste basket' nor by any other more sophisticated erasure software. The most useful find was Robert DuGresson's list of personal contacts and diary as well as recent emails, all kept conveniently on Outlook software. He downloaded all that, as well as all the archived files onto one of a number of memory sticks he had brought with him and reset the logs so that his download was not traceable. He did find paper printouts of bank statements and correspondence, but a quick check confirmed that most of the Group's banking was done online and the statements were available there. He did, however, note the presence of a small wireless network. The answering service had been erased – or never contained anything. He would have to ask Madame DuGresson about that.

He had never really thought that it would be easy, so he next turned his attention to finding the any other computers. Oddly, that proved to be very easy indeed. The combination supplied by Madam opened an incongruously old fashioned safe in Robert's office it contained a slim tablet PC, together with an expensive digital camera, a passport with a large bunch of other personal documentation. What he took to be backup CDs and quite a lot of cash – about twenty thousand Euros – completed the contents. Smith left the money and put all the rest into his briefcase. If these hid anything then he would need solitude, his own computers and a glass of whisky to find it.

It was obvious that the rest of the apartment could contain all sorts of stuff, but he had no great confidence in his ability to find anything quickly that had been concealed at length. If that were necessary, it would a problem that he could lay on his client's desk. So, he contented himself with a cursory glance around the bedrooms. In his limited experience men tended not to regard bedrooms as places to hide things, unlike the few women with whose bedrooms he had acquaintance. Similarly, with locations for suicide, he thought. He found nothing of obvious significance and turned back downstairs. He put his head around the office door without turning the light back on to perform some sort of perfunctory check. The room was shuttered, and therefore fairly dark. Had it not been he would probably not have noticed very small flashing green light behind Mademoiselles Brique's desk.

Modern offices are full of lights like these. Even when they're not being used, most machines are kept on standby and conventionally a blue or orange light shows this. Green lights show that something is actually on and working and the presence of one here in an office that was supposed to be closed was slightly unusual. Moreover, it was flashing periodically. Smith immediately recognised that it was a modem traffic light and, more than that, periodic amounts of data were passing through it. Sure enough, he found the modem that had been placed unobtrusively but not necessarily hidden behind some files on a bookshelf behind the PA's desk. The flashing was not continuous but every ten seconds or so there was a small burst of activity. This was a modem maintaining its link to a computer. More importantly, a computer that was on rather than off. Looking at the modem it was obvious that its wireless capabilities were relatively limited. It was the sort that's usually used for a wireless network within a house. This house or at the most next door. The two PC's in the office and the one of Robert's desk were certainly all off. Smith fished the tablet out of his case. So was it. He tried to boot it up. The tablet fired up but was password protected. This was not going to be a problem for him, but he did need some software that was on his PC at home to break it quickly. He sat for a moment, idly turning the tablet over and over in his hand and thought about the problem. There were no other PCs in the house that he could see and another portable computer, left on charge, for instance, might be time consuming to find. Then it occurred to him. No-one had mentioned finding a mobile phone, nor had he found one. Robert must have had one. If fact, given the aggressive modernity of much of his life, there was a very good chance that he had a iPhone or the latest smartphone that combined telephone, email and internet functions. 'Now, if I'm lucky and it is not turned onto silent...,' he thought.

He quickly booted up the nearest PC and checked for Robert's mobile number. Using his own mobile he dialled the number, got a connection and walked out into the hall and listened for a telephone ring tone. Nothing. However, when he climbed the first flight of stairs he could just hear a muffled ring that stopped almost immediately. He checked and found himself being asked to leave a message. He rang off and back. The noise was coming from Robert's bedroom. He stood in the doorway and listened more. It took another call before he found the machine in the inside a drawer in the stand beside the bed. Needless to say, it was the latest iPhone. The device had been left to charge – possibly the reason it had been left there and not found on Robert's body – but not switched off. It was connected to the wireless network. The wire for the charger had been led out of the back of the bedside cabinet. It was a slight sense of triumph that he slipped the device and its charger into his pocket and returned to the ground floor office.

He had done all he could for the moment. He needed the quiet of his own study and his PC to investigate what he had found further. He turned everything off, gathered up his belongings, reset the alarm and left the building, taking care to lock up fully behind him, and set off for home. He had taken just under half an hour.

He had just climbed the Rue de la Calade and was rounding the top of the Arena when his own mobile rang.

'Monsieur Smith?' The non-accented voice was instantly identifiable. 'Chief Superintendent Blanchard, here,' it said unnecessarily. 'Are you free for a late supper?'

The chosen venue was one of those basic but comfortable café brasseries that used to be widespread throughout France but more recently have become rarer as the pressure to feed demanding but undiscriminating tourists has grown and the requirement for decent but extended business lunches has reduced. The Bistro Central on the Place Lamartine outside the northern gate of the city wall had been built just behind the spot where Van Gogh's famous Yellow House had stood before it was bombed by the US Fifteenth Airforce in June 1944 under the impression that they were destroying the Arles railway bridge across the Rhone. The daily menu at the Bistro Central was good sound food, well-cooked from fresh ingredients every day and representing excellent value for money. There was always a set of a la carte choices available, but anyone who knew the qualities of this type of establishment invariably didn't consult it, preferring instead to leave their sustenance in the hands of the cook and the plat du jour. So it was for Blanchard and his guest. The only deviation from the norm was the choice of a bottle of Château Cissac negotiated from off the wine list.

Blanchard looked slightly sheepish.

'I apologise, Monsieur Smith. I'm afraid that I have not yet developed a taste for the local wines.'

Remembering some of the wines he had drunk over the last few days he was minded to point out the Chief Superintendent's error. But that might have led to more of an exchange of information than Smith wanted. He just smiled politely.

'How can I possibly object to one of the better crus bourgoise in this excellently bourgeois café, Monsieur.'

'I gather that you are now associated with Madame DuGresson, Monsieur Smith.'

Smith decided not to pursue the question as to how Blanchard knew so quickly.

'If by that you mean that I'll be doing some consultancy work for her company, then yes.'

'Quite,' he replied with a condescending smile, 'A consultancy.'

The first of three courses arrived. A simple *salade nicoise*, to be followed by a *magret de canard* with a ginger sauce and a pudding – inevitably a choice of fruit salad, a tarte or a crème caramel. Plain fare but good.

Blanchard took his first taste of wine, grimaced slightly as if it was not up to his expectations and looked across at Smith.

'I wish to ask for your help. Monsieur.'

'Oh God,' thought Smith, not another one. Blanchard continued:

'And in order to try to persuade you, I feel that I should probably explain what is going on.'

'That would be nice.' replied Smith with the faintest whiff of sarcasm.

The smile that crossed the Chief Superintendent's faced definitely forced. He was not at all at ease and he paused before continuing as if waiting for Smith to take the conversation on a little for him. However, he was disappointed. Smith was in no mood to make any of the running.

'Firstly, I should confirm that I'm indeed a Chief Superintendent of police but not of the local force, as you have rightly concluded. I work for Department SC4 of Europol, the European Union police force.'

'SC4?'

'The department that deals with serious financial crimes. Although the headquarters are in the Hague, for the moment, I'm operating through a liaison office in Paris.'

He placed a small, leather-bound wallet on the table presumably containing an identity document. Smith made no effort to look at it.

'Not Cellarini, I'm afraid,' he commented, with a wry smile as he replaced it in his jacket pocket. He continued:

'The basic facts are these. For the last three years I have been leading a small team investigating the theft of very large amounts of money from the funds that the European Union distributes for the repair and maintenance of ancient buildings. In all the Commission gives grants to its member countries amounting to billions of Euros each year. Much of this money, of course, goes to the correct recipients but each year a proportion goes missing. A small proportion, perhaps but actually a very large amount of money. We estimate in the region of five hundred million Euros annually. My investigations brought me here six months ago because not only is Arles a substantial recipient of funds, we received information that it is the centre for the administration of this Europe-wide fraud. My job is to try to identify the people who are doing this and where the money is going. I believe that Robert DuGresson was at the centre of all this and somehow something went wrong last week.'

Smith thought it was time to join the party. 'Presumably your ridiculous story of a suicide was put together in order to stop the local police investigating the murder and thus getting in your way.'

'Yes. I certainly didn't want a load of local police with

possibly very local loyalties trampling all over what had been three years of very careful work. After our first meeting I was confident you would either not be interested or understand what was going on, in principal if not in practice.'

'And so why are we having this meal together?'

'Quite simply, we are interested in whether Madame DuGresson's family is involved. We have little information about them, and they seem protected by the local community that's very reluctant to give a Parisian policeman any information at all let alone confidential details about the activities of one of the oldest and most powerful families in the region. You seem to have gained their confidence and I want you to help us. Before you ask, we have had Robert's house under watch for more than a year. We saw you visiting earlier and leaving with a brief case that was obviously heavier than when you went in. In terms of getting close to the family, you seem to have achieved more in a week that we have in three years.'

Smith was angry with himself for not realising that the office was under surveillance. He had to sharpen up. Although there was not real reason why he should have been on his guard, he felt it had been a mistake.

'Presupposing I was even remotely interested in doing so, why on earth should I?' he replied. 'I have a strong dislike for the institutions of the European Union in spite of supporting it's aims in a wishy-washy sort of way. I dislike policemen and I certainly dislike all politicians of whatever hue with a passion that's difficult to express. I regard them all as self-serving parasites and I would shoot the lot. If a bunch of criminals wants to rip the system off, I find it quite difficult to work up much indignation. I knew a European politician once and, apart from being a complete arsehole, he was more of a rip-off artist that any Camargue gangster. I'm contracted to Monsieur Aubanet's company to provide them with a marketing strategy and that's that. I've signed a confidentiality agreement with them and have absolutely no intention of breaking it. My personal loyalties are to my family, my dog and myself in that order and my professional loyalties are to my client.'

'Especially when she is handsome, rich and powerful,' Blanchard added with a smile.

'To that I can either say 'don't be ridiculous' or 'precisely'. I'm not sure if I care which.'

'Monsieur, perhaps you are being a little defensive?'

Partly because he wanted to and partly because he felt he should, Smith decided to get angry. In any case he had suddenly become bored by this clever young man. He actually wanted to start digging around in Robert's computer and he felt he was wasting his time here. His anger was only partially forced.

'Defensive or not, at present I'm not remotely interested in you or your bloody investigation. You pissed me about when I was in hospital, expecting me to be satisfied with a story that wouldn't pass muster in a children's nursery school and now you think that just because you are some jumped up European Union official with a taste for expensive suits and a large expense account you expect me to accept gratuitous insults because you buy me a cheap dinner. If you really want my help, then all I can say is that you are going the wrong way about it. Money might help. Until then, all I can say, Blanchard, is that you can shove your smooth Parisian sophistication somewhere, as they say, where the sun doesn't shine and bugger off.'

With that, Smith took his napkin from his lap, dropped it onto the table, got up and walked out of the restaurant leaving a completely bemused policeman surveying an empty table. He was clearly taking a risk treating a senior European policeman in this way, but he decided that the time had come for people to be straight with him or not to bother. He guessed he would either be arrested within the next hour, left alone or have a further meeting with a slightly more accommodating Chief Superintendent sometime in the future. As he actually thought that he still had not done anything wrong, he was really quite relaxed about which.

He walked home briskly. Slightly to his annoyance there was

no pursuit and he arrived home to the customary greeting from Arthur. Flouncing out was not something that he was particularly proud of, but it should bring something – anything – to ahead. He had no desire to help with a police investigation, particularly if he was not being paid.

The expected call came less than half an hour after he got home.

'Monsieur Smith. I can only apologise. You are, of course, quite right. There is absolutely no reason why you should help me, and I was wrong to assume that you would. I do, however, still need your help and I'm prepared to pay for it. I don't expect you to go beyond your confidentiality agreement but I'm sure that we can find some way to work together that will be mutually beneficial. I would be grateful if you would give me another chance.'

Blanchard paused, as if hoping for some sign that he was making progress. When none came, he continued:

'Perhaps by way of an apology and in the hope of persuading you to assist my investigation, you might consider having dinner with me and my wife tomorrow evening at L'Oustau de Beaumanière? My much-maligned expense account can probably stretch to that.'

Smith smiled at the reference and found his anger fading as he appreciated the cleverness of the invitation. The inclusion of the wife indicated that talk of business would be limited, unless, of course, she was another policeman. An invitation to L'Oustau was one that he was very unlikely to turn down. Nestling in the valley below Les Baux, it was not only arguably the best restaurant in this part of Provence, it was one of the great restaurants of France and, as such, well outside his budget. He had been only twice before and remembered the food as if it was yesterday not fifteen years ago. With a great effort he delayed his reply in the hope of giving the impression of some sort of internal debate and reluctance.

'Very well, Chief Superintendent. I accept both your apology and your invitation. However, I should warn you again that I won't help you in any way that would cause me to compromise my business relationship with my client. I'm fully aware that you may have the power to force my cooperation but until you are prepared to use those powers officially, you must respect my judgement as to what I choose to discuss with you.'

Blanchard sounded genuinely pleased. 'I'm delighted and I understand your position. Can I pick you up at about seven thirty?'

'I appreciate the offer, Chief Inspector, but I would rather drive myself, if you don't mind.'

'Of course. Shall we say eight o'clock at the restaurant?'

'Yes, that would be fine.'

Ordinarily, Smith would have taken a little time after the phone was put down to think about this latest turn of events. However, he was anxious to get back looking into Robert's tablet and iPhone. It had taken the half hour between returning home and Blanchard's phone call to get everything hooked up together and talking to his PC. He also had to reinstall some of the more useful but not exactly legal software in his collection that would enable him not only to get into places that he shouldn't but also allowed him to disguise his presence. Hacking into computers and across networks is nowhere near as difficult as is generally thought. Most passwords and security firewalls are relatively simple to break and most of the commercially available encryption systems have similarly available decryption systems if you knew where to look and had the money to pay. A few years ago, Russia and Balkan websites used to be a good place to look. Now it tended to be China. No, getting in was not the problem. Making sure that no-one knew you had visited was more difficult. He had begun to get the feeling that he might also have to poke around in his client's system and he certainly didn't want her to find out about it.

Given that it was probably his constant companion, Smith left the iPhone second. Sure enough the laptop yielded very little of interest. It was password protected but it took no more than an email to Madam to obtain it. It contained all the records, correspondences, cash flow projections, draft accounts and so on, that one would expect of a Financial Director. The internet log was equally anodyne. Robert had used online banking for both business and personal use, downloaded eighties pop music, modern jazz and pre-Bach chamber music. He followed Paris St Germain football club, booked flights, theatre and opera tickets online and a whole host of other things that all seemed perfectly normal.

Possibly more disappointing was the lack of anything hidden. Microsoft's simple deletion process does not actually permanently delete anything, it just pretends it does, but there was nothing exciting to be found when Smith recovered a random selection of deleted files. The temporary files were intact as was the internet history. As no effort had been made to delete or disguise them, Smith felt that, at this early stage at least, it was probably a waste of time to investigate further. There was no evidence of encryption software nor of professional deletion software. Even Robert's emails were intact with the archived data transferred to the company server as part of a weekly routine. A quick glance at the current email files all looked normal. He would have to ask Madame to check them as well as Robert's contacts list for any unusual entries as, at this stage, he was incapable of distinguishing between a legitimate business contact and any other sort.

The iPhone was a slightly different matter. Given the portability of these devices, they are built with a higher level of security that the common laptop. Fortunately, the entry password was not difficult. Dugresson's phone used the usual four-digit code and hadn't been setup with fingerprint or face recognition software. A four-digit code only has ten thousand possible combinations and going through them was only a matter of time. It may take a human a long time to so, but Smith's software could do it in seconds. The standard iPhone security that is supposed to erase the phone data after ten unsuccessful attempts is also easily bypassed by fooling the mechanism that updates the ten tries counter. After a few moments was in.

The iPhone email contact list was almost twice the size of that on the laptop. Again, they were completely unknown to him, but he downloaded it. Perhaps it might prove to be something that he could pass on to Blanchard at an appropriate time and for an appropriate reason. The laptop also contained considerable numbers of emails, documents and spreadsheets all encrypted. What was most interesting was that a sweep of the hidden installed programmes showed up that someone had installed keylogging software on it. Smith could think of no good reason why Robert should put it on himself so it would be interesting to find where the system was programmed to broadcast the keystroke log.

'All in good time.' He thought as he immediately disabled both the laptop and the iPhone's transmit facility and removed the SIM card from the phone. Smith set his software running and left the machinery to read to logs and therefore identify the full range of passwords and encryption keys that Robert had used. This, Smith thought, was going to be easier that he thought.

By the time he looked out of the window he realised it was completely dark and well past midnight. The strong yellow glow from the Amphitheatre floodlights tended to fool him a little. As usual when he settled into work with computers, time vanished. Sorting the key log was going to take his PC some time so he left it to its work and, having let Arthur out into the garden for a last pee,– an opportunity spent, as usual, looking balefully around the tiny space for something small and furry to kill, closed up the house and went to bed.

5. Investigations and Good Food

The computer was still running when he got back into his study at seven thirty the next morning after Arthur's walk, so, having made himself his usual very large espresso from the wildly expensive Italian machine he had treated himself to a few years ago when he couldn't afford it, and swallowing the usual quartet of blood pressure pills, he sat down at his desk in the little room at the top of his narrow, four story terraced house and set to work. Madam had arranged a meeting for him with Mademoiselle Brique for the next morning at Robert's office and she enquired as to his progress, and he was pretty sure she was not talking about marketing. The report on his findings took him an hour to write but essentially it read: 'nothing much yet.' He wanted at least another day and the meeting with Blanchard before he was confident in deciding what parts of the information, he was beginning to learn he chose to pass on.

He emailed the list of appointments around the various businesses to Madame with a request to make the arrangements and then realised that until his PC had finished number crunching and Madame had made his appointments, he was at a bit of a loose end and it was still only 9 o'clock in the morning. His emails contained the usual collection of rubbish but also a couple of newsy contributions from his daughters. Exile in France was made all the more pleasurable by the fact that his relationship with his daughters has survived the domestic upheavals of the last couple of years. They visited and emailed regularly.

Suddenly he had one of those Wind in the Willows moments. 'Bugger this,' he thought, 'what I need is a long walk.' The thought lacked the elegant exasperation of the whitewashing Ratty in Wind in the Willows, but the sentiment was the same. The day was cooler than usual, and the air was crystal clear. From his study window he could see well past the Abbey of Montmajour across to the Alpilles some ten miles away. In fact, this was to be one of the first opportunities of walking there as the network of footpaths that crosses and re-crosses the mountain range had been closed for much of summer months in the annual attempt to prevent the regular fires that broke out across the mountains during the summer as a result of visitors' cigarettes and picnicking lovers' passions.

An hour or so later he had parked the VW Polo at one of the many parking places at the foot of the hills. This one was near the old Roman reservoir to the north of St Remy Glanum. It was mercifully quiet, as it often was on a Monday the week. Most of the tourists were stumbling around the remains of the mental hospital where the troubled Van Gogh spent a year, having been forced to leave Arles. Arthur's utter delight at the prospect of a long walk shamed him, as it always did. There was no reason why he should not do this more - only his infinite capacity for finding other things to do prevented him. He strapped a very small knapsack somewhat self-consciously on his back; he definitely wasn't a knapsack sort of person. He justified this now however by the necessity of carrying a supply of water and a drinking bowl for Arthur and a chilled half bottle of Crémant in an insulating jacket for himself to be consumed at an appropriate moment during the walk. He knew perfectly well that this was not exactly the correct beverage when taking physical activity, but he had never really understood water, either for drinking, or for swimming in. Whisky, his garden and showers were the only places he felt truly comfortable seeing water. In any case, he could share Arthur's if necessary.

The Alpilles are not really mountains at all. They just look like it. They rise steeply in a short line that starts just north of Arles at St. Gabriel and continue roughly east west for forty miles to Cavaillon where they get lost in the more expensive extravagances of the Luberon and then the Alpes Maritimes. They rise only to just short of four hundred metres to the north of the richly agricultural Plan du Crau and therefore present no great challenge to the professional mountaineer. However, for Smith, they had something of the true Provence about them. He loved this place. The mountains start with low grass pastures filled with sheep, goats and somnambulant horses. A few, expensive villas cluster protectively around their swimming pools. But very soon as you climb the vegetation get harder until the cypress and oak forests give way to umbrella pines and hard little shrubs and wild lavender. Higher still and the mountain just grows rocks.

On top it is arrid and almost perpetually windswept, but the views are spellbinding. Face south and the Mediterranean lies in the distance across the Crau and the Camargue. Turn around and one can see a vista that extends from the Cévennes to the north west, Avignon straight ahead, and as you turn east past the Mont Ventoux sometimes you can glimpse the Alps themselves. One the right day, it is a breath-taking place and this was one of those days. Days this clear are rare in the summer. You tend to need a northerly Mistral to clear the heat haze and if you have one of those it is often too strong to stand up, let alone mountaineer. Winter is a better time to come. But Smith felt elated as he walked up the steep incline that was to take him to the Tour de Guetl TV relay station at the top. Dead financial directors vanished completely from his mind.

The problem of fires in the mountains during the summer had been dealt with very effectively by an extensive and intricate network of narrow gravel roadways that criss-crossed the entire mountain range and connected the villages at the foot of the mountains with the fire watch towers and the microwave relay masts at their summits with all parts of the mountains. There were maintained to a high level as they were there to give access across the mountain to firefighting trucks in an emergency. Huge, underground cisterns had been constructed at intervals along these roadways to give reservoirs of water when fires had to be fought. The result was twofold. Not only did the fires no longer ravage the countryside and endanger the influential owners of those swimming pools, but these roadways provided an extensive and intricate spider's web of walks for the public. Smith felt a lightening of heart as he struck upward with a purpose.

An hour later and after a number of stops to top up the dog, he stood at the Tour. He sat in the shade of a thwarted bush on a rocky outcrop and looked about him. Arthur, like most greyhounds, was never one to sit when he could stand, and he laid his chin lightly on Smith's knee. Smith opened the crémant and took a careful swig to avoid the lively contents going in through his mouth and out through his nose. That easy indignity avoided, he looked around him. There were many reasons he came to live in this bit of Provence. For a start it was the only place he knew he could afford a house after the divorce. Nowhere in England had held any ties anymore and a choice of somewhere to live would have been utterly arbitrary. In any case, he could not have afforded to buy anything even had he found somewhere he wanted to live. He had been coming to Arles since his teens and had always loved it and the countryside around it. He liked the people. They were as hard and unyielding as the countryside he now sat in. It was not a rich area. The opposite. This was not the middle-class Provence of the Promenade des Anglais and Peter Mayle; the chatterers. It was also not the Provence where waiters hear your bad French and reply in English. It was better than that. Much better.

Below him and to the left lay the Plateau de la Caume, a flat plain populated with olive trees from which came the olive oil that actually is as good as any in the world. Down to the south west he saw the outline of Les Baux, tottering on its hilltop some five miles away. It was only then that he remembered that his present rustic fantasy would be exchanged later for a more sophisticated episode in one of France's great restaurants. Reality, of a sort, pushed its way in.

He had no idea what the time was. His new life in Provence had been marked by a number of changes, one of which being that he no longer wore a watch. On this occasion, he had also left his mobile in the car which, given the possible proximity of his next heart attack, was not a really clever thing to do. There was no 'up' to head towards, so 'down' was the only option. He found that the mechanical champagne stopper he had brought was unnecessary, as always, and he set off down the mountain, a grateful Arthur by his side. Long periods of introspection were clearly not his thing.

As usual, the downward trip was both harder and less interesting. Smith had always thought that there must be some significance in the fact that humans are built better for climbing than descending. Rather like cows being able to walk upstairs not down. Feet and ankles seem to work better going up than down. However, he arrived, before too long, back at the car and was surprised that it was nearly four o'clock. He had been walking for hours. It was only then that his legs started to ache.

Insofar as Arles had a rush hour, he arrived back in the beginnings of it. However, once he had fought his way past the streams of determined locals and confused tourists, he found a parking place on the Place de la Major.

His computer had finished its work, but he decided not to get into all that. He only had a small amount of time before his dinner appointment and he simply didn't feel like it. The time was more than filled by domestic chores, feeding Arthur and a long, leisurely shower. At just after half past seven he drove slowly out of Arles retracing some of his route of earlier that day and found the road that went past Montmajour and through Fontvielle, then ran along the southern edge of the Alpilles until the turn north to Les Baux. As he drove, he anticipated with relish what lay ahead.

Smith had always been a bit of a Darwinist when it came to restaurants, especially good ones. He used Red Michelin Guides that were still the best guides to good food in spite of many competitors, although they were always more fallible on hotel recommendations. He used ones were at least five years out of date, preferably longer. The principal was a simple one. Any restaurant that was listed ten years ago for the quality of its cooking, no matter how modestly, that was still in business and listed ten years later had to be doing something right. The policy meant that he invariably missed, of course, that regular but changing constellation of rising star eateries that twinkle in many towns across Europe. New restaurants in Arles, like elsewhere, came, impressed, got written up, adopted by the local foodies and well-heeled tourists and then sank without trace a year or two later, sharing their fate with the high fashions boutiques in the Rue de la Republique who blossom briefly for a few high season months and then sell up and vanish. Arles is only superficially rich in the summer and it takes real quality rather than show for businesses to survive the long winters.

L'Oustau de Baumanière had been alive for longer than he and for many of the years since its foundation in 1942 it had held a full hand of three Michelin Rosettes for many years before subsiding to a more realistic two and, while it has had a very uneven reputation as a hotel, and some time ago had been scarred by an infantile and totally ridiculous olive oil scandal, its restaurant remains one of the greats of the region. It was with a sense of anticipation that he drove the dented and very dusty Polo into the gravel car park and parked proudly between a new Bentley Brooklands and Ferrari 599 GBT on the stroke of eight o'clock.

He was met at the door by the maître d'hôtel. 'Good evening, Monsieur Smith. Please come this way.'

Impressed, Smith followed the man through the stone vaulted dining room. At this relatively early stage of the evening, it was only half full. Their journey stopped at a small round table at one side of the room. Blanchard rose and came around to the front to greet him.

'Good evening, Monsieur Smith. Thank you for coming.' He turned slightly. 'May I present my wife, Suzanne?'

Smith walked around the table and took a confidently proffered hand and was please to feel his firm handshake exactly reciprocated.

'I'm delighted to meet you, Madame.'

'And I, you, Monsieur. Please do sit.'

Suzanne Blanchard was a slim young woman, dressed expensively but plainly in a high-necked, dark blue silk dress with a single string of pearls around her neck and a plain gold Piaget watch on her wrist. She wore her dark hair short but elegantly coiffeured.

'I have heard a lot about you, Monsieur Smith,' she continued.

'Oh dear, Madame.' Smith smiled.' Then I fear that your impression will not be particularly positive.'

'Quite the contrary. I've also walked out on him - from restaurants from time to time,' she added hurriedly.

At this point, the Chief Superintendent decided to re-join the conversation.

'Perhaps you should know, Monsieur Smith, that my wife is also my boss.'

'Good heavens,' Smith replied with a straight face, 'I have no idea what lies above a Chief superintendent.'

To judge by the amused looks on both their faces, the image was not lost on any of them. Both giggled slightly uncharacteristically. Smith found himself warming to the pair in spite of himself.

'Actually, my wife is an Assistant Commissioner in Europol and my department comes under her jurisdiction.'

Smith saw with delight how easy it was to come to terms with the European Union gravy train when he was about to become its beneficiary.

'Monsieur Smith,' Blanchard continued, 'I really must repeat my apology for my remarks yesterday. They were uncalled for especially as it was my intention to ask for your help.'

Faced with the imminence of one of the best meals he had had for ages, Smith was minded to be gracious. He embraced both of his hosts with his reply:

'Please, it's forgotten. I'm happy to help you insofar as I can and it doesn't conflict with my arrangement with Madam DuGresson - unless, of course, this whole matter is put on a much more official basis, in which case it would be duty to inform my employer. Clearly if this happened, my source of information would probably dry up immediately.'

It was Madame who replied.

'I quite understand. At this stage we also would prefer for our relationship to remain unofficial.'

'But hardly confidential, Madame,' Smith replied looking

around the rapidly filling restaurant.

'Yes, I'm afraid that's impossible. Our suicide explanation is no longer credible, and it wouldn't be entirely fair if I didn't point out that the association is not without its risks for you personally.'

'That has occurred to me as well, Madame, but I can't see any way of avoiding it. Like it or not I'm involved, and it is my choice.' He continued in an attempt both to lighten the atmosphere and to change the slightly uncomfortable subject. 'As long as someone takes care of Arthur should anything happen to me.'

'Of course, Monsieur, I would be delighted, but I suspect that Monsieur Aubanet would get there first.'

'God,' thought Smith, 'they could all be in this together, for all I know.' He turned to the much-anticipated pleasure of the menu.

'Monsieur Smith,' the Chief Superintendent, 'the purpose of this meal is twofold. Firstly, to apologise for my inept handling of our first meal together and secondly to try a little to get to know one another. If our relationship is to be an unofficial one, this is important because most of the time We'll simply be doing favours for each other. I can assure you; I don't intend that this should be a purely one-way process. You will be well rewarded for your cooperation. However, there will be plenty of opportunity to talk business at other times and in other places. We are looking forward to this meal as much as, I hope, you are, and it would be wrong to ruin it with talk of murders and criminal fraud. I therefore suggest that we talk no more of the business that has brought us together and simply enjoy the food and each other's company.'

'Willingly.' Smith's smile was broad, but he did find himself wondering when on earth Blanchard was going to get around to talking about what he wanted.

The meal was spectacular as anticipated and the conversation was surprisingly relaxed. The Blanchards seemed to talk freely about themselves and their careers and how much they had come to like Arles. Smith, for his turn, found it was relatively easy, in a limited sort of way, to talk of his life in Arles and how it came about. He was less forthcoming about his past on the grounds that they had probably already found out some of it and the rest was none of their business. At this stage he particularly wanted to keep his IT expertise out of the conversation. But the shared admiration of what was put in front of them to eat was always pre-eminent.

The food was sublime. Smith chose truffle and leek ravioli to start. Grilled red mullet with basil and thyme flowers was followed by the restaurant's legendary leg of lamb en croûte. The vegetables were, as expected, cooked to perfection. A modest expedition into the cheese selection, fresh but certainly imported from regions further north, left just enough for the soufflé crepe.

The choice of wine was made by his host and was gratifyingly unconventional. A 1999 Chateau Grillet, that tiny AOC hidden near Vienne on the northern Rhone accompanied the starters and fish. Arguably the best of the crus bourgeois, Chateau Cissac was again chosen to go with the meats and the cheese. The 1990 was memorable. The pudding was accompanied by 2001 Chateau Lafaurie-Peyraguey. All three declined coffee and a digestive. Smith still had half a glass of the Sauterne and he was happy to finish by savouring that. The maître d'hôtel came up to Blanchard and whispered in his ear. A slight frown crossed his face.

'Please excuse me for a moment. There is apparently a telephone call for me. I apologise but my instructions were not to be disturbed unless it was truly important.'

With this, he left the table. Smith was impressed by the fact that, unlike a number of their moronic fellow diners, Blanchard has not used a mobile in the restaurant. The changes, when he returned, were subtle but nevertheless it was pretty clear that something had happened. The conversation, about the annual opera performances in the Antique Theatre at Orange, continued but no-one's heart seemed to be in it. Sensing that, after a reasonable time Smith finished his wine.

'May I thank you for the most pleasant evening? It was a great treat to eat such food again and I'm very grateful for your invitation and your company that I have enjoyed immensely. However, if you would excuse me, I have a dog to walk when I get home and, in my retirement, I'm not used to late nights.'

Madame replied: 'Thank you for coming. We too have enjoyed the evening. I hope we can do it again before too long.'

With that, the three rose from the table – Smith noticed there seemed to be no question of a bill to be presented - and went out past the smiling maître into the car park. As they approached their cars, Blanchard stopped and placed his hand lightly on Smith's arm.

'My remarks about the possible risk to you personally from all this appear to have been well-timed. That telephone call informed me that Robert DuGresson's secretary, Mademoiselle Brique, was killed by a hit and run driver in Tranquetaille about an hour ago. At this stage I don't know whether this is anything more than an accident but until I find out, I suggest that you take care crossing the road - amongst other things. I'll telephone you in the morning.'

'Thank you for the warning,' replied Smith as he shook hands with his hosts and turned towards his car

---

By the time he got home the memory of a magnificent meal had been pushed aside the death of a woman he had not met, and now never would. He had never really met a coincidence. A bit like boredom, he didn't really know what it was. However, no one in his business life before had died, for any reason, the day he was going to meet them.

It was eleven thirty and Arthur needed walking. Only half way round his usual short circuit across the Redoute, down the montée Vaubin, north along the city wall on the Boulevard Emil Combes, back into the town and up the steps back to the Place de la Major, that he suddenly thought that walking unescorted around the town at almost midnight might not be the most sensible thing to do. The result of all this was that, by the time they got home, he was wide awake. He poured a very large but modestly strong whiskey and went up to his study, sat at his desk and drew a pad of paper towards him. Before tomorrow came and his inevitable telephone conversation with Madame, he had to have some information.

The effect of all the number crunching was that Robert's iPhone was a relatively open book. After about half an hour, he had listed four items that needed investigation. Firstly, the contact list was very small indeed, containing fewer than fifty names and contact details. Secondly a full calendar of appointments. Point three was a full log of emails. Fourthly, the sweep had identified the IP address to which Roberts laptop key log was regularly transmitted.

Keylogging is simply the listing and storing of every keystroke that's pressed on the computer. They are widely used - much more widely than is generally acknowledged - in business to keep track on what employees are actually doing of their computers. Everything that has even been typed on the keyboard can therefore be read by anyone with a sufficient mind to do so. Laptops tend to be particularly vulnerable because, for some reason, people in general protect them less well than PCs.

Another trick less generally understood concerns the anonymity of individual computers. Smith knew that it is generally assumed that people who used computers also assumed that their presence on the internet is invisible. This is very far from the case. Every computer has its own identifying number known as an Internet Protocol Address and it is very easy using publicly available tools to find out where that address is. The easiest information tends to be the latitude and longitude of the IP address holder, but town, street and house details present no great difficulty to those with a little perseverance.

Within a few minutes Smith found that Robert's activities on his laptop were sent daily to Madame DuGresson's office network. Madame obviously wanted to check up on her divorced husband, but Smith found the discovery more interesting than suspicious.

The contacts list on the phone only contained initials of people and email addresses, and when he compared these with the longer list from the laptop and was slightly surprised that very few seemed to correspond. More surprisingly, there were no telephone numbers or addresses. The former were, however, in the telephone memory. One thing did catch his eye. All the contacts were identified by two initials. Two contacts only were identified by one only, a 'G' and an 'S' and they seemed to be the recipient of at least half the emails. The calendar showed a frequent appointment with someone also called 'G', often on Wednesday lunchtimes; fewer with 'S'. These stopped with last Wednesday, and there were none in the future from that date, although the next month or two were filled with appointments almost every day. The Wednesdays were, however, blank.

He controlled his immediate desire to hack into Madam's electronic calendar then and there. He could do it relatively easily but disguising intrusions into networks was a lot easier when the network was busy and preferably when Madame was herself using her system. Two o'clock - good lord, was it that late, he thought - in the morning when there was no electronic chatter to hide in was not an ideal time.

The iPhone's document files contained only a few documents, copies or airline and train timetables, personal details like clothes sizes and credit card numbers. However, there were also traces of small files that had been regularly created and then deleted. They had been deleted by a much more sophisticated deletions system and were, for Smith at least, gone forever. The question was, of course, was where they had gone. The answer was either that Robert didn't want to keep them at all or that they had been exported to some external medium. A thought occurred to Smith and, sure enough the outgoing logs showed almost daily transmission to one IP address at the same time every night, rather like the keystroke log. This time however the transmission was to a commercial internet backup service or the Cloud as it is known as. 'Bugger,' Smith thought, knowing full well that hacking in there would be very difficult unless he had better equipment. He would have to rely on the keystrokes, and he remembered that reconstructing spreadsheets just using keystrokes was extremely tedious.

He was beginning to think that, in spite of his cracking what passed for the security of Robert's machine, he wouldn't find anything particularly exciting. Bed was definitely calling. But a last look though the unscrambled files in Robert's documents files did show a something interesting, an empty spreadsheet template of the sort that comes up when you fire up Microsoft Excel for the first time. This template was more interesting as it contained column headings along the top and dates down the rows. It was set up vertically for a month and was arranged like a bank reconciliation form. Nothing strange there, thought Smith. The guy was an accountant. What caught his eye was the template's name: 'Girondou'. 'Girondou?' though Smith, 'G? Ho Hum.'

6. Gentry, Bonafides and Swimming Lessons

Tuesday started normally. Arthur started making noises just before his alarm went off at seven and he had completed the usual preliminaries of a forty-minute walk followed by a mug of very strong coffee before the telephone rang.

'Smith? Gentry.'

One of the peculiarities of their relationship was that, in common with many of their British similars, surnames were used a sign of affection. They both regarded the current generation's unauthorized and almost universal use of Christian names as both frivolous and disrespectful. He was delighted that his children, now in their mid-twenties, had marked the transition from child to adulthood by changing from calling him 'Daddy' and his ex-wife 'Mummy', to 'Pa' and 'Ma'. Peter and Geraldine would have been impossible. If anything showed that they had been properly brought up it was the fact that neither of them had had to be told.

'Coffee?'

The two men did get together from time to time to chat at one of the less reputable cafés in the town with which Arles was particularly well stocked. Almost invariably the topic was cricket where they both followed England or rugby at which they were sworn enemies, Smith having Welsh connections that allowed him to support the principality. Never politics nor their shared past. Smith would always accept the suggestion as would Gentry had it come from him, but coming so soon after their last chat, there was no question.

'Certainly.'

'I'll come by at ten thirty.'

The line went dead. Gentry was never a man to use two words where one would do. But this was brief even by his standards. Normally they would meet at the café. Whatever he had to talk about, it was not just the latest test cricket debacle against India. He obviously didn't want to talk about their destination either. A cold shudder ran across Smith's shoulders. Suddenly the past felt nearer.

He was standing outside his house a minute or so before half past ten, looking around for his friend walking up into the square, when a quick toot on a horn directly behind him made him spin round ready with the usual scowl that he usually gave to local drivers who did alarming things near him in their motor cars.

To his surprise it was Gentry at the wheel of what can only be described as his motor. It was not the first time that images of Toad of Toad Hall came to mind where Gentry was concerned. The car only reinforced the metaphor. Smith had no idea how many Morgans there were resident in Provence but given that Gentry's British Racing Green version of a 1986 Roadster was the only one he had ever seen, probably not very many. It was an unusual car for someone who valued his anonymity so greatly but as Gentry had remarked when Smith said so, people looked at the car not him. Gentry leant over.

'Get in.'

Smith lowered himself gingerly into the narrow machine and Gentry had it moving before he had swung the tiny passenger's door closed. Gentry's driving style matched his car. Idiosyncratic and perilously fast and without further exchange they drove out of town on the old road eastwards past Pont de Crau towards Salon de Provence. Smith made no attempt to ask what was going on. He learned not to question Gentry years ago and, in any case, with the hood of the Morgan was down - in fact it had been removed completely - the wind and the car's exhaust would have made any conversation impossible. He did notice, however, that Gentry was observing the rapidly receding Provencal countryside in his mirrors with more than usual diligence. After about ten minutes they reached Saint Martin de Crau and turned off the main road into a small side street and then again into the rear cark park of a small café.

They sat at the back of the café and Gentry waited until Smith's large espresso and his own noisette were put in front of them. Smith knew that the reason for this unexpected excursion would come out in time, so he didn't ask. When it came, Gentry was brief and to the point.

'Much of it you know already. It seems that Robert DuGresson was a major figure in a criminal fraud that was stealing money from the EU. The recipient of the money is the criminal fraternity based primarily in Marseilles. The main man, as they say, is called Girondou although there is some suggestion that other of the so-called families also benefited.'

He looked directly at his friend.

'These are not pleasant people, Peter. Not as nasty as some you have dealt with successfully in the past, I'll admit, but we were both younger then and, although it sometimes felt like it, not really alone. Robert was the scheme's accountant, as it were. Or at least he seems to be the man who, shall we say, moved the money around. As far as I can see the scam has been going on for some time and is very successful. Blanchard is a relatively senior Eurocop investigating the fraud; not very successfully, it seems.'

'Madam DuGresson is the only daughter of Emile Aubanet, the current head of one of the most powerful and long-lived families in the area. When I say powerful, I mean it. Very little happens around here without their say-so and that of a few similar families, most of whom are based in the Camargue. They call themselves Les Frères - the Brotherhood - if you like. Given that this society has been in existence in one form or another for a couple of thousand years, their influence over local events is hardly surprising. There is also a history of difficulty between Les Frères and the Marseilles lot although there are signs that an agreement was worked out between the two after the Second World War and they tend not to tread on each other's toes too much.'

Smith interjected: 'Do I infer that Les Frères operate on both sides of the law?'

'Insofar as they acknowledge any law other than their own,' replied Gentry 'Yes, the word is that they do although I have never heard that they are actively criminal. In fact, I rather think they are not. They just exercise virtually complete control over much of any significance in the Camargue and in the town.'

'The local politicians..?'

'...are a joke.'

'Police..?

'The same, I'm afraid. There don't seem to be any rumours, wild or otherwise, about who actually killed Robert or why. In fact, there seems to be a marked reluctance to talk about it at all which, as you know, is very unusual indeed in this part of the world. I did pick up on some suggestion of sexual impropriety but given the number of years that he was separated from his wife and the usual indulgence granted towards men who stray from the straight and narrow whilst married, I hardly think that had much to do with it. Must be something to do with the fraud, I suppose.'

Gentry broke off while the waiter brought two more coffees. He was amused that he had seen no signal requesting them from Smith. Given the past, this didn't entirely surprise him. Smith had always been able to do things like that and, in the much wider context of their work together, it was a skill that had served them both well. They both glanced quickly around the café, each automatically scanning the view in front of them. No one had entered or left. There were still only eight people in the café including the barman. Gentry continued:

'Finally, I came past earlier this morning. There are certainly two people watching your house. I could not pick up on who they were. The French plain clothes police seem to dress like the homeless, so I don't know if they were police, goons from Marseilles or some of Madam's people but whoever they were, they certainly weren't very good. However, I thought it better to have this chat out of town. Although it means that I'm pegged but at least we'll not be overheard. I wouldn't trust your phone either. If Blanchard thinks that you are involved and he is even vaguely competent, your phone will be tapped.'

They both sat in silence for a moment. Gentry looked across the little table at his old friend.

'Knowing you as I do, you're not going to let all this fade away and not get involved, are you?'

'No, David, I don't think so. I'm not particularly happy to be assaulted, interrogated by police, followed and spied on by miscellaneous Marseilles ruffians without doing something about it. What interests me is primarily why everyone is so interested in me, as it were. Someone must be worried about something. If what you say is right, and I'm sure it is, then other people's attentions will not stop just because I want them to. In any case, I sniff the opportunity of making some money which, as you know, wouldn't be unwelcome.'

Gentry's concern was evident.

'You omit the beautiful widow, of course. But you're mixing with some pretty odd people, some who may not as gentle as you might hope. And before you remind me, I know that you used to be one of the more skilled at staying alive under trying conditions - the fact that I'm here at all proves that, but you are not as young as you were in those days, my friend.'

'I'm not thinking of going to war, at least not just yet, but it does seem inevitable that, irrespective of what others like Madam DuGresson might want, I have to sort something out. I'm not going to spend the next few years looking over my shoulder.'

'I had a feeling you might say something like that.' Gentry took a deep breath.

'OK, you do what you want. I'll ride point. I owe you at least that. Do you still have a gun?'

'Yes.'

'Do you want anything from me?'

'Well,' he replied after a moment's thought. 'Perhaps a new phone with the usual encryption gismos might be a good precaution.'

Gentry just nodded. They drove back a good deal more sedately than they came. They took a circuitous, if scenic, route back to Arles. They left St Martin going north towards Mausannes les Alpilles through some of the rich agricultural land that starts the Plain de Crau. Then they cut back toward Arles via the remains of the Roman aqueduct that once brought water to the city from the mountains and re-entered the town via the Montmajour road. Smith had a feeling that the route was more to do with finding a scenic way back than avoiding what was some highly unlikely observation. There seems very little more to say. Smith felt that old familiar comfort of having Gentry silently running things in the background. He relaxed and just watched the countryside pass.

By the time they were driving back under the rather bleak, low railway bridge over the Avignon road made famous in one of Van Gogh's many Arles pictures, it was very nearly lunch time.

'Please drop me off when we get through the gate,' said Smith, 'I need to get some bread for lunch.'

Gentry nodded and pulled over as soon as they had rounded the Place Lamartine and gone through the Porte de la Cavalerie that formed the northern gate into the old city. Smith got out and stood on the pavement.

'Thanks, Gentry.' He was rewarded with a slight nod of the head before he roared off into the maze of little streets that somewhere housed his much-prized garage.

Madam in the bread shop was as cheerful as usual, greeting Smith with a broad smile and her habitually bustling demeanour. He received the usual admonition that she had not seen Arthur recently, handed over his usual *gros pain* and accepted the one euro with another broad smile. Smith had no idea how she managed to remain so constantly cheerful give the ridiculously long hours she and her husband worked. She was completely unflappable even when faced with a crush of waiting customers that would have a British health and safety inspector enter cardiac arrest. The daily bread ritual was one that he looked forward to.

Loaf in hand, he started the climb through the Place Voltaire and up to the arena. Rather than taking the direct route onto the Place de la Major he turned left up the little Rue Renan, a steep little cobbled alley that cut up to the back of the Place.

They stood out like the proverbial sore thumbs. The square was used for mainly for parking, so it wasn't difficult to spot two men sitting in a battered silver Renault Clio, elbows slung casually out of the open windows, smoking. These were not professionals. He made a point of walking past the car close enough to brush past one of the men's elbows and knock his loosely held cigarette into his lap. A significant commotion ensued inside the car while he walked on oblivious and went into his house. Like all the best gestures it was pretty meaningless, but it was an effective way of letting whoever it was know that they had been spotted. Smith picked his digital camera out of the sideboard drawer returned to the car park and walked up to the Renault and very deliberately took a photo of the car, its registration number and the two occupants. The look of surprise on their faces registered clearly. Smith rightly surmised that as they were on surveillance, in theory a least, he wouldn't be challenged. The message would get back to whoever sent them and that was the object of the exercise. Smith was beginning to get fed up.

Lunch over, he decided on a siesta for an hour or so. Try as he might, he could not seem to fall properly into the siesta routine. He accepted that it was the best way to spend a traditionally very hot couple of hours in the middle of the Provençale summer's day. But he had never been able to sleep properly then. He hated that disorientated feeling when he woke; rather like coming out of a cinema while it was still light. He never felt rested in any way and often felt dreadful. However, he tried it from time to time, hoping that his body would finally come to terms with it and he might get some benefit rather than just a feeling of a simple waste of time. This time, however, he was woken by the telephone; never a good start for anyone and for someone who disliked the thing as much as

Smith, a dreadful one. He made a point of never having a telephone of any sort in the bedroom and the small circle of people from whom he was happy to receive calls knew when to call him and when not. However recent events had added a couple of people who had yet to learn the rules and the telephone continued to shrill. He checked his clock and realised that two thirty was a not unreasonable time for anyone to call. He clambered out of bed, put on his towelling dressing down, and set off up the flight of stairs to his study, his irritation increasing with every step until he slumped into his desk chair a slightly grumpy person.

'Yes?' His tone was less than polite.

'Monsieur Smith, have I caught you at a bad time?'

'No Madame. I apologise. I had rather a late night and I was trying to catch up some sleep with an attempt at a siesta.'

'Ah, then I'm sorry to have woken you.'

Please don't worry. I was not being particularly successful. How can I help?'

'Perhaps you have heard that Mademoiselle Brique was killed in a road accident yesterday evening.'

'An accident?'

'That's what the police are saying but...'

'Quite.'

So that will make interviewing her a little difficult'.

'Yes, it will. I have had to agree to give the police access to the office,' her voice trailed slightly.

Answering the unspoken question, Smith replied: 'I have Robert's laptop here, Madame. I wouldn't worry about the police visiting the office, although I would have a lawyer present just in case their enthusiasm takes them places where they shouldn't go.'

'Yes, I have already arranged just that. Did you come across Robert's iPhone, by any chance?'

His instant reaction, of course, was to deny it. He would have preferred a little more time to look into it. However, he remembered the destination of the keystroke log and saw that it was pointless.

'That's what kept me up so late, Madame,'

'I'm glad it wasn't the food from L'Osteau.' she replied with a teasing laugh.

'As usual, Arles proves to be a much smaller place than I imagine, Madame.'

'Yes, especially if you are involved with us, I'm afraid.'

'Blanchard said he would telephone me this morning, but I can't believe the accident to Mademoiselle Brique it was a coincidence. He and his wife want me to help their enquiry into Robert and the possibility that he might be involved in some sort of fraud to steal EU funds meant for the preservation of ancient monuments.'

She snorted down the telephone. 'Yes, I know all that. Monsieur and Madame Blanchard have been blundering around in our private lives for some time. However, I thank you for telling me. It appears that your assurance of your loyalty to your clients was true.'

'I would be pretty unhappy if you doubted it, Madame. You clearly don't know me as well as you think you do.'

'That's both a justifiable rebuke that I accept, and an intriguing thought, Monsieur.'

Smith let that hang.

'OK. I need to visit some of your businesses over the next few days. Perhaps you could make the appointments for me? I would be happy to start this afternoon.'

'Of course. Let us hope they don't suffer the same fate as your last appointment.'

'If they do, then you will have a need of a larger personnel department that you currently have.' Smith had always hated the ridiculous modern expression: Human Resources.

'We don't have one of those.'

'Precisely.'

Smith could not help warming to this woman who, he was beginning to think, was almost certainly up to her elegant elbows in whatever was going on. He could see a serious chat with her and her father looming before long. Madame's email arrived a couple of hours later.

His later afternoon was spent happily enough at a large rice storage facility just outside the town. The place was very like the usual grain handling and storage plants that littered his native East Anglia and was staffed by the French equivalent of the British grain merchant whose main skill was playing not buying and selling grain but manipulating the European Union intervention fund system. While this may be regarded by those, like Smith, who thought that the Common Agricultural Policy was a huge, international, institutional legal fraud designed to keep incompetent farmers for whom society has no use in business at the expense of the non-farming tax payer, Madam DuGresson had at three of these monstrous facilities in her portfolio. This was certainly European Union fraud, Smith felt, on a grand scale but all perfectly legal. He was very well behaved and showed as much interest as he could muster to the kindly, enthusiastic man who showed him around. Obviously, any friend of Madam's had to be treated like royalty. However, this place needed no marketing. Demolition, perhaps, but not marketing. Rather like an old acquaintance of his who was an owner of marinas on the Thames in England and got away with doubling his rich customers' mooring fees by remarking dryly that they could hardly take their gin palaces home, the local rice farmers were hardly in a position to get their product to the supermarket shelves themselves. In fact, judging by the lack of presence in even the local Arles shops, the Camargue rice farmer seemed to survive completely without retail sales. It was a situation that would have warmed the cockles of the Brussels bureaucrats' hearts, and probably did. However, the rice storage bit of his report wouldn't take too much writing.

He got home at about six, hung out his washing, checked his emails and the details of England's attempts to avoid defeat at cricket, and settled to make some notes on his afternoon. The telephone rang.

'Your answering service seems not to be switched on, Monsieur Smith,' Blanchard's tone seemed to indicate that he was slightly put out.

'On the contrary, Chief Superintendent, it cannot be switched on as I don't have one. And before you try, I don't have one for my mobile telephone either.'

'Are you not afraid that you might miss something important, Monsieur?'

'No.'

The answer hung emptily between them.

'I promised to inform you about the death of Mademoiselle Brique. I'm afraid that we have very little information. She was struck by a car outside her grandmother's house in Tranquetaille. No one seems to have seen the incident and she didn't regain consciousness before her death in hospital an hour or so later. I have no indication of foul play, but I also don't believe in coincidences.'

'Well thank you for your call. I'm not sure what to do with the information but thank you, nevertheless. However, I'm pleased that you called because I find I have no idea where to send my thank you letter to you and your wife for last night. It was a most enjoyable evening.'

'Monsieur Smith, such a thing is not necessary.'

'Yes, it is, Chief Superintendent.'

'Very well, Monsieur. Suzanne and I rent an apartment on the Boulevard Hausmann. Number seven. However, concerning the other matters, at this stage, I feel that I should warn you that you might be getting into dangerous company.'

'Yes, the thought had occurred to me as well. I very much appreciated not diluting last night's meal by talking business, but perhaps we should have a word in private, and given that it seems that it is impossible to go anywhere in Arles without everyone knowing, why don't you come here for an aperitif. Then at least the men you have parked outside my house can take care of you while you are here.'

It was a wild stab but, as it turned out, a very accurate one.

'Ah, you have noticed them. They have been somewhat be embarrassed. Yes, I think that would be a good idea.'

'Seven o'clock?'

'Yes, that would be fine.'

It gave him an hour or so to collect his thoughts and having set himself down on the sofa beside a slumbering Arthur he was slightly amused to discover that he didn't have any - or, at least, nothing specifically on the mystery. Apart from the fact that he was completely unable to tell the good guys from the bad, insofar as there were any of either type or even a distinction between the two, the whole thing was making little sense. Robert was obviously up to something. Madam was keeping track of his every move. Blanchard and his wife were on a mission from Brussels that, by their own admission, was going nowhere. Someone bumped off Robert and possibly his PA for no obvious reason. Whatever Robert was doing, he had no idea who would get sufficiently angry about it to kill him. Unless Mademoiselle Brique kept information in her bottom drawer, he could see little reason for disposing of her unless her killers were simply taking out insurance. That was the point that he ran out of inspiration, so he turned his attention to one of his current books, Jaques Aymard's splendid three-hundred-page essay on hunting in ancient Greece and Rome. He was still engrossed when the doorbell raised both him and Arthur from their respective reveries.

'Good evening, Chief Superintendent. Please come in.'

A surprisingly dressed-down Blanchard entered. Jeans and a Ralph Lauren polo shirt, a sweater tied loosely around his shoulders and the inevitable Gucci loafers at the other end. Arthur greeted him with his usual enthusiasm and much to Smith surprise, Blanchard seems as impressed with the dog as had been Madam DuGresson a few days before.

'Now I can see how you seem so content with your solitary retirement in Arles,' he said, making a genuine fuss of the dog. 'He much be a splendid companion. One day our lives will settle down sufficiently for Suzanne and me to have some dogs.'

Arthur accepted the adulation with his well-practiced ease and then, judging that seating was going to be a priority, leapt back onto his sofa and sat down with an emphatic thump.

'What can I offer you to drink.'

'A whisky, please. Ice but no water thanks you. I feel that I should apologize, to you, an Englishman, for this American taste.'

'Please don't. I drink my whisky with both ice and far too much Perrier water to be acceptable in the correct circles. However, that had never concerned me unduly. However, if it helps, I'm Welsh, not English, by parentage, at least,'

'Ah,' Blanchard replied, 'I'm sure that explains a lot. But what exactly?'

'I haven't the faintest idea,' came the rejoinder with a chuckle, 'but I'm sure it must, so I thought I better say it.'

Blanchard was obviously thoroughly relaxed, even before his whisky. This, Smith thought, might be an interesting interview.

'I must first apologise for not having a range of indigestion-making little bits and pieces for you to eat as is the habit in France. My only excuse is that I cannot resist eating more than I should of the damn things, I'm already overweight and I tend not to keep any in the house. If you are hungry a little later, I can quickly make something to eat if you wish.'

'Thank you. You are most considerate. I too have little time for nuts and bits of Arles sausage.'

'Ah yes one of the great over-hyped delicacies of the region. I really don't like it very much, but I have discovered that if you cut it into very small pieces and fry it with some olive oil, onions and white wine it can make a passable dressing for pasta or in a salad. Now where do we start?'

'Well perhaps you could tell me what you think of this whole business and then I can try to fill in any blanks and then perhaps we can progress to how we might be able to help each other.'

With that Blanchard settled back into his seat at the end of the sofa, laid a finely wrought hand on Arthur's head, draped conveniently for precisely that purpose over the arm on the adjoining sofa, and looked expectantly across to Smith.

'Well, I tend to look first for the simplest explanation. Robert DuGresson was the financial brains behind a scam to steal large quantities of EU money meant, amongst other things, for the preservation of ancient monuments. He was officially involved in the patrimony of Arles and was in a very good position to do such a thing. Although I have not tried it myself, it can't be too difficult given the tens of thousands of people and institutions that do it legally, let alone illegally. He presumably was associated with others, possibly all over the world. Something went wrong, either with the system or with Robert himself and he was killed by his associates who were pissed off. He might have been killed by outside agencies wanting, as they say, a piece of the action, although I think that unlikely given that he seems to have been in the best position to get hold of the money. Killing the golden goose, and all that. His PA was probably killed for insurance. My experience of good PAs is that they tend to know entirely too much about their bosses. You and you wife are trying to catch these evil doers but have run up against something of a brick wall here in Arles because no one here speaks to outsiders. You presumably suspect Madame DuGresson and her father of some sort of involvement, as do you the rest of the very closed community here in Arles and especially the Camargue. There is Mafia of sorts here, Gipsies with more money than Croesus and the sort of traditions and secrecies dating back over centuries that make for unexplainable loyalties and hard investigations. My involvement is fortuitous for you because for some reason that I don't understand either, Madame or her father have come to considerable lengths to involve me. I'm uncertain whether you want me to spy on her or she wants me to spy on you. Probably both. From a personal point of view, I'm quite close to getting very pissed off with the lot of you. However, it must be said, following your previous remarks about my person safety, I'm more inclined to put my trust in the Aubanet family's ability to protect me than the local, national or European police forces. Of course, there is also the possibility that Robert was mugged for his credit cards and Mademoiselle Brique was killed by a lunatic driver of which there are hundreds of thousands in France. That's about it.'

Blanchard nodded. 'A very good summing up of the situation we find ourselves in, Monsieur. Before adding my bit, perhaps you might like to speculate on any other explanations that there might be.'

'Well,' replied Smith, 'Those are endless. Robert could have had a jealous lover who killed him over some domestic tiff. He could have been involved in something totally unrelated but equally criminal. His ex-wife may have wanted him back and killed him when he wouldn't come. I could have killed him for some reason that either of us could create. The list could go on with increasing unlikelihood. Good Lord, he could have even committed suicide, which is, as they say, where we came in.'

'Thank you. I think that you have covered most of the possibilities, but I favour your first suggestion. In fact, I'm embarrassed to say that I have little to add. We are pretty certain that the fraud was going on and that Robert was, so to speak, its Financial Director. Before you ask, we don't believe that the Aubanet family was involved, at least not directly. It is a family of some principal and their position in the community over many years would make this sort of thing unlikely. Not impossible, mark you, but unlikely and, possibly more importantly, unnecessary. They don't need the money. As far as I can see they have no criminal connections of any magnitude except, of course, to acknowledge that they are connected in some way to almost everything of significance that happens in this part of the world. Again, you will have seen that many of their businesses seem to be run primarily to support the local community not to fleece it. I also happen to know that the family has been a major influence in keeping other criminal organisations out of the area. We thus have some evidence of the fraud but little proof. In fact, just before Robert's murder we were on the point of giving up here and looking elsewhere for a weakness in the scheme. Robert's death gave us some hope that, by persisting here, we might be luckier. I'm personally not completely convinced that Robert's death was actually related to the fraud, but I cannot afford to let the possibility go un-investigated. Then, of course, you came along.'

'So, what do you want with me?'

'I want to offer you a job.'

Smith got up and replenished their glasses. 'Oh Hell, London busses and all that.'

His guest looked genuinely puzzled. 'I'm sorry, Monsieur, I don't follow.'

'Oh, just an old English joke. You wait for ever for a bus to come and then two or more arrive together. Except in this case it seems to be jobs not buses.'

'Ah, I see. Well you would seem to want to earn something from all this, and I'm quite happy to pay you for information.'

'We seem to have covered this ground before. I already have an employer and I suspect that both her cooperation and the money would dry up immediately she thought that I was telling you any secrets. If that happened, of course, my usefulness to you would end simultaneously.'

'No. no. I'm quite happy to rely on your judgment as to what you might pass on.'

'There is another matter, Chief Superintendent, that perhaps ought to be clarified before we go.'

'Oh yes, and what is that?'

'Well I haven't any real idea of who you are. I know what you say you are, and you have a nice official - looking identity card. But other than that, and with respect, your declared identity and its documentation could easily be as false as a van Meegeren Vermeer.'

'Ah, I see. You wish me to establish my credentials, as they say.'

'Under the circumstances, I don't think that's entirely unreasonable, although I have to admit that I haven't the foggiest idea of how you might do it.'

'Yes, I see the problem.' Blanchard paused for a moment although it was difficult to know whether he was actually trying to solve the problem or whether he was just trying to avoid creasing his immaculately smooth forehead. Probably the former as it was half a minute before he spoke again.

'Is there anyone you know personally in the British police or legal system who you trust to be honest with you.'

This was a more difficult question than Smith would have chosen to admit, or, indeed, Blanchard might have imagined. Throughout most of his life he had tried to avoid having any contact whatsoever with police in any form. No policemen figured in his modest collection of current friends. Then he remembered. Some years ago, he met and gone game shooting with a very high-flying young policeman who was in charge of the bit of the East of England's police that did all those things that you now see in American films. Insofar as Norfolk needed people to dive into ponds and run around the countryside with guns, he and his little group did it. He seemed to remember that the man retired at an obscenely young age on a full pension and embarked on a thoroughly remunerative second career advising ex-colonial police forces in warm and comfortable parts of the world how to implement all those things that the British tax payer had paid him to learn. The Bahamas was the last place Smith remembered.

'I certainly used to know a Chief Superintendent, like yourself. I think he has now retired and when I last heard of him, he was working with the Bahamas police force as a consultant. His name was Chris Borrowash. He retired from the Norfolk police in the UK about five years ago. If you can find a contact number for him, I can talk to him and ask him to confirm who you are.'

'Of course. May I use your phone?'

If Blanchard was a fake, then he must have had some pretty good connections for it took one quick call from the Chief Inspector and a wait of about fifteen minutes for someone to call back with the required number. He took out a small business card from a plain silver case, wrote the number on the back and handed it across.

'That's the number of the Royal Bahamas Police Force. I gather that your friend has an office there.'

'Thank you, I'll call him later.'

'As you wish.'

Blanchard glanced at his watch. 'Perhaps you can call me

when you are satisfied. In the meantime, I'm expected home for dinner.'

With that he rose, turned towards the door. Smith extended his hand.
'Please give my regards to your wife,'

Smith suddenly thought it was worth a try.

'Chief Superintendent. In your investigations have you come across a group of people called Les Frères - 'The Brothers' or possibly, The Brotherhood'?'

Smith thought he might have seen a slight flicker of recognition, but he could not be sure.

'No, I don't believe I have. Are they important?'

'I don't know. It is just something I came across,' Smith replied, hoping that he had struck the right note. At the moment he had no idea whether it was important or not, but he certainly didn't want to give the policeman the idea that he thought it was.

With that Blanchard walked down the front steps, walked briskly down the hill towards the now floodlit Arena, and turned the corner out of Smith's sight.

Somehow each time he met Blanchard, the less impressed he was with him. In three of conversations he had gained very little new information and that was not just because Blanchard was being clever. It looked as if his actually didn't know much. It was pretty obvious that his so-called investigation had got nowhere as it was looking increasingly like Blanchard and therefore presumably his wife were just another couple of people on the European gravy train.

No, the answers, if there was one, would come from the laptop or, the iPhone. He had already failed to find any actually on either of the computers. He could have another computer hidden away, although he thought that highly unlikely. People don't often double up of these things. No more likely was they were buried somewhere on the internet and the key logs would, in time, yield their location. However, it was not the sort of job you started at that time of night when dogs and humans needed feeding and walking. He would return to this in the morning.

It is a commonly held misconception, especially amongst people who know less than they might about computing that there is a place called 'cyberspace'. Normally it seems to exist as a sort of Bermuda Triangle for electronic data when it is lost by people who have no real idea of what their PC actually does. 'My email must have got lost in cyberspace' is the modern equivalent to 'my letter got lost in the post.' It is a way of shifting the blame either for sending it to the wrong place or, like the proverbial cheque, not sending it at all.

Cyberspace doesn't exist. All the increasingly infinite amount of data that wings around the internet at close to the speed of light travels along as radio waves, in bits of wire and bendy glass rods. It ends up, possibly temporarily, at real, solid computers called servers and on whizzing magnetic discs - glorified vinyl singles, really, - where it sits, ready to be recalled at a nanosecond's notice. These computers are not mythical. They hurt if you hit your knee on them. There are just an awful lot of them connected together electronically and they exist all over the globe. The system that joins them all together is called the Internet. The internet is only a filing system. Big, certainly; very big actually, but still a filing system with more than a few similarities to the modest and much unloved filing cabinet.

It you want to get the data stored in your office filing cabinet; you first have to know where it is. You may take for complete granted that you know where your filing cabinet is but try using getting hold of that latest letter from your bank manager if you have filed it and then forgotten where your filing cabinet is. You need to know.

The internet is no different. Data doesn't vanish, it just ends up in a 'server' somewhere in Albuquerque or Beijing or even Ulm.

Wherever. The secret is to know where it has gone so you can get it back if you want. Lose this particular set of filing cabinets and you are completely buggered. Internet search engines like Google, and those interesting blue underlined words that make your curser arrow turn into a hand are simply someone telling you that they know where the data you want is. Click it and you find the right filing cabinet in Bejing - as long as you have asked for the right file in the first place, of course. Computers are just fast idiots. It does what it is told. If it goes wrong, it is usually your fault, not it's.

Thus, the Internet is doing not more than offices have done ever since there were offices. The only difference is that the filing system is bigger, and retrieval of the data is faster.

Retrieval is the key. However, the impression is that if your data is in a filing cabinet in Beijing then is somehow secret or secure. No one can get hold of it. This is the biggest myth of all. What the internet does is bring the Beijing filing cabinet into your office the millisecond you ask for it. All you have to do is know where to ask for the data and prove that you are entitled to have that data. This is where the Internet's biggest weakness lies. The Internet only works because the system can identify every bit of data on it, which is impressive given the unimaginably large amount of data that it holds. If the 'system' can identify where to look and what to look for, so can anyone. If you have enough money you can buy every Visa number and all their attendant details. A few years ago, the source was China. Now it is one of the 'istaans'.

The problem then is that the more difficult you make the access systems to prevent someone who should not access the data, for getting hold of it - and you can concoct some alarmingly elaborate systems for doing this - the more difficult they are for ordinary humans to use. Remembering four-digit PIN numbers defeats many people. Carrying twenty-digit alpha numeric passwords in one's head is next to impossible.

Thus, if you decide that a set of spinning discs in Saskatchewan is the best place for you to store your innermost secrets, your secrets are as only as safe as the much unloved username and password. Not very. Almost all major institutions and business back up their data regularly over the Internet and often store it in places like Saskatchewan - although they don't actually know it is Saskatchewan, of course. They don't care, of course, as long as they can get it back when they want. Earthquakes in Saskatchewan may be a problem, of course, but there are solutions to this as well.

If you really want to keep your data safe, then the usual advice is store it in code - encrypt it, to use IT-speak. Unless you are the CIA or Her Majesties Government or another of the Establishment acronyms, and most private individuals aren't, this is complete rubbish. Most commercially available encryption programmes are easily crackable in spite of the sales jargon festooned with comfort words like algorithms. This makes them of very limited use for private individuals. Most people who try encryption systems give up. They take too long on a standard PC. The whole point of a computer is that it is the fast idiot and you don't want to have to wait around for. If it works slower than you do normally then it's a dead loss. Good encryption takes time or expensive computing and software to run on it.

Given that Smith had found nothing stored on the Aubanet server, nor on his laptop or iPhone, it was a fair bet that he had used the internet to keep his records. So, Smith had to find three things. An IP (internet Protocol) address to locate the files, user name and password once he had found where the data was. IP addresses are stored in the computer's memory as well as other useful bits of data called cookies. Unless considerable care to erase all this, somewhere on your hard disc, every IP address you visit can be discovered. The usual erasure devices offered by Microsoft are about as useful as the Trash Bin system; not at all to a competent hacker.

Addresses that appear regularly, especially in conjunction with encryption software use would be even easier. Robert was an accountant not an IP nerd. His username would be exactly - that a name. Fewer than two percent of people use numeric usernames although there is no reason why they shouldn't. Something to do with the word 'name', Smith supposed. Also, fewer than one percent of people use different usernames for each purpose. A search for an odd name in the keystroke log that occurs regularly would also not pose too many problems for his computer. Finally, a password. In spite of regular advice to use "strong passwords" most people have a very basic approach. People take comfort in thinking that 'my son's birthday backwards' is a good approach. They don't realise that a birth date is a birth date and the fact that it is their son's is irrelevant. It does not make it less detectable. It just makes it more memorable to the user. The twentieth century only contained thirty six thousand five hundred and twenty five separate birth dates – give or take – twice that if you use the American date format as well and whether expressed backwards or forwards to the computer it is just a number and a half decent PC can crunch the relevant birth date numbers in seconds.

Finally, Robert either worked with his files remotely, not downloading them, in which case there should be a record of substantial time spent online to particular IP addresses, or, more likely, he downloaded the files and worked with them locally before uploading them again when he was finished. That should leave traces on either the laptop or iPhone, unless he laboriously cleaned his discs after every use. Some people do, but very few in reality.

Robert probably have used his laptop to access his files. The IP address of his archive would be buried in the downloaded key log and, given the very recognisable format of the address, a simple, if lengthy, scan will find it. Looking for usernames and passwords is similarly simplified by the fact that will almost invariably follow the dialling into the archive. If you are going to access a secure website, you tend not to dial in to the log-in page, then go off and type a letter or some other task before entering username and passwords. It tends to happen all in a string and therefore simple software can recognise the sequence. It is unlike anything else.

Smith loaded up the raw key stoke logs and set the parameters of the scan. As with all codes, the Achilles heel, as Smith knew well was the repeat. If this sequence only happened once, then needles and haystacks come to mind. However, this sequence was used regularly and frequently. It was very, very unlikely that Robert changed his username and password every time he used the archive. Who does? Repeats are manna to the code breaker and computer searches are no different.

The raw data took a bit of sorting, but Smith was only looking for IP addresses with their own unique logins. All the others that shared usernames or passwords could be discarded. Having removed hundreds of duplicates, he ended up with four candidates. Three of the IP addresses were commercial, on-line archive sites. The fourth got him immediately to the private client page of the website of the Banque Générale de Berne.

He downloaded everything he could from the three archives. Two were in clear text, a third was encrypted. The less time he spent online the better. Having taken all the data, he erased the archives. Access would be automatically blocked in any event soon when Robert's monthly payment failed to appear. 'Best form of security,' Smith thought grimly. 'Don't pay your bills.'

He accessed Robert's bank accounts. A local Arles account at the Société Général was obviously where his salary was lodged. There was a standard current account and a solid if unspectacular savings account. There were also two Swiss accounts. One had been opened almost eight years ago and the balance was currently some fourteen million Euros. A second started four years ago and contained a further eight million. Smith thought for a moment what he could actually do with that amount of money, then realised that he actually hadn't the faintest idea. One million he could use. Fourteen, he couldn't. He left it all intact and decided against even downloading a transaction record. Banks are better than most at security and it was highly likely that any departure of data would be logged, as was his current enquiry. However, the news of Robert's demise had obviously not reached the bank and given the dubious and completely secret nature of Robert's funds, the site would probably remain open for a little time at least.

The downloaded data proved to be a complete record of what Robert had been up to. Every criminal project he had been involved in, how much had been siphoned off through inflated contracts, bribes to obtain contracts in the first place, kickbacks to EU officials, slush funds, plain thefts from funds, together with full details of who received the funds, what bank accounts they used, what and when money was moved about. There was also a full list of contacts of those involved. Smith was relieved to find that the name Aubanet didn't appear. However, the name Blanchard did. The Eurocop had been receiving a monthly 'retainer' of ten thousand Euros for the last five years.

Smith turned his attention to the third, encrypted folder. Without really looking closely before he started, Smith set his decryption software to work. Robert had used a simple, very cheap, commercially available system that really had more annoyance value rather than anything else. What did surprise him, however, was the time it took to unravel. It was the best part of fifteen minutes to clear. Then he understood. These were large, high resolution, picture files, hundreds of them. Pictures of naked children, most having sex with adults, many with Robert.

He felt sick. These were not images that Smith wanted to view and he closed them down as quickly as possible. He also found another database in the folder, presumably of fellow paedophiles. It was also obvious also that Mademoiselle Brique had indeed, procured children for Robert. It was completely sickening stuff and Smith closed that down as soon as possible as well. He didn't even bother dialling up some of the other websites. He had a nasty feeling that he knew what he would find.

He suddenly felt very tired. Without noticing, he had been sitting in relative immobility for some time and, looking at the computer clock, he was surprised to see that it was nine o'clock in the evening. Arthur had to be fed and the evening walk would be a good way of clearing this collection of muck if not out of his mind then at least to the back of it.

Unusually for that time of year, it had clouded over and the evening was somewhat darker than usual. It was still not night time, but a western sun was very low, shining yellow just above the horizon. It just got in under the cloud and the whole of Arles was bathed in a blood orange light. It was an uncharacteristically harsh skyline that matched his mood. His walk started as usual across the Hauteur and then descended the steps that dissect the Jardin d'Ete and give onto the main Boulevard des Lices. There was still a good smattering of tourists although the main evening promenade usually happens a little further down the road nearer the centre of town. Instead of turning down his usual route along the city wall, he felt he needed a much longer walk.

He walked directly across the road and continued almost due south through a small residential area known as Les Alyscamps after the Roman necropolis situated at one end. It is a quiet section of town of relatively small town houses each with pretty walled gardens. Most of the buildings are late nineteenth and early twentieth centuries with only the occasional incursion of some monstrous institutional concrete blocks that so despoil many of the France's towns.

One of the virtues of this route was that there were seldom any tourists and not too many locals. Equally importantly there were precious few other dogs. Arthur had never really liked other dogs and certainly would object violently if they interrupted his walk. Smith thought through the consequences of what he had just learned. In a sense, although he had learned much more about the dead man personal life, it didn't really take him further on. It all just confirmed much of what he had suspected. However, that proof brought its own dangers. The bad guys presumably knew of his investigations through Blanchard who was now obviously connected with the fraud. In fact, that sort of intelligence was almost certainly Blanchard's main function. That in itself was not entirely satisfactory. However, Smith now had a full set of names and details. That made the whole thing much less calm.

Whatever happened he had to make himself secure from their possible wrath should it get out that he had enough information to put the lot of them away in prison for a long time. That simply meant that the records had to be put somewhere that was safe and from where they could be made public should any misfortune befall him. In the world of the internet, this was actually not too difficult to achieve. The files could be hidden very much as Robert had tried but very much more successfully. Their location could also be given to anyone who had an email address and that certainly goes for any police force, newspaper or government in the world. Their transmission could easily be made to activate automatically unless

Smith was around to prevent it. Perhaps it would be prudent to set something up as soon as he got home.

His leisurely perambulation continued in a wide arc, taking a westerly direction past the town sports stadium and on towards where the AutoRoute sliced through the town northwards on its way towards Nîmes. He cut up towards the remains of the Église de Carmes at the bottom of the Boulevard George Clemenceau and on up towards the Rhône. None of his trip had been done at more than ambling pace so by the time he reached the river under the new bridge it was dark. Well past eleven he thought. He very soon caught up with the place where the previous night he and Madam had started their walk along the riverbank towards his home. This time however he had somewhat unsettling thoughts rather than a beautiful woman for company. The same lights that the previous night had looked romantic, lightening their path in a magical glow, tonight just looked menacing and inadequate for the purpose of lighting his way safely home.

He shuddered slightly, mentally scolded himself for being stupid and set a stiffer pace back up the river, out of the Roquette, under the old Tranquetaille bridge and on past the Baths of Constantine and the Réattu Museum. The path was relatively deserted. The odd pair of tourists came towards him from the direction of the mooring point of the large river boats with their tourist hoards already locked up and tucking into food and drink on board that had been paid for before they ever left wherever they came from. Many of the restaurants bars in the town would probably be half empty. A few late-night dog walkers wandered about in that halting way you have to adopt when allowing a dog to interest himself in the sort of things in which dogs interest themselves. The river was still slack and there was still just enough light to see across the sharp bed where the river turns abruptly north towards Avignon and Lyons.

It was pretty obvious that they weren't tourists, neither were they a pair of chums, gay or otherwise. Two men were walking towards him in a manner that seemed to Smith to be both casual and odd. The good thing was that they were relaxed. As Smith knew all too well, people who were relaxed were also unprepared. At that walking pace he had time to plan. It was at least thirty seconds before they would come together. The topology was interesting and potentially useful. The river walk along the south bank of the Rhone was built up on both the river and the street side. From the river, a high rampart has evolved over the years. Running along the entire outside of the river it was built to protect Arles from the regular flooding that occasionally affects the river on the narrow right-angle bend. At low water in the river, it is a ten meter, virtually sheer, paved drop into the water. A low wall separates the high pavement from the drop, less than a metre high. This, Smith noted, was well below most people's centre of gravity. On the inland side, the pavement dropped about fifteen feet down to the road lined now, as usually, with parked cars.

The two men were within two meters, the one on the river side, very slightly in front of the other. They were young, well-built and not taking the whole thing very seriously, or so it seemed to Smith. They were also looking at Arthur, not him. Smith let go of Arthur's lead and dropped into a half crouch. The front man had just opened his mouth to say something when he was hit by Smith's left shoulder on his hip, very hard and without warning. He hit the wall and was immediately toppled over into the river. Less than half a second later he was alongside the second man whose hand had just begun to move towards the inside of his jacket. One foot behind the man's right leg and a sharp punch with the heel of his right hand into his upper chest and the man was on his back on the ground. As Smith dropped to a squat with one foot on the man's neck, he felt contempt for anyone so badly prepared. He pressed down with his foot, took the gun from the man's shoulder holster and tossed it over the wall into the river with a flick of his wrist.

'Monsieur. You are less than two kilos of pressure from having your throat crushed and you dying. You have a choice. You can talk to me or you can die. Which?'

Smith quickly glanced in both directions along the pavement. At least these two idiots had chosen their moment properly. There was no one in either direction for a couple of hundred yards. To anyone looking on, he was doing no more that bend over to help someone who had fallen down. Arthur, never a dog to take offense or be remotely aggressive to anything with fewer than four legs, just stood back with an air of detached curiosity. Nothing to do with him.

The man made a gargling noise. He wanted to talk. Smith shifted his foot slightly so that his heel was across the man's Adam's apple.

'Let me explain. My heel has a steel cap. It will kill you in less time that it will take you to blink. You will answer my questions exactly and quickly. You have no options. Do you understand?'

The man nodded slightly. Smith took some of the weight from his foot. Considering it was the second time he had done this sort of thing in as many days, he felt perfectly calm.

'Who do you work for?'

The reply was a whisper. 'Monsieur Girondou from Marseilles.'

'What were your instructions?'

'To bring you to meet him in Marseilles.'

There was little point in any further questions. The man wouldn't have known much more, and Smith didn't want to show his own ignorance by asking silly questions.

'Well, you can tell your Monsieur Girondou that if he wants to talk to me he can telephone me and arrange an appointment. You can also tell him that I don't take kindly to this sort of thing. Do you understand?'

The man nodded painfully.

Smith took his foot from the man's neck and helped the man to his feet his feet. A quick glance in both directions confirmed that there was still no-one close enough to take much of an interest in what was happening.

'Can you swim?'

The man nodded again.

'Good.'

The man followed his colleague over the river wall and Smith turned to continue his walk home leaving the dull splash behind him.

Things were beginning to hot up, Smith thought. It didn't actually worry him unduly. He had faced more difficult circumstances before. However, given that he was now firmly on the radar of a serious Marseilles criminal, it was probably time to take some precautions. He took his mobile phone from his pocket and called Gentry. It was answered immediately.

'Yes?'

'Smith. Can we meet?'

'Your house. Ten minutes.'

'No. I need to do something first. Half an hour would be better.'

'Very well.'

With a sense of some urgency that Smith got home and went straight up to his study. The episode on the river had convinced his that he did indeed need a little insurance. He was just finishing transferring what he had obtained from Robert's archive onto a memory stick and making a copy when he heard Gentry letting himself in. By the time he got downstairs again, his friend was sitting in his usual place, Arthur was accepting his customary attention with his customary good grace and the two whiskeys had been poured.

Without preliminaries Smith recounted everything that had happened since the morning. It was a skeletal briefing, no embellishments or explanations and took less than five minutes. Gentry listened silently. Smith finished.

'What can I do?'

'In my opinion, I'm only in any danger from the people from Marseilles. Blanchard is not the sort of man to get involved in violence of any sort. At worst he could be an annoyance. The Aubanet family has had more than enough opportunity to do something if they harboured evil thoughts.'

Smith handed over one stick.'

'There is enough on these to put the whole lot of them plus a lot of others in prison for a long time. Please get this can get these safely out of the country. I'll lose the files on the internet as well and set them on a failsafe. Unless I'm well enough and able to cancel the instruction regularly, they will be emailed to a number of national police forces. Once Girondou knows this it should insure he leaves us leave us alone.'

'Stopping the email regularly will be a pain in the arse for you.' Gentry was no fan of computing.

'It does not have to be done that often, if at all, really. It could be daily or monthly. As long as the ungodly think it is daily, the deterrence is the same.'

'And this memory stick?' asked Gentry. 'Any preference as to where they go?'
'No, not really. Maybe one of your old chums in the department. There must be a lot of them who owe you. You know what is needed?'

Gentry nodded.' You are going to have to find a way of telling Girondou the good news. Any ideas?'

'Yes, I thought I might call him and invite him to lunch.'

'You don't change, Peter. You never climb in the back window when you can knock down the front door.'

Gentry sighed, shook his head slightly and reached into his inside jacket pocket. He handed a piece of paper across to Smith who raised an eyebrow.

'Girondou's address and telephone number.' Smith burst out laughing.

'Yet again, you are ahead of me, old friend.'

'So, when do you intend to issue this invitation?' Smith glanced at the clock above the fireplace, reached for the telephone and dialled the number.

'No time like the present.
It rang three times then was picked up by a voice that had clearly been roused from sleep.

'Yes?'

'Monsieur Girondou. Good evening. This is Peter Smith.'

To give the man credit, he recovered quickly. His voice was immediately calm and level.

'Monsieur Smith. How nice to hear from you.'

Smith allowed a small chuckle to make its way down the wire to Marseilles.

'I gather you were hoping to have a word with me. Perhaps you would accept my invitation to lunch at my house. Perhaps tomorrow at about noon?'

The recovery continued for after only the shortest pause the now fully awake gangster accepted with some grace.

'How very kind, Monsieur Smith. I shall look forward to meeting you tomorrow. By the way, might I ask how you got this number?'

'Until noon, then.' said Smith and rang off.

Gentry looked over at his friend with an amused concern.

'Well you will have an interesting lunch although I wouldn't like to guess whether it will be with a major French gangster or a couple of his of his hit men.

'Don't be silly, Gentry. If Girondou had wanted me dead, he would have done it already. A long shot alone the river wall this evening, for instance. In any case, he has no reason to. It is much more important for him to find out what I'm up to and what I know.'

Gentry poured himself another malt. When he next spoke, it was in a serious voice that immediately caught Smith's attention.

'From my point of view this all seems to be getting a bit messy. What started off as an innocent murder – innocent from your point of view, that's – has now developed into an international financial fraud involving bent policemen, Marseilles criminal gangs, local families that seem to have more power and influence than is good for them, one of who just happen to be probably the most attractive woman you have met in some time, to say nothing of your now uncovering some highly deviant and immoral sexual practices. At any time in the last week you could have opted out but haven't. If I didn't know you better, I would say you are enjoying yourself. Or perhaps I do, and you are. You seem to have got everything out in the open with you in the middle. Do have to remind you that this approach has got you into trouble before – on a number of occasions.'

Smith smiled. 'Well it has certainly made life slightly more interesting; I agree. However, might I remind you that I operate best under pressure and in the middle. You were the one who needed the calm anonymity of the shadows.'

'I think the word is 'operated' – past tense. I remind you that we were both a lot younger then.'

'Oh, come on. Where is your sense of adventure?'

'I had rather hoped to have left it behind in England. If you had any sense, you would have done the same, especially after what happened.'

The memory of Somalia came back to them both and they sat in silence for a while. Gentry was the first to pull himself back to the present.

'Time for a gun, Peter?'

Smith took a little time to consider.

'No, I don't think so. If you start using one of those, so do the opposition and I don't quite know who the opposition is yet. As I said I think there is more curiosity than anything else at present. Girondou needs to know what I know and that gives me the opportunity to reminding him of the dangers to him in taking too precipitous a course. I really can't see too much danger from anywhere else at the moment.'

'Perhaps you're right. Just keep it handy in case. However, let me remind you of Seffradi. Let me give you some background.'

For the next half an hour, Gentry spoke quietly and fluently as only a man experienced in giving detailed briefings could. By the end, Smith knew as much as necessary about crime in France and Marseilles in particular. Who controlled it, how it was organised, and where, in particular his prospective guest stood in the system? Rather high up, apparently. That had always been Gentry's strength and why Smith had strenuously rebuffed, on one occasion violently, any attempts to poach him by other colleagues in the Service. Gentry knew that what Smith needed in the field doing what he did so well were certainties, right or wrong. And Gentry was usually right.

When he had finished both the briefing and the bottle, Gentry got up and made his way with complete stability out into the street.

He looked up at Smith.

'Have a nice lunch.' And walked away.

7. Gangsters and Grandmothers

'Prompt, if nothing else,' Smith thought as the bell rang precisely at noon. In his book that meant polite. He had almost never been late for an appointment in his life and he failed to understand why others could not observe what was, for him, a common courtesy. He put a slightly annoyed Arthur out into the garden and because he had given the matter some thought he was not surprised to see a well-dressed but extremely large man standing at his door.

'Ahah,' he thought. The monkey,'

Sure enough through what was left of his view out of house, he saw two more men standing in the street below. One as large as the one who was currently blocking out the sun, - another monkey - while the other was small, dark and immaculately dressed in a light summer suit, pale blue shirt and matching tie. Highly polished mid-brown loafers with the inevitable tassels.

Smith took a pace forward as usual causing the large man to take an involuntary and slightly surprised step back and addressed the well turned-out organ grinder.

'Monsieur Girondou, I'm delighted that you have accepted my invitation. However, the invitation was for you alone, and not for your – shall we say – colleagues. I'm perfectly happy for this gentleman to come into my house to verify that the entire French police force is not hiding under my bed, but if you wish to talk with me then he and his friend should go off and enjoy the delights of Arles for a couple of hours.'

To give him credit, his guest hardly hesitated. A sharp nod of the head saw the sun coming back to Smith's doorway and the small man climbing the four steps up to the house. Smith shook his hand firmly then stood aside to let the man in.

'You are welcome in my house,' Smith offered the traditional Arab greeting to a man whose rule over much of the North African based crime in France was apparently legendary. The man smiled broadly at the compliment.

'May Allah bless you and your .. daughters,' came the traditional, if slightly modified response with only the slightest hesitation. He looked squarely at Smith. 'I too am blessed with daughters.'

'Yes, I know.'

'Monsieur Girondou. It's not too hot yet. Shall we sit in the garden or would you prefer inside?' He was conscious that the climate might not be the only consideration for this man.

'I'm sure that the garden would be fine and if that means I can meet your beautiful dog then that clinches it.'

They sat at the table and Arthur greeted their guest with his customary enthusiasm. Smith was delighted to see that it was returned. In fact, it was some time before he could attract his guest's attention to ask his preference for an aperitif.

'Thank you, a Pastis, please.'
'I have Ricard or Bardouin.' said Smith, referring to that most Provencal and expensive brand. It was meant as a compliment and Girondou understood.

'Ah, that would be a very great pleasure. It is my favourite. You may not know that I was born in Chateaurenard where it comes from.'

They settled into the warmth of the early afternoon and looked at each other. Smith felt he should start with an enquiry.

'How are they?'

Girondou smiled broadly.

'They suffer from little more than injured pride but are wiser men,' his guest acknowledged with a slight smile. 'Hopefully they will never underestimate their elders again. You might well have taught them a lesson that their parents failed to.'

'Good. I'm glad they were taught at least to swim. They seemed to be a bit young to die from inexperience.'

'Unlike us.'

'Indeed.' he answered a touch grimly.

'Monsieur Girondou. We obviously have business to discuss, but I suggest we eat before we do that. I have no great pretension to being a good cook but I would prefer to separate eating and business. I feel that the idea of a business lunch is an insult to both business and lunch.'
'I agree.' He man said smilingly, taking off his jacket and draping it across his chair. Smith caught a flash of the label. Another customer for Saville Row he thought.

The meal progressed with some ease. He produced a simple salad with sautéed pear slices, walnuts and a warm Roquefort and crème fraiche sauce followed by veal *scallopine al limone* with a tomato salad and fried potatoes. Bottles of both red and white vin de table were within easy reach for both of them. The conversation was very general and completely relaxed. On the two occasions Smith had to leave the table to cook, his guest followed him to the kitchen, glass in hand, to continue the conversation. They both carried dishes to the table. Each asked about the other, their families and their background. They both seemed to find it easy to avoid potential areas of difficulty and they tended to focus on things that they both enjoyed. They found easy agreement about the inherent superiority of French and Welsh rugby over English, French and Italian cooking over anyone else's, Provence over anywhere else on earth. The found they shared a passion for Mozart and Cézanne but disagreed about Thomas Mann. It was an effortless and genuinely enjoyable conversation.

'The modern gangster is an odd, sophisticated, fish,' thought Smith, 'No wonder the police have difficulty catching him.

The main meal over, he put cheese and fruit on the table, replenished the glasses and replaced the bottles of wine. Pudding could come later. Again, Smith started.

'I gather you wanted to talk to me.'

'Yes. I wanted to find out what your part is in all this.'

'You mean in the suicide of one of Arles prominent citizens a week ago? I might wish to ask you the same question, Monsieur.'

Smith sensed that his guest was not used to this sort of exchange and was having some difficulty in remaining entirely calm. He decided, not for the first time, that the most direct approach would be the best. He continued:

'One of us has to stop beating about the bush and come directly to the point. Preferably both of us, Monsieur. As I'm you host, perhaps I should start.'

Girondou sat back in his chair and took a good swig from his glass and Smith took a mental deep breath that he hoped wouldn't show. He decided on brevity.

'You are stealing millions of Euros from the European Community from its fund from the renovations of historic buildings. You may well be doing this throughout Europe but all I know for certain is that you are doing it in Provence. Robert DuGresson, as the local administrator of the EC funding, was the man who actually stole the money and passed it on to you. You are also probably getting kickbacks from the contractors for the work itself but Robert was not involved in this and that's my speculation. You have bought a Eurocop called Blanchard to make sure that no investigations come your way. I have no idea whether you have bought his wife as well, but I rather think not. I appear out of nowhere on the day Robert is killed and you have no idea who I am and why I'm poking around in the story. The whole thing is probably a relatively small part of your activities but is an easy way of making money and much less risky that your traditional way of doing that. However, you are one of the pioneers, if that's the right word, of organised cybercrime in Europe and any real investigation could leave you vulnerable. You wish to know more and hence this meeting.'

Smith stopped and looked at his guest. His glance was met with a level and utterly unflinching gaze, neither friendly nor hostile. That look explained why this charming little man occupied the position he did. He hoped his momentary flash of doubt didn't show.

'Do you have any proof of all this?' There was no denial. The man was clearly a pragmatist.

Smith reached behind him and produced an envelope he had put in the flower box before his guest arrived and handed it across the table. Girondou opened it and unfolded the single piece of paper. It was a printout of a page of Robert's spreadsheet that contained a recent monthly record of payments made to one of Girondou's accounts. Smith looked across at his guest and said quietly:

'You know that if I have that, then you know I have the rest, too.'

Like most silences it was probably not as long as it felt but it seemed an eternity before the man from Marseilles raised his head from the piece of paper with a look of marble.

'And what, Monsieur Smith, do you intend to do with this knowledge?'

Smith had anticipated this moment It was inevitable, and he was prepared for it. It was a bit like shooting a pheasant. If the bird comes towards you from a long way away and you follow it throughout its journey there is a very good chance you will miss it when it finally comes in range. Better to close your eyes, delay until something tells you that if you don't open your eyes instantly, the chance of a kill will be gone. You do and the bird is dead. The longer you leave it, the better your swing though the path of the bird and the better your chance of killing it. Smith metaphorically closed his eyes and felt the strength of his position building until to wait any longer would undo it all.

'Nothing.'

'Nothing?' His guest also knew the effect of a dramatic pause.

'No. Unless you do something that I imagine as being thoroughly uncharacteristic, I intend to do absolutely nothing.'

Answering the unasked question, Smith continued.

'While many will almost certainly disapprove, I really don't care much what you and your friends get up to. I have no all-consuming sense of morality that drives me here. In this particular case, I have complete contempt for most politicians of whatever political colour and for the many thousands who have climbed aboard the European Community gravy train. To find that you are ripping it off as well make little or no difference to me. Whatever you get up to might well offend me if I thought about it too much, but it doesn't particularly interest me. All I want is to live here in my retirement and for the world more or less to leave me alone.'

'So why did you get involved in investigating the suicide of one of Arles most prominent citizens.'

The irony wasn't lost on him.

'Firstly, because someone hit me over the head and I rather take exception to that and secondly because a beautiful woman asked me to.'

'Ah. Madam DuGresson. Perhaps, Monsieur, there is more to her than meets your English eye.'

'That, Monsieur Girondou, is one of the things that makes her beautiful.'

His guest allowed himself a calcified sort of smile.

'You understand, Monsieur Smith, how it might be dangerous to possess this knowledge?'

'Dangerous, Monsieur? To whom?' To you, perhaps? I don't intend to pass this information on to anyone, Monsieur Girondou. I much prefer to have you as friend than an enemy. That's the reason for this lunch.'

Girondou nodded as if in agreement but paused as if a slightly disagreeable thought just occurred to him.

'What would you say to some of my colleagues who might not be as, shall we say, relaxed about this arrangement as I am?'

Time to get nasty, Smith thought.

'I have located all of Robert's records and have tucked them away in a bit of the Internet that I assure you, you will not find. I have set them up so that unless I personally cancel the instructions on a regular basis, they will be emailed simultaneously to a number of police forces around the world. I can imagine any number of promotion-hungry policemen being most enthusiastic about coming after your hide.'

'In case you imagine that these records might be found in the same way as I found Robert's, I can assure you that I'm very, very much better than he was at this sort of thing. I have also placed a complete set records containing all the data somewhere out of the country subject to a very similar set of instructions. I would suggest, Monsieur Girondou, that you and your chums have an interest in ensuring that I and those close to me remain well and very alive.'

'I'm beginning to see, Monsieur, that the two I sent to fetch you last night, had little chance of success. Please forgive my mistake. So what do you want in exchange for your silence?'

'I think that you continue to misunderstand me, Monsieur. I don't want anything. This isn't blackmail, nor am I particularly interested in seeing you stop whatever you are doing. I don't want to interfere in your life at all. However, I don't wish you to interfere in mine either.'

Girondou nodded slowly.

'Very well, Monsieur Smith. You will understand that I need to consult my colleagues but from my part we have an agreement – albeit a slightly unusual one.'

'Of course. However, before we finish our meal, I might offer you a small piece of information by way of a goodwill gesture.'

Girondou looked only slightly interested. 'Yes?'

'You are not the only recipient of the European Union's largess. One of your, shall we say, colleagues, a Signor Giacomo Seffradi, also has his hands in your till.'

Smith found himself instantly faced with a very different Girondou. His erstwhile relaxed and urbane luncheon companion leant forward stiffly; his face was transformed into something very nasty indeed. It took Smith a substantial effort of will not to react. Girondou's voice was very quiet and thoroughly menacing.

'Are you completely sure.'

'Yes.'

There was a pause while the man's fate was settled.

'Does it concern you that you have probably signed this man's death warrant, Monsieur Smith?'

Smith looked his companion directly in the eyes. 'Not in the least. It is probably an elegant way of stopping the bloody man coming after me.'

Girondou nodded and let a pale smile return to his face.

'You are an unusual man, Monsieur Smith. Perhaps we can talk further when this current matter is, as they say, resolved?

Smith returned the smile and continued:

'Possibly. Pudding?'

They finished their meal with a couple of pastries from Madam LeNoir, the legendary patisseuse in Arles and a glass of one of the Smith's Loupiacs. His budget didn't run to anything more exotic. Their conversation reverted to pleasant generalia and by the time they had finished, it was past two o'clock. The temperature had risen significantly in the garden in spite of the shade afforded by the grape vine and jasmine and they both had run out of things to say.

Smith opened the door to let his guest out and as he went out into the waiting attention of two now thoroughly overdressed minders, Girondou turned.

'Is there nothing I can do for you, Monsieur Smith?'

'Perhaps you can let Blanchard know how things stand. He does, after all, work for you, more or less. Other than that, perhaps one day you can introduce me to Marseilles cuisine. I know little of it and I have always imagined that there must be more to it than just tourist bouillabaisse.'

'I would be delighted. I suspect we are destined to meet again. It would seem that, possibly literally, we cannot live without each other. I believe it was Sun Tzu who originally said, 'keep your friends close but your enemies closer. I wonder which you will turn out to be, Monsieur Smith?'

'Ah,' smiled Smith, 'I prefer to think it was Machiavelli, but time will tell, I think. Goodbye Monsieur.'

A firm handshake concluded the meeting and the gangster started down the steps. After a couple he turned.

'You never told me how you found my telephone number.'

'No, monsieur. I didn't.'

Girondou frowned slightly then shrugged and turned away. The two goons escorted their charge into a silver Peugeot 607, and they slid smoothly off towards the AutoRoute back to Marseille.

It was indeed too hot to sit outside any longer, but he had too much on his mind to think of an attempt at siesta. He sat down beside Arthur on his sofa and let his lunch settle. Whatever he did for his living, he found Girondou quite beguiling. The man was civilised and sophisticated. That he was a criminal with a long track record didn't affect Smith either way. He had meant what he said and saw no particular reason to go rushing off to the authorities. He could not remember the authorities doing anything for him. Whatever he thought privately about the morality of the world he was simply too tired to be interested. In truth he was not sure that he ever was. Even as a student he had found it difficult to get really involved in anything. Every time he had tried something went wrong and he ended up getting up getting his balls slapped. It was usually his fault - or so others said - and that was the sort of pattern that had continued throughout his life.

From childhood he had become progressively more and more self-reliant as the years went by not particularly out of choice but because usually there was no one around to help. He knew enough about business and many of the people in it to know that criminality up to and including murder was not the sole preserve of those against whom society had actually passed laws. It didn't take too much tweaking of societies rules to turn the desultory light of morality in a very different direction. Not that he could actually care less about Girondou and his activities, unless, of course, they started to impinge on him. When that sort of thing happened, he got very involved and he tended not to give up. It was an attitude that got him involved in all this in the first place. They should never have hit him on the head.

In spite of himself, he had enjoyed the lunch. Girondou was a very modern gangster; smooth, sophisticated, intelligent, very good company; only allowing the nasty side to show occasionally. In many ways Smith felt a kinship. However, most importantly, he had probably removed Marseilles as a source of personal danger - or at least lessened it. If he had actually succeeded in enlisting Girondou's protection, then that was enough to make the lunch a success.

However, he didn't seem to have made much progress on

finding out who killed Robert. If Girondou or any of his colleagues were involved, then he had done a very good job of disguising it. Rather than consider the major developments, he began to wonder about some of the loose ends for there were a few of them. Mademoiselle Brique's death in a hit and run was one of them. It may, of course, have been perfectly genuine, but for both the occupants of the offices in the Impasse Balze to have died within a day or so of each other was a very long shot indeed. However, he still couldn't see very clearly why anyone would want to kill Robert's secretary. Any murder carries risks of being found out and there is usually a good reason for doing it. It was, indeed, a loose end.

Then he remembered that her grandmother lived in Tranquetaille. He found his telephone directory but failed to find a listing under Brique, but a quick call to Gentry and a five-minute wait came up with an address across the river in Tranquetaille. Taking Arthur in hand he struck off down the hill towards the bridge across the river.

The house was in a terrace, but it had escaped the bombs of the liberating Americans. A classical facade of four windows arranged either side of a substantial front door rose four stories. The whole building was in excellent condition. He thought it was about five o'clock so he knocked firmly on the door and stood back a pace or two.

Her face was the colour and texture of a walnut. He hadn't really given the matter too much thought but given that her late granddaughter was about forty, he was expecting someone in their seventies. The lady who peered around the heavy door was considerably older than that and tiny – less than five feet tall.

'Yes?' The eyes, however, were bright and piercing.

'Er, good afternoon, Madam. I'm looking for Madam Brique?

The door opened little more and the woman looked up at him with an expression that indicated that she had made this particular speech before.

'If you mean my daughter, she died ten years ago. I'm Madam Durand, Genine Brique's grandmother,' her face fell slightly. 'or was until recently.'

'I beg your pardon, Madam. Please accept my sympathies. I'm Peter Smith and…'

She cut him off.

'Yes, I know who you are, Monsieur. Madam Aubanet told me you might be calling.'

Smith sighed. Madam was ahead of his again. He was going to have to up his game. He also noted the use of the maiden name. She motioned him through the door.

'Come in.'

Smith could not decide whether it was an invitation, a request or an instruction. He decided on exaggerated courtesy.

'I was just calling to see if there might be a convent time when I might talk to you.'

The old woman remained direct.

'What's wrong with now? I'm doing nothing of importance. Bring your beautiful dog. There are no animals in the house. Genine didn't like them.'

With than she turned and walked slowly but without hesitation or unsteadiness back into the hall of the house and then off to the right into the main sitting room.

'As you see I have spent much of my long life in the Provençale sun and I now try to stay out of it. I'm much more comfortable indoors these days.

She indicated one of two high backed chairs set either side of a large stone fireplace. 'Let your dog off his leash and then please sit down, Monsieur.'

He did as he was asked. His host sat on one end of a sofa that formed the final side of the square and patted the settee beside her. Needing no bidding, Arthur hopped up beside her and lay down, instantly at home, his head on her lap.

A broad smile took residence on her lined face.

'Madame Aubanet told me that he likes to lie of sofas.'

Smith smiled and wondered what else his employer had told this old lady about him. After a few moments stoking the dog's head she got up and went out of the room. Smith headed the sound of glasses being clinked together. He looked round him. The high-ceilinged room was furnished with considerable elegance. It was much more Parisian in feeling that Provençale. The furniture was antique but comfortable, a difficult combination to find in usual French interior décor. The full-length shutters that obviously opened into the garden were latched a few inches apart letting only a small amount of light creep into the room. Wall lights supplied the rest of the illumination. The floor was carpeted and some good - Smith thought surprisingly good – eighteenth century portraits and small bucolic scenes decorated the walls. It was a comfortable and somewhat distinguished room.

Madam Durand returned carrying a small tray on which there were two beautiful cut glass tumblers each holding a generous measure of whisky. A matching jug held some sparkling water. The surface of the whiskey was rock steady in her hand. Smith took a glass and topped it up with water. His host put the tray down on a side table beside the other armchair and raised her glass, without, Smith noted, adding water.

'Your health, Monsieur.'

'And yours Madame,'

This had all happened so quickly that he had really not thought out what he was going to say. However, characteristically, she started first.

'I can save you some time, young man.'

He smiled. It had been some time since he had been called that. She continued:

'I'm ninety-three years old and for almost all that time I have been a friend and a servant of the Aubanet family. I was Monsieur Aubanet's nurse and then became the housekeeper and a friend to his daughter, Martine. My daughter, Genine's mother, left the Camargue to work in Paris where she married a businessman and had a daughter. They lived in Paris but came to visit regularly. After only a few years my son-in-law died in an accident and my daughter and granddaughter came to live with me here in Arles. At one stage all three of us were all in service with the Aubanet family.'

'Ten years ago, my daughter died from breast cancer and Genine started to work for that man.'

There was a new, more contemptuous tone to her voice. The expression in her eyes changed from a distant wistfulness while she was telling the story to a much harder, almost fierce look now.

'That man changed her. I felt it from the beginning but only found out how much a year ago.'

She broke off. The façade cracked and she started crying silently. Arthur looked up, slid off the sofa, stood to one side and put his head gently in her lap. She looked down and laid a veined hand on his head. Smith sensed that they were straying into difficult territory.

'Madam please don't go on if this is painful'. She gave him a look that was defiant. This was not a woman to shirk from pain.

'It may be difficult – and it is in ways that you don't realise at present – nevertheless you are helping Madam Aubanet and therefore I'll try to help you.'

Smith was suddenly conscious of an intensity in her voice, still not that of a frail old ninety-year-old. The connection with the Aubanet family was clearly deeply important; important enough override any personal feelings she might have about raking over her family history. In a catholic region of France where the family was of great importance, especially to someone of Madam Durand's age, this was highly unusual. Smith felt that it was now time to ask a few questions.

'You say that Genine worked for Monsieur DuGreson for about ten years.'

'Yes. She started as his secretary when he married Madam and came to work at the Mas.'

'And she continued with him after he moved into Arles?'

'Yes, they got on well together and she found the work interesting. She was always good at figures and would have liked to train as an accountant.'

He wanted to ask how Madam had reacted to DuGresson leaving her so soon after they marriage, but something told him that he wouldn't get a useful answer. Madam Durand's daughter must have died at about the time her granddaughter started to work for DuGresson. However, he was conscious of looking at a very old woman who had seen her daughter and granddaughter dead before her; something that might go some way to explaining the quiet intensity of her seeming loyalty to the man's widow. He also sensed that he had yet to get to the centre of things with Madam Durand. While he was wondering how to get at that, he was unexpectedly presented with the truth. He felt he should offer his sympathies.

'Madam, I have not offered you my condolences on the loss of your granddaughter.'

The ferocity of her reply took him aback and startled Arthur to the extent that he turned and lay defensively down on the carpet at

Smith's feet.

'She is better dead,' she spat.

Smith was astonished and was completely unable to think of anything to say. But she continued, her eyes blazing. The sinews on her thin hands stood out whitely as she gripped the arms of her chair.

'He made her into a terrible person. She wasn't like that before. She was a sweet girl, hard working. But bit by bit she became a monster. It was all his fault. He was a disgusting person. Oh yes, he seemed very nice and cultured, but he was a devil. I'm glad he is dead. I rejoice at it. I told Madam Aubanet so. She is free of him now and she can have a life again.'

Her voice dropped to a whisper.

'Genine is better dead too.' Smith sat very still and said nothing. It was not long before Madam Durand regained her composure enough to continue. She looked up at Smith.

'What I haven't told you, Monsieur Smith, is why I think this. Robert DuGresson was – how do you say? – he liked to abuse children.'

'A paedophile, Madam?'

'Yes, a paedophile.'

As gently as he could, Smith probed further. 'And Genine?'

'He made her find the children for him. Always when he was away on business either in France and abroad. Then she started going with him and….'

Her voice became almost inaudible, 'finally she became one too. May God forgive her because I cannot.'

They both sat in complete silence. She had fallen into a reverie and Smith certainly didn't want to leave her like that. He made a bit of a fuss about draining the last mouthful of his whisky and set his glass down on the table with a slight click. The manoeuvre worked and his host looked across and very rapidly pulled herself back to the present.

'What am I thinking about?' she scolded herself. Without consulting him, she rose, took his glass and disappeared into the kitchen only to return a few moments later with the glass refilled and topped up with Perrier. She set it down on the table and with a glance that said that she was grateful for the artifice.

'Madam told me you liked whisky and soda. I prefer it without water. My doctor told me that I should not drink more than one glass each day, so I tend to make it a large one and have it in the evening like this. Doctors have been telling me what to do for fifty years now. I have been ignoring them for as long.' A slight smile crossed her face. 'Most of them are dead before me.'

Having escaped from the topic was obviously nothing to be gained by going back to it. He wanted to ask her if she knew anything about Robert's business activities, but this was not the time to return to him. Given her obvious feelings about her granddaughter's employer, there would be plenty of time for that. However, was also not prepared to leave her at the moment. Another topic.

'Madam. Can you tell me anything about a group called Les Frères?'

'Yes, I can, Monsieur.' She took a sip of her drink and, shaking off the recent devils, warmed to a task of recounting some Camargue history, a task that she obviously relished.

'It used to be simply a society of people who have been and who are involved in farming on the Camargue. You have probably found they seem to be a bit of a secret these days, but this has not always been the case. You must be under no illusions about Les Frères. Originally it was emphatically not a society of menadiers, of owners. It is a society of farm workers and could be thought of as one of the oldest trade unions in the world. It can trace its origins to the peasants that raised and sold meat and grain to the Romans when they occupied Arles two thousand years ago and has been in continuous existence ever since. Les Frères are the men who have sweated their working lives away here in this difficult land ever since. When I was a girl on the Camargue it was still like that. Farming has never been easy here and we have had to rely on each other in the many difficult times. It was one of the few groups who resisted the Nazis when the occupied Arles. The Camargue was too difficult to them too.'

'After the last war, farming became even more difficult as people have been reluctant to pay for good local produce when there is cheap imported rubbish to be found in supermarkets. Farming has become more of a business in the hands of a small number of families. Occasionally people like me are invited to join. It is the greatest of privileges. Without these men, we would have nothing here.'

Smith kept his silence in the hope that she would continue; as she did but only briefly.

'I have lost touch a little with what is going on now. My contact is only through Madam Aubanet who is very kind to me.'

Smith wanted to know a little about the current, less romantic, sort of Les Frères that he had experienced recently. He asked:

'Is the brotherhood still active, Madam, since so few people are left farming the land?'

The old lady looked a little wistfully.

'I'm afraid that many younger Camargue farmers are still finding difficulties in living in a world that no longer seems to need them. Education, in the traditional sense, has never been too much of a priority for the working farmers and the last generation or two has tended to stray a little.'

'Towards the more rewarding life of Marseilles crime,

Madam?'

'Yes,' she nodded sadly, 'I'm afraid so.'

The old lady was beginning to look a little tired at the end. Smith felt that it was time to leave.

'Madam, I can only thank you for your time and your hospitality. I'll leave you now but perhaps you will allow me to call on you again?'

'Of course,' she replied getting to her feet. 'It is not often that I have an eligible young man coming to call. I make only one condition and that's that you bring your beautiful dog with you when you come. I must make sure that I don't make Martine jealous, though.'

Smith found that he was slightly flustered by her gentle mockery.

'I'll telephone you first, Madam.'

'Yes, of course. To telephone would be polite, of course, but not necessary, Monsieur. I don't go out very much, these days. If I'm out when you call, it will not be for long.'

She bent down to pat Arthur as Smith fastened his lead, then led them both to the door.

Once outside Smith turned to her.

'Madam, I hope you will forgive me, but I think that you should try to be careful about talking too much about this. My feeling is that there are some unpleasant people tied up in all this and I wouldn't like to see you harmed in any way.'

'Your sentiments do you credit,' she smiled. 'Monsieur, and I thank you. But, as you see, I'm quite good at looking after myself. I also have the protection of the Aubanet family. That means much here. More than you might understand. Perhaps you have it too. I don't know. No, I think that you have more reason to look after yourself.'

He held out his hand but found that she didn't release him from the handshake. She drew close and looked up directly into his eyes.

'I sense that you are a good but dangerous man, Monsieur. Martine says that she trusts you and I agree with her. She needs someone at the moment. You will find her a talented and very competent woman. She is a member of a much loved and respected family. But Robert made her life hell for ten years. There are many in our community who can never forgive him for that and who rejoice, with me, at his death even if they didn't know about him and his disgusting ways. But take care, Monsieur, that you bring no further sorrow to her life. She has had too much of that. If you do, you will answer to me.'

Her gaze never wavered and the grip on his hand had tightened until it was almost painful. In an effort to be released he inclined his head to her raised hand and kissed the air a few millimetres above it. The old woman smiled, let go of his and retreated into her doorway. She turned back.

'Madam Aubanet also said you were a bit of a flirt. As usual she was right.'

With that the door closed.

By the time they got back across the river and arrived home, he felt somewhat leg weary. He fed Arthur and decided that he really couldn't be bothered to cook. In any case, after lunch, he didn't feel very hungry. The fridge yielded the makings of a simple salad endive, tomato, a few finely chopped shallots. He found a small tin of tuna fish and shredded that in and moistened the whole with a light French dressing. Had he thought about it he would have picked up a baguette on the way home but now he couldn't be bothered to go out again. He took the salad out into the garden with a glass of cold rosé.

It was difficult to know what to feel about the old woman. To have lost a daughter would have been bad enough. The Aubanet family clearly had taken care of her. But then to witness the perversion of her granddaughter to the point where her death was a relief was, for Smith, beyond imagining. Yet she seemed relieved, pleased, even. Certainly satisfied. There was an intensity about her that was unnerving. To approve of the death, possibly the murder, of her own granddaughter took a level of moral certainty that he could hardly imagine. Whatever her beliefs were built on they were absolutely rock solid.

What to do next/ Well he had to find out more about the fraud and Blanchard was his only real way of doing that. He also had to find out a little more about the Aubanet family. Now there were a number of ways of doing that. He could always ask Madam, but he was not altogether confident of getting the truth, or at least anything useful. Graveyards. That was it. It is surprising how much you can learn from dead people if you know where to look, and he had a feeling he knew where to look. He went inside the house and returned with his 1:25,000 scale Michelin map of the area around the Mas des Saintes. The nearest place he could find that had a church was Le Sambuc about five miles away from the farm. So that was tomorrow morning sorted. Blanchard next.

He finished his supper, put the plate down on the ground for Arthur to pick over and went inside. Picking up Blanchard's business card and looking at the kitchen clock, he did a quick mental calculation. Nine o'clock here will be three in the afternoon there. He picked up his phone and dialled the Bahamas.

He felt that surprise that many people of his generation felt when they were suddenly connected to talk with someone on the other side of the world.

'Chris Borrowash?'

'Yes.'

'Peter Smith, from, er, England. I'm not sure if you remember me but it is good to talk to you again. How are you?' It all came out in a bit of a rush.

'Good Lord, Peter,' came the gratifyingly friendly reply, 'How on earth are you? Where are you?'

'Well it is a very long story and one that I can't really afford to tell you as the call would bankrupt me, but it is certainly nice to hear you again. But I'm afraid, on this occasion, before getting into reprising the past, I need a favour.'

The voice five thousand miles away suddenly became business-like.

'OK. Go ahead.'

Smith gave his old friend a very abbreviated account of what had happened and what he wanted. It only took a few minutes.

'Hum, I'm not sure if I like the sound of all that. Dead bodies are just that, dead bodies, and, having seen more than my fair share of such things, I tend to think that the further away you can stay from them, the better. An odd opinion for a policeman but nevertheless true, I believe. However, I can certainly check up on your Brussels policeman if you wish. These days computers never sleep, and it will certainly not take me more than ten minutes. Let me call you back. What is your number?'

Smith barely had time to give his telephone details before the line went dead.

It was eight minutes rather than ten before his telephone rang.

'OK. Your Blanchard certainly seems to be the real thing,' came the reply without preamble, 'he is who he says he is, and he certainly works for Europol. Has done for more than ten years, rather successfully, according to record.'

'Do you have any other details - any personal details - stuff like that?'

'Very little unless I do a further search and that might alert attention. Although Blanchard has told you that you can make enquiries about him, but others might not be as happy. Let me see. I have some basic details, all pretty normal as far as I can see. Standard education, university to read sociology - got a first - straight into the police force and then on to Europol.'

'Where does he come from?'

'Er, the file says he was born in Lille.'

Smith felt a small frisson up the back of his neck.

'Do you have anything about his wife?'.

'Yes, she is a very highflyer. Fast-tracked out of University and, in my opinion, looks destined for the very top. Does not seem to have been operational for very much. More a politician than a policeman.'

'Yes, certainly, that's the impression I get as well. Any biography?'

'Er, yes. Born in Toulouse, educated locally then in Paris. Married Blanchard ten years ago. No children - probably in the way of her career.'

'Anything else?'

'No, not really. A bunch of pretty anonymous bureaucratic postings. Let me just track back a little. No nothing obviously significant. Her first job after graduating university was back in Toulouse. Pretty good one, too. She went straight in with the rank of Inspector. All right for some. Yes, here it is, Inspector Suzanne Aubanet. Must have been before her marriage.'

The frisson suddenly moved from his neck and hit Smith's gut.

'Are you sure? Her maiden name was Aubanet?'

'Yup, or so my tin brain says. Why?'

For absolutely no reason that came to mind, Smith fell short of passing over more information that he had.

'Oh, nothing really. I just wanted to keep my notes in order.'

God. It sounded as lame to him as it obviously did five thousand miles away.

'All right. It's up to you. If there is nothing else, I can do for you I had better get back to doing what Her Majesty pays me for. For God's sake take care. People who go around murdering other people don't, in my experience, stop at one. Good to hear from you again and keep in touch. Call me again when you have time to chat.'

'Many thanks, Chris. I much appreciate your help.'

Smith laid his phone down thoughtfully. It was just past nine and there was still a little light in his garden. What to do next?

A call to Gentry was next.

'I found out that Blanchard's wife's maiden name was Aubanet. Could you find out for me whether this is a coincidence or not?'

'I'll text you, later. It may be tomorrow now. I'll have to call in a favour at the Mairie.'

'OK. Thanks.'

He tidied up the small amount of washing up and did the usual circuit of window and shutter closing. After the exertions of the day, Arthur showed no real interest in anything further. So, in spite of the relatively early hour, he went to bed.

8. Le Sambuc

For many people, other than those on a tour of the eastern Camargue, the main real reason for travelling down the road to Le Sambuc is that it takes you to the well-known, if idiosyncratic, restaurant of La Chassagnette. Under its founding chef, Jean Luc Rabanel, it achieved a Michelin rosette or two, some including Smith would say, by elevating the creation hors d'oeuvres to a very fine art indeed. No choice and a long succession of exquisitely prepared small - sometimes tiny - courses, each accompanied by a tedious and completely compulsory lecture, the memory of each utterly precious mouthful fading instantly with the onset of its equally exquisite successor. A cross between tapas and haut cuisine, Smith felt. It was the sort of cuisine what these days win plaudits and for which a working set of teeth is completely unnecessary. After a while, Rabanel moved himself and his Michelin stars closer to the larger wallets of Arles, but his successor is grimly following a similar course.

The village of Le Sambuc is, for most people, the traffic lights at which you turn around when you have missed the restaurant. It is a small, slightly scruffy place of about five hundred souls located predominantly on the eastern side of the D36 running south from Arles to Ports St Louis just before the turn west to the Mas des Saintes. The area around it is given over mainly to the rearing of bulls and the cultivation of rice. Most of the village extends dustily for about half a mile either side of a single narrow road, that goes almost to the Rhône. The few shops are clustered near the main road south so one has to go almost out of the village past single lines of unmemorable, single - story white painted houses to find the little church dedicated to the Nativity of the Virgin. Established in the seventeenth century at the same time as a number of small villages in the Camargue received churches at the order of Monseigneur de Barrault the then archbishop of Arles, it is the closest to the Mas and was, Smith guessed, likely to be their family church. Churches and graveyards can often be a useful source of information.

The church proved to be as undistinguished as the rest of the village - although perhaps modest would be a more appropriate description for a church. It was locked, of course, but an enquiry at a nearby house, soon elicited they key and the attentions of a concierge who enthusiastically led Smith through the limited highlights of the church furnishings. The south wall had a series of small but carefully sculpted memorial tablets dating between sixteen fifty and eighteen twenty. All bore the name Aubanet, or at least predictable variations of it. The concierge remained enthusiastic, but his tone became more dignified. Yes, the Aubanet family had been here longer than the church and were universally loved and respected. They had a family tomb in the cemetery on the opposite side of the road.

The church had only four small windows, two each on either side of the nave. Three were plain but one was of stained glass. The concierge explained that the old windows had been shattered by an errant Second World War bomb, meant for the port to the south. The coloured window showed a traditional picture portraying the birth of the Virgin. Along the bottom of the window ran a dedication inscription saying that the window was a gift, a thanksgiving for the peace and liberation for Nazi occupation in 1944. The last word on the dedication, after the date, was the name of the donor. Smith half expected to read the name Aubanet but he was disappointed. Somewhat more intriguingly the window had been donated by 'Les Frères.'

Turning again to the concierge, Smith continued: 'Who were Les Frères?'

'I'm afraid I don't know who they are, Monsieur,' said the concierge glancing down to his left. Smith silently noted the use of present rather than a past tense.

He was about to press further on the matter, then suddenly thought better of it. He had the feeling that enquiries on this particular topic wouldn't be met with any great enthusiasm and he didn't want the concierge reporting back to his boss that someone was showing interest. It also occurred to him that there was a very good chance that any record of that service of dedication would most likely be held in archives in Arles not here in a church that was empty and locked most of the time. Smith decided to put his faith in

French bureaucracy and not to press the man further. Instead he remarked on another, completely insignificant, item of carving on the opposite wall and, as anticipated, his guide resumed his enthusiastic discourse.

Ten minutes later, he stepped out into the bright sunlight and the midday heat. He thanked his guide and offered twenty Euros for church funds, although he did wonder whether it would end up there.

He paused at the war memorial outside the church for long enough for the concierge to disappear back into his house. The memorial, oddly, just listed those from Le Sambuc who died during the First World War, making no mention of the Second. However, the memorial still listed some twenty one names, a significant number from a community that at the time probably numbered no more than one or two hundred at most. Five of the surnames were Aubanet. Thoughtfully he walked across the road into the tiny walled graveyard. It was typical of thousands of similar across France. Graves, of all sorts and sizes were ranged side by side with little or no space between All were immaculately tended. The traditional and rather touching enamelled photographs of the occupants of the tombs were all clean and polished. Graveside decorations, little chain fences, gravels, statues of angels were all maintained with loving care. Fresh flowers abounded and there was so sign of dead or dying ones.

The Aubanet family tomb was by no means ostentatious but it was still the largest one in the cemetery. It was a low enclosure with a single stone obelisk. At the base was mounted a line of stones that encircled the tomb bearing a long list of family members whose ashes had been buried there. The list went back three centuries and continued the sequence from inside the church. The last name on the list, Pierre Jerome had been buried eight years before, aged ninety-three.

For the first time Smith began to get the feeling of what he was involved in. He sat down on the front edge of the tomb contemplated the scene. This was very much more than just a modern family with a large modern business with a large modern problem. There was a sense of place around him. Not just the memorial in the church nor the tomb. The list of names on the war memorial was poignant but no more than many similar memorials in small villages the length and breadth of Europe that documented the obliteration of almost entire families on the battlefields of Flanders and elsewhere. The Aubanet family was just like thousands of families decimated by the twentieth century's stupidities. No, this was a family whose roots went deeper even that the local church. They were surely not going to be embarrassed by an errant employee no matter how big was the fraud he was involved. He made a mental note to ask Blanchard exactly how much Robert was supposed to have stolen. Perhaps it was very much more than he had imagined. Even so, the chances of whatever he was involved in doing damage to a family like this, or the businesses they ran seemed to Smith to be remote. In this he felt reasonably confident that he could answer the question posed by Monsieur Aubanet.

As for the question of who did it, he didn't feel as if he was very much further towards answering this particular question. Perhaps he needed to spend a bit more time ferreting about in Robert's iPhone although he was pretty sure he had got everything.

After a while he got up and slowly walked around the tiny walled cemetery. It was by no means a sombre place. Unlike the gaunt institutional urban cemeteries and the increasingly regimented and iconographically sterile country churchyards in England, it was intimate and very personal but certainly not sad. Not actually dignified in the accepted sense of the word. The little pictures on the tombs did it. Faces of past loved ones look back at him, serene and confident, as he passed by reading the inscriptions one by one. These were not dumb memorials to people who ceased to matter the second the wake was out of the way. They were members of living people's families and in some odd way were all the more familiar for that. Not alive, obviously, but certainly not as dead as Smith's British predecessors seemed to feel. Not that he had been particularly close to any of them but the fact that his father's cremated ashes had been scattered to the four winds over some nameless bit of a Yorkshire moor did make the process feel very final indeed. Lost and gone forever, as they say. Out of sight, out of mind. Dreadful.

In fact, it was more than that. He had no roots and no

memory of a relationship with either parent. Quite the contrary, in fact. To say they didn't get on was something of an understatement and he had long since got used to the unpleasant memory of it all. He had been getting used to it since he was in his mid-teens so there was certainly no sense of sorrow. Mild regret possibly. The brutal reality was that he disliked both his parents for entirely different reasons for most of their lives and the feeling was mutual.

Well, the residents of this little place were certainly not erased from history and he felt a little jealous. Their tombs were cared for by loving relatives and they remained looking out at the world even when the world was not actually looking at them. Death, with all its supposed miseries, Smith realised, possibly for the first time, was about the living not the dead. He completed his circumnavigation with a surprisingly cheerful heart.

Without really thinking much about it, he left the cemetery and walked back to the junction with the main road. The village shop had a very modest selection of flowers and be bought a small, squat bunch of the brightest he could find. They were all local, Candytuft, Violets and some bright red Anemones. He retraced his steps and placed the flowers in a small, chipped green enamel tin vase that was one of a collection of similar of various sizes on a shelf just inside the cemetery entrance. He filled it with water from a rusty tap just under the shelf and placed it without due ceremony or particularly profound thought at one corner of the stone apron in front of the Aubanet family tomb.

A low bleep on his mobile phone signified that Gentry had found some information. The text message was terse.

'Cousin.'

He left, got back into his car and started back up the lane toward the main road and home.

He had just turned north and was passing La Chassagnette when he saw it was not as surrounded by cars as one might expect for a Saturday lunchtime. He was tempted to stop to see what sort of a fist Rabanel's successor, Armand Arnel, was making of the restaurant. He had heard that the food had become slightly less idiosyncratic, based on what was always the restaurant's great strength, its own fruit and vegetable garden and the new administration was making a great virtue of a necessity and hopped on the organic bandwagon. Reports had been good. The prices had become considerably more reasonable, too - for lunch at least. Dinner was still expensive. However, it was an exploration that he would like to share with someone a little after the season and thus thought better of it for the moment.

Lunch therefore was more prosaically a *gros pain* in the garden; a decision that pleased Arthur who lay at Smith's feet in the expectation, rather than just the hope, and, as usual, found that expectation fulfilled.

Smith cleared the lunch table and settled into the relative cool of his sitting room while Arthur somewhat perversely preferred to digest his lunch in the direct hot afternoon sun, flat out in the garden. Smith glanced in the direction of the supine animal with a fond smile. In spite of his recently found and rapidly expanding circle of acquaintances, the dog's undemanding companionship was one of the rocks on which the contentment with his retirement into the pleasant exile of Arles was based. He had had dogs all his life; lurchers mostly. All had given much more than they ever took, and he had wept over each when he buried them. Burying Arthur would present more of a problem in that regard as divorce had reduced his previous twenty English acres to thirty square French metres. However, he thought, dismissing the rather disagreeable matter, hopefully there would be some time before that had to be addressed.

Just as he reached for his book the telephone rang. Unsurprisingly, he felt, it was Madam.

'Monsieur Smith, I hope you don't mind the interruption. I think you once said that you don't take the siesta.'

Smith felt a genuine pleasure in the interruption. In fact, the combined effect of the sun and the lunchtime rosé made him uncharacteristically frivolous.

'Of course not. I was just sitting here slightly thinking of you.'

It was a simple falsehood; not really worthy of being called a lie. To give her credit she recovered quickly and chuckled her reply.

'Oh, I'm sure that's not true, Monsieur.'
Smith thought it was worth one more exchange. 'Ah Madam, you will never know.' The voice remained amused.

'Monsieur Smith, you must have had a good lunch.'

Smith sighed as he felt the moment dissolve.

'Oh dear, the last time I talked to someone who could make good guesses like that, I was married to her.'

'Well Monsieur, I'm not calling to offer you that, but I was wondering if we might dine again this evening. I have some charity meetings this afternoon in town and if you are free..'

Her voice tailed off with the sound of someone who already knows the answer to her question.

'I would be delighted,' he replied as that was precisely what he felt.

'Good. Our usual time and place?'

Smith took pleasure in the fact that she made a routine out of something that had only happened once before.

'Of course.'

The phone call ended but he didn't return to his book. He forced himself to think again somewhat more analytically about what was going on. This was clearly not a simple dinner invitation no matter how much he hoped it was. Madam Aubanet was much trickier than that.

Smith poured himself another cold Rosé and went back into the garden. Much of the picture was reasonably clear but all the bits, however well focussed, were still not exactly connected. He had found no evidence that Robert DuGresson's murder would in any way harm the business. Nor could he really believe that the Aubanets were part of the fraud. There was simply no reason for them to be so. They hardly needed the money. The fact that Robert was paying off two Marseilles families could provide a key. Perhaps he got in the middle of some sort of internecine strife. Girondou looked genuinely angry when Smith told him about Seffradi. The picture was no clearer. It suddenly occurred to him that what he probably lacked was a simple connection that would tie everything together.

On an impulse he picked up his phone and dialled Blanchard. The policeman answered neutrally.

'Yes?'

'Blanchard? Smith,'

The policeman was instantly defensive. Clearly, he had talked with Girondou. His voice was an unusual mixture of contempt and fear.

'What can I do for you, Monsieur?'

Smith decided to dispense with formalities, niceties and all of the other usual preliminaries.

'Does your wife know what you are up to?'

There was a long pause while Blanchard decided how to proceed. In the end there was just a monosyllabic: 'No.'

A man in Blanchard's position, in conversation with someone who could ruin him with a telephone call, is unlikely to start lying. Smith realised that he knew the answers to any other questions he might have and therefore rang off without saying anything further.

Suddenly he felt like doing something else for a while if for no other reason that he found himself getting bored with the problem. The ingestion of the modest amount of wine rendered the choice of what book to read academic as he fell asleep in the shaded warmth of his little garden.

Another hot day had turned gradually into a very warm evening. The kitchen clock said six o'clock and having pushed himself through that disagreeable feeling of waking while it was still light, he set himself to preparing himself for the evening. The problems of the late Robert DuGresson were set firmly at the back of his mind. He had the usual and more important things to think about. What shirt to iron was important, as was whether or not he had clean underwear? Arthur was fed, watered and walked. Smith took a long shower and got dressed. At ten to eight he was walking, ambling really, in the warmth of the early evening again along the elevated pavement along the Rhône. The water was slack almost to the point where it was difficult to see any flow at all around the sharp bend at the narrowing of the river that was the main reason for the first Roman settlement here in the first century BC. Crossing the Rhone and thus accessing the Languedoc to the west and thence into Spain was as much of a problem then as it is now. Between Arles and Lyon, a hundred and fifty to the north had been only one Roman crossing of the river, at Avignon. The town of Arles grew up around this crossing where it could also service a maritime business with access to the sea down river.

He ducked under the new bridge between Arles and Tranquetaille and, after a hundred yards or so, cut away from the riverbank into the Roquette and arrived at the restaurant promptly at eight.

As before, Madam was there before him and greeted him with broad smile. To his delight, she took both his hands in hers and offered her cheek to receive the first of the traditional Provencal three kisses. Smith had always thought that three was a bit excessive but not for the first time he found that Madam Aubanet, as he now thought of her, was changing his preconceptions. She was in a sort of business dress, presumably because of her earlier meetings. Grey silk blouse and beige linen trousers. Modestly heeled shoes and a grey linen jacket completed the picture. A single string of pearls and her Camargue cross for jewellery with a small red flower in her buttonhole adding a start of colour. She led him back to the same table they had had before.

'How was your meeting, Madam?' It seemed like a pretty lame way to start. Judging by the look on Madam's face, she thought so too.

'I'm on a number of committees that concern themselves with charitable activities in the region and we meet from time to time. Unfortunately, there always tends to be more talking than action.'

'Most meetings are like that, Madam, in my experience. I have tended to avoid these as much as I could for precisely that reason.'

'Well I'm glad that you didn't avoid this one, Monsieur.'

'Oh, this is entirely different.'

'Why exactly?'

He decided to risk seeing if her remarks about flattery were true.

'Only a complete fool would avoid having dinner in an excellent restaurant alone with a beautiful woman. Even the prospect of having to talk some business should not be allowed to deter him.'

'Well thank you. More Welsh flattery. Well, I suggest that we talk business quickly over an aperitif and then we can get it out of the way.'

The Crémant arrived as before.

'So, how are you getting on.'

'As I'm sure you know already, your businesses are in excellent health, judged, that's, by your own slightly unusual criteria.'

'What do you mean by that?' she asked looking interested.

'Well while most of your businesses either make profit, or at worst, break even, some run at a loss and have done so for years. Some of the small hotels, for instance. I get the impression that you maintain your interest primarily to support the families that either run them or derive their livelihood from them. If that's the case, then business development, other than a minimum to ensure survival, isn't a priority. The other major profit centres are in agricultural and this is a sector that has never been particularly susceptible to marketing. I have a number of specific suggestions to make but other than those, I would be wrong telling you that there is a lot more work to be done.'

'And Robert?'

'Chief Inspector Blanchard believes he was involved in stealing EC money and was killed because of some deal or other that went wrong. As he is now dead, Blanchard will be leaving.'

'Does he have any evidence of this?'

'I don't think so, Madam.'

'And do you?'
'No. I can continue to look, if you wish. I still have the laptop and iPhone.'

'Perhaps, monsieur. I would like to be sure that whatever he was up to, it will not come back to haunt us.'

A passing thought that Madam's seeming reluctance to let dead husbands lie was allowed to keep on going. Smith was not going to let the matter spoil what was about to be an enjoyable hour or so.

'Very well, Madam.'

The meal started with pan fried duck fois gras. It had more taste that the usual force-fed goose product. Smith thought he would start but there was no surprise in the fact that he was beaten to it.

'Now, Monsieur. Please tell me a little about yourself. I'm interested to know a little about you.'

'Well, Madam, I'm not sure what you want to know.'

'Well,' she replied. A little about yourself. I seem to know very little about you.'

'It is all pretty boring. I started teaching art history after universities in England and America. Stuck at that for about ten years. Moved into business, because I started getting fed up with dealing with students who were getting both more stupid and less interested in working as the years went by, and then spent the next twenty-odd years travelling the world for various companies and working for myself selling stuff to unsuspecting foreigners. Finished with that a couple or three years ago, had the usual businessman's small heart attack and decided to retire here to do essentially nothing. Two ex-wives, two beautiful daughters with the second, numerous dogs, a passion for cricket, Mozart and Provence. That's it really.'

'Yes, but why Arles in particular?'

The fish course arrived but rather than a piece of fish, a small pile of linguine was covered with a sauce made up white wine, cream and tellines, a tiny clam found around the Camargue beaches, particularly at thoroughly inaccessible places like Beauduc. Accessibly only via a long and completely unmade roadway, you need air suspension on your kidneys to get there to the sand. It is a form of small shellfish, akin to a small Cockle, found regularly on Arlesian menus but usually it served in shell, necessitating a continuous struggle to extract enough meat to taste, let alone savour.

Smith hated having to work hard for his food and usually avoided dishes that required it. Happily, on this occasion they had been de-shelled. The sauce has a hint of aniseed, Pastis, perhaps. It was, like all great food, stunningly simple and utterly memorable.

'Well, I'm not sure if I can answer that briefly,' he continued. 'Firstly, I love the area, I don't know a lot about the Camargue and its history, but I love going there and just poking around. The little tour of your farm with you and your father the other day was more of a pleasure than you can ever imagine. As I think I said to you before, I like Arles itself because it is a real place. It has real people doing real jobs. It has a thriving life whether culturally or socially. It is a poor town with a long proud history. Its monuments are stupendous, the food is simple but exciting. The climate is almost perfect, hot in summer, cold in winter, but, above all, predictable. The people here are unpretentious and welcoming. The town is small enough to be intimate but big enough, so people leave you alone. I could go on.'

He looked across the table.

'Your turn.'

'Well, I was born here on the farm and spent all my childhood here. I went to the village school in Le Sambuc and later in Arles. I stayed here until I was nineteen when I went to University in Paris. That's where I met Robert. When I graduated, I came home, primarily because, although my father is a good farmer, he is not good at good business. Someone needed to take on the business, and that job fell to me. Since then I have continued to work at developing our businesses. My mother died ten years ago leaving my father and grandfather at home. Robert came back on the scene about twelve years ago when we felt we needed a financial director. We had kept in touch off and on since our days in Paris. To cut a long story sort he joined the business and within a year or so we were married.'

'It was a very good thing from the point of view of the business,' she continued. 'Robert was very efficient and got the whole thing running on a professional basis. He laid the basis of the businesses you see now.'

She hesitated for a moment and they both ate in silence for a moment. Smith waited for her to continue. He had a feeling that this was going to be the hard bit.

'I realised that the marriage was a mistake almost within months. Robert hated the country. He was a townie and spent most of his time away from home. Don't get me wrong. When he stayed away it was always on business. But he did stay away rather a lot. He never spent much time in the office but was hard to develop a home life when your husband is never there, Monsieur Smith.'

Smith let that one go. It was entirely too close to the bone. There was a pause for the arrival of plates containing beef filet with a black olive tapenard and caviar of zucchini. After a preliminary mouthful, she continued with the air of someone reluctantly talking about something that she would much prefer would remain unsaid.

'It turned out to be an ideal arrangement.' Her tone became quietly bitter and a tear formed in the corner of her eye. 'We found out simultaneously that I couldn't have children and Robert could not stand the idea of having them anyway. I tried to persuade him that we should adopt but he refused. Within a few weeks he had moved out into Arles. Divorce was not an option, of course, so we settled into what can best be described as a working relationship. Robert did his job and for the rest he had his own life.'

Smith felt that he should be more than just a sympathetic ear. For some unaccountable reason he didn't wish to see this attractive woman sad on account of his wish to know more about her.

'I'm sorry to hear that, Madam, very sorry. From what little I have seen of it, the farm and your family would make an excellent environment to bring up children, whether they were born or adopted. Ideal, actually.'

'Yes. I thought so too. But it was not to be. Robert was a mistake personally, but I never had cause to find fault with his work for the business. The systems he put in place work very well, the accounts were always prepared accurately and promptly. He got on well with all our people, he visited the businesses regularly and they all thought well of him. We paid him well, but I can honestly say that I have no idea what he did with the rest of his life, outside the business.'

She raised he head and looked across the table at him with a touch of defiance.

'All I know is that's didn't include me.'

'In that case, he was an idiot.' She smiled her thanks.

'And I'm not just being polite.' The smile reached her eyes.

A change of subject was obviously in order. Right, apart from your father and the farm, what do you like?

What do you mean?'

'Oh, the usual stuff, interests? hobbies? What do you like doing?'

'Oh, I'm involved with a number of charities in the region, I enjoy the theatre and music, of course. I'm a trustee of the Marseilles Opera. I used to travel a lot but seem not to have the time anymore. I think that my greatest pleasure is working on the farm. Especially with my father. It is what the family has done for centuries and all the traditional things, the service for the Gardians on May the first at the Church of La Major in Arles, the day we brand the bulls, the two Ferias in the Arena. It is all part of the history and culture of what we do here, and it is very important to me. The natural life of the Camargue is also important, and I'm involved in many conservation projects. And what about you? You seem to lead a rather solitary life, if you don't mind my saying so.'

Smith chuckled. 'You are not the first person to stay that. Actually, don't really see it like that. I'm very happy in my own company. I can be selfish and do what I want, when want to. I have never seemed to be very good at making and keeping friends, so a long time ago I learned to make do without them. So here, like you, I enjoy music and the theatre, reading, going for long walks in the

Alpilles with my dog. I also like walking around the town and looking again for the umpteenth time at the little, unimportant places as well as the great monuments and museums. An old professor of mine once said that he was going to spend his retirement learning more and more about less and less. Spending my time looking again at buildings that I thought I knew well or re-reading books that I thought I had long done with is, I find, a good way to spend my own retirement.'

'And, of course, you have your family; your daughters at least.'

Smith had hoped to keep off that subject given what Madam had just said.

'Yes. I enjoy when they come to visit. Perhaps you would like to meet them when they next come?'

'Yes, I think I would like that very much, Monsieur.'

The main course was cleared away. A couple of pieces of cheese that Smith knew better than to try to identify and then a plain but anything but simple raspberry tart. Glasses of wine to match. The conversation drifted off into minutiae, enabling Smith to enjoy the informality into which their relationship seemed to have drifted and, of course, the not unsubstantial pleasure of simply being able to look at her. He knew that she was about forty. But he had never really understood what age actually was. He had never certainly never seen any connection between the age he was and the way he felt. She really didn't look any particular age. She certainly looked good to him, though. Dark hair that had that sort of uneven lustre that meant it was clean not coloured, piled up on top of her head to expose a slim, unmarked neck. A completely clear complexion and a light coffee skin tone that came from a life in the open but not from exposure to the extremes of sun and wind that could often be found on the Camargue. Dark brown eyes and slightly pronounced cheek bones. An attractively wide mouth. A minimum of makeup around eyes and mouth. Sitting across a very small restaurant table from her was by no means a hardship.

The meal annoyingly drew to a close, but he was delighted

when she said: 'Monsieur Smith. Is not the moment when we usually take a final stroll along the Rhone?'

'I believe it is, Madam,' happy to accept the suggestion, 'tradition is very important.'

They thanked the staff and went out into the warm night. This time she didn't wait until they reached the river before slipping her arm through his. Jean - Marie again trailed them by fifty yards in the black Range Rover. Again, the river gleamed with the reflected lamps along its banks and their easy, if inconsequential conversation continued.

They approached the point at which he would turn up into the town and she would get into the Range Rover and go home.

'Monsieur, I have a favour to ask.' 'Please ask it, Madam.'
'Tomorrow evening I have to attend the opera in Marseilles. I'm a trustee and it is the opening night of our latest production. My presence is expected, although I should admit that it is not usually a hardship. I enjoy these occasions. Normally my father accompanies me but, on this occasion, I know he would prefer to be at home to attend to some farm business. I apologise for the short notice, but would you perhaps be prepared to stand in for him? That's if you are not busy.'

As it happened Smith would be at his habitual loose end, but in any case, he could not imagine anything that would prevent his accepting – including his own demise.

'Madam, I would be delighted.'

She squeezed his arm. 'I'm very pleased. I shall ask Jean - Marie to pick you up early enough so that we can have an aperitif at the Mas – about five?'

'That would be fine.'

'One more thing. It is a gala night so dress will be formal.'

'White or black tie, Madam?'

She laughed. 'White. We are rather old fashioned here in the South.'

'What makes you think that a retired old man like me has a full evening outfit in his wardrobe?'

'Have you?'

'As it happens, yes, I have.'

'There you are then' she said triumphantly. 'I'll look forward to it, Madam,'

He saw her into the rear seat of the Range Rover.

'Thank you again for a delightful evening,' he offered through the open window.

'I also enjoyed it, Monsieur.'

He took her hand intending to do the usual and rather unsatisfactory hover above it by way of a farewell gesture and was slightly taken off guard when he was pulled firmly towards a proffered cheek. He was delighted to negotiate safely for the second time that evening the potentially hazardous ritual of planting the traditional three kisses on alternating cheeks. Reluctantly he stepped back from the car and she leant slightly towards him.

'Oh, by the way, thank you for the flowers, Monsieur.'

He was flummoxed. Perhaps there was some ritual that he had missed? Perhaps he should had brought flowers? He didn't think she was particularly sarcastic person. Then he saw. She had raised her hand to her lapel and was gently touching the flower in her buttonhole. It was a bright red Anemone.

9. Grandma and Puccini

The next morning after dog walking was whiled away on domesticity while various thoughts passed around his mind until, as he was beginning to think about lunch, an idea came to him. He took is phone out and dialled the number for Madam Durand. The phone was answered on its second ring.

'Yes?'

'Madam Durand. This is Peter Smith. I'm sorry to disturb you again so soon but I would very much like to talk to you again. I need your advice.'

'I would be delighted to help if I can. Why don't you bring your dog here later this afternoon after lunch? We can take a short walk together as long as it is not too hot. About three?'

'Until later, Madam, and thank you.'

So it was after a relaxed lunch in the garden with the usual half of his *gros pain*, pate and camembert going down Arthur, put on a lightweight linen jacket and took his straw hat and his dog down to the river and across the road bridge to Tranquetaille.

'You're very prompt, Monsieur.' she said as she opened her door to them. I appreciate punctuality although it not a virtue much prized generally in Provence.'

'Thank you, Madam. I have noticed since I came here that time is slightly more elastic that in other places further north.'

The sun was still well in up in the sky, but the old lady had clearly forgotten her professed antipathy to going out in the heat of a Provençale September day. She was dressed quite formally in rather an elegant, flowing floral day dress. Soon they were strolling under the shade of the plane trees than grow along the Quai Saint Pierre beside of the northern Rhone embankment towards the bend where the river swings north. Considering the age of his companion, their pace was by no means slow, just a proper amble by two people who didn't wish to let the negotiation of kerbs, bollards and other impedimenta divert them from conversation. She too had linked her arm up into his and seemed to be taking considerable pleasure in talking about the town they passed by it. Arthur strolled along at Smith's side, content to amble too but always looking about for something to kill. He obviously felt that this was good cat country and, as usually, he was right.

'Your dog seems beautifully mannered, Monsieur.'

'Thank you, Madam. I can't abide a dog that cannot walk to heel properly. Would you like to take him for a while?'

The old lady smiled delightedly.

'Oh yes, I would. Thank you.'

The lead was passed over and Arthur continued to walk steadily at the pace of his new owner, close to her side, the short lead hanging in a shallow loose curve between them.

'That's wonderful, Monsieur. Did it take a lot of training to do this?'

'Actually, for me, not at all. I got him as a rescue dog after he had raced for a couple of years. An important part of greyhound training is going for very long walks on leads, usually with a number of other dogs. He simply got used to not pulling and walking at the general speed that everyone else was going. That, together with their gentle nature, is what makes then such wonderful pets after they retire.'

'Unless you are a hare or a cat, I presume.'

'Er, yes. That can sometimes be a problem.'

'I don't think so. I don't like cats and I cannot recall ever seeing a hare in Tranquetaille. Does he ever run off the lead?'

'Not really, Madam. In town, of course, he can't and when I walk him in the countryside we're usually up in the Alpilles and he would probably injure himself if he started seriously chasing something up there. In training they only run free when they are racing, and they are quite happy on a lead. Obedience is not a priority in training, and he would almost certainly not come back if he started to chase something – at least he would come back in his own time. They also much prefer to lie down rather than just sit and will usually do that when asked. I do, however, sometime take him for a run in the Beauduc beach in the winter when most of the tourists have gone. He enjoys that.'

She looked down at the long sinuous back undulating slowly beside her. Arthur was large, even for a greyhound, and Smith thought that there was less than eighteen inches in height between them both.

'It's many years since I have the pleasure of walking a dog, Monsieur. I'm grateful to you both. You should ask Emile to let him run over the farm. They do still have the occasional rabbit there although the local hares of my youth are gone now. I can see that he'll trouble his beloved bulls much.'

They reached the main bend in the river and the old lady gestured at one of the shaded seats that were regularly spaced along their route.

'Now, young man, what is it that you want? You surely didn't come just to enjoy my company.'

'Actually, Madam, normally I would be delighted to do just that. I'm very interested in your memories of the town and your life in it. I have only just arrived here and would like to learn much more. However, as you rightly say, on this occasion there is some specific help that I would like to request, although I would understand if you felt you didn't want to give it.'

'I'll help where I feel I can, Monsieur and not when I don't.'

Smith smiled. This old woman may be well into her nineties, but she was as sharp as a knife. He would have to be alert.

'Last time we met you kindly told me a little of Les Frères. If you would allow, I would like to know a little more.'

'What, in particular, interests you Monsieur?' She had turned her head away from looking down at Arthur who had collapsed to lie onto his side in the shade beside the bench to look up at her directly and steadily out of one eye.

'You gave me a little of their history, Madam. Now I would like to know a little of their present. Their authority and influence. I would like to know of their morality and their relation to the Church. I would like to know about their relationships with the politicians in the area and the police.'

'Ah, I see. What you are really asking is whether they still influence life here, possibly even control it.'

'Yes.'

'Then the short answer is yes, but not quite perhaps in the ways you might think. Until recently, at least, Les Frères have never been a simple group in the way political parties or secret societies join together to exercise power and influence the way people live. It is more subtle than that and possibly stronger because of it.'

Smith sat quietly, marvelling at the clarity with which Madam Durand spoke. He knew that Arlesian women were renowned both for their beauty and their longevity – Madam Jeanne Calment, at the time oldest woman in the world, had died only a few years ago at the age of one hundred and twenty two – but this little bird of a woman expressed herself clearly and unfalteringly. He very much doubted that he would do the same in the highly unlikely event that he attained a similar age. She continued:

'What you have to understand is that we - the people from the Camargue, that is - have a particular way of life and have had for two thousand years. We are proud of our traditions, but we keep ourselves to ourselves. It is not that we don't like outsiders, but no one has done us any favours over the years, and we have got used to taking care of our own. We have our rules and if the outside world does not enforce them for us, we do it ourselves.'

'What about the Church, Madam. Where does the Church stand in all this?'

'We have been good Catholics for as long as Christianity has been here. Since the fourth century. Even the young. It takes no effort. It is the way we are. The way we always have been.'

Smith asked the question that could well be a key to the last few days.

'What happens when the interests of the people of the Camargue don't coincide with the teachings of the Church?'

'Then, Monsieur,' she replied with a small rather hard smile in her eyes, We must all be guided by our own conscience for we'll all one day stand before the judgement of God and we'll be called to account for what we have done.'

'Unfortunately, as I have lived so long my interview with the Almighty will be a long one, I suspect. But,' and her voice lowered perceptibly, 'I think he will understand.'

Smith thought it was a good moment to change the subject.

'Madam, have you heard of two called Claude Chadriol and Jean Mistraux by any chance.'

She frowned in a sad sort of way.

'Ah. I haven't personally met either of the people you mention but I know of them and I know their families well. They are typical of many farming families not just here but all over France. Although the government tries to protect small farmers it is difficult these days for them to survive. The older ones carry the problem with the same courage that they have faced difficulty for generations. It is more of a problem for the younger ones. They either work for the big farmers or they leave the Camargue. I believe that these two are some of those who has been unable to find a solution. I gather that Monsieur Mistraux met with a recent misfortune, but I think that you know that already, Monsieur Smith.'

With that she rose to her feet, took a firmer grip of Arthur's lead and they continued their walk around the bend in the river and back towards the centre of town passing in front of the cemetery. The conversation moved on to more general topics and before too long they arrived back in front of her house. She handed Arthur back and, having unlocked her door, she turned back to him.

'I have enjoyed our little walk together and the pleasure of having your dog as a companion. I have also enjoyed talking to you and I hope I've been some help. I ask only one thing of you, Monsieur Smith. When you judge us, as I have a feeling that you will be doing very soon, try to remember who we are, how we have had to look after ourselves for a very long time. We have lived by our own rules and if they are not the same rules as yours, that does not make them wrong. It just makes them different, Right and wrong in the Camargue is not the same as in Paris. Take care of yourself, Monsieur Smith. I sense that you are not always the charming Welshman that you seem. There is a streak of evil in you Monsieur. However, Martine tells me that she thinks that you are loyal to your friends and loyalty more than anything that's what she needs now.'

As if to dispel the solemnity of the moment, she smiled up at him.

'Come and see me again, soon, Monsieur.' Smith took her offered hand and was delighted to see that the old lady tilted her head in that way that invited the first of the traditional three kisses. It was a sign of his acceptance by her that he suddenly felt was important to him.

'I shall, Madam. I shall.'

The Range Rover arrived promptly at five. Jean-Marie was obviously not in the mood to chat. Smith wondered if he ever was. Perhaps he didn't like Smith sitting in the front. However, he was content to watch the familiar countryside sweep by and to wrestle with a problem. When Madam had invited him to the opera he was delighted to accept. He wasn't exactly overburdened with female company or social engagements and he had increasingly been looking forward to the occasions when they met. He certainly wasn't going to let a small matter of a personal dislike of Italian opera in general and a loathing of Madam Butterfly in particular stand in the way of a evening out with a beautiful woman. His love of opera, and it was a profound one, stopped after Mozart. Being honest, it didn't really start until Mozart either. That limited him to twenty-odd operas, of which only seven are regularly performed, and a very few other odds and sods of dramatic works and incidental music.

He had always thought Puccini a writer of great tunes and magnificent pieces of theatre, but he had always come home from performances of Tosca, Turandot or Bohème entertained but not satisfied. Butterfly he always thought of as particularly silly. Grand opera is replete with unbelievable characters, but he thought Pinkerton one of the least credible. Also, the whole story hardly interested him. However, it didn't take too much thought to decide to keep quiet, at least until he learned Madam's thoughts on the matter. They swept into the Mas and he jumped down from the Range Rover. Monsieur Aubanet greeted him with a very warm handshake.

'Nice to see you again, Monsieur Smith. Please come in.'

They walked together to the house and into the sitting room. Without asking, Smith had a very large whisky and soda pressed into his hand.

'Madam Butterfly.' he whispered, 'You're going to need this.'

Smith took a sip. Monsieur Aubanet was clearly not going to run out of soda any time soon.

'Martine will be here in a moment. She says she is still getting ready, but I think she wants to make an entrance. She has a new dress.'

After a few moments the door opened. Yes. A dress. And what a dress. Heavy black silk with a narrow but deep Vee neck. It was very tight down to mid-thigh when it fell heavily to the ground more fully. It was a black dress sparkling with black light. Virtually every square inch was covered in faceted black jet beads embroidered into complex and detailed patterns. The whole thing shimmered as if it was alive.

Her hair was piled onto the top on her head. Black jet drop earrings and a similarly embroidered choker tight around her neck. The only other jewellery was a small diamond inlaid Camargue cross on an almost invisible silver chain around her neck. She looked completely devastating and knew it.

'Gentlemen,' she said with a smile, 'You may now both close your mouths. I take it that you approve.'

Her father took her by the hand. 'My dear, you look quite wonderful.'

She did a slow pirouette on his hand and looked at Smith.

'And you, Monsieur?'

'Yes,' he said quietly, 'Quite wonderful.'

Evidently satisfied with the affect, she took a sip from her father's drink. She looked at a small clock at the side of the room.

'We must go,' she said. She held a similarly jewel-encrusted short jacket out to Smith, and he held it for her. It weighed a ton. It was a long sleeved, very waisted jacket, rather on the style of a matador's bolero jacket. A very small black bag completed the ensemble.

'Au revoir, Papa. I should be back about midnight.'

He managed to beat Jean-Marie to the Range Rover door to escort Madam in, but it was a close-run thing. Disapproval was shown by the fact that the wheels were spinning slightly before

Smith closed his own door behind him. They started at high speed towards Marseilles. After a few kilometres she turned to him.

'Peter, I wonder if, for tonight at least, you could possibly call me Martine. We are not at work and some of the people we have to meet tonight might think it a little odd if my escort for the evening called me Madam DuGresson all the time.'

'Of course,' replied Smith, delighted with the familiarity. She continued:

'Thank you for coming this evening. I must admit that Madam Butterfly is not my favourite opera but I'm a trustee of the Marseilles Opera and it would be impolite not to attend these gala opening nights.'

'I'm delighted to be invited,' replied Smith, rapidly thinking of a way to avoid the subject. 'I have never been to the Marseilles Opera before. I'm looking forward to it.'

Madam laughed. 'That was elegantly done, Peter. I have never met a man who actually really likes Madam Butterfly. There is something about the story that men seem to find difficult to relate to, I think. Probably because Pinkerton is such a bastard – from a woman's point of view, that's. However, I hope to enjoy your visit to our opera house. It used to be rather grander than it is now. The original Salle Bauveau was constructed in the late eighteenth century, but it was virtually destroyed by fire in 1919. It was a great house in those days. It even staged the French premier of Aida. Now it's a smaller theatre, but it still has a good season. Placido Domingo made his French debut here too. Now, I'm a trustee so there will be a few people to meet and talk to. Like many opera houses these days we rely on sponsors and they have to be looked after. We are doing the Italian version of Butterfly rather than the American one so there will be only one interval, but we'll have to socialise then. But I've said that we can't stay for the party after the performance. I certainly don't really want to go, and I suspect it is not your sort of thing either. I would be grateful, very grateful, if you stayed with me during the intervals. I don't like this bit of these occasions and often find myself needing to end conversations and having with me someone that I need to introduce around will make extracting myself from time to time slightly easier.'

'Delighted to serve as a diversion when required, Madam - sorry, Martine.'

She reached across and found his hand and gave it a squeeze of thanks. He was a little disappointed when the hand was withdrawn. The rest of the journey took about half an hour and they talked a lot about nothing in particular. The Range Rover swept up to the front of the opera house and they were absorbed into a world of red plush, gold paint and spectacularly costumed guests. Madam slipped her arm lightly through his and he lost count of the people he was introduced to.

Inevitably they were in a box. He hated boxes. Everyone in the audience spends most of the time looking up playing a 'spot the bloated plutocrat' game. Being looked at enviously was not something he relished, especially in this land of revolutions, guillotines, baskets and old women knitting. In any case the view of the stage is usually terrible. You are often closeted with a bunch of people you hate, who talk all the way through the performance and you're usually forced to stay with them during the intervals rather than rushing off to consume as much gin and tonic as you can as quickly as you can in the anonymity of the crush bar. Instead you are condemned to drink gut-wrenchingly bad champagne in an even worse company.

This time, however, there were only two chairs. People in the audience looking up would see him with the best-looking woman in the place. He didn't like the opera, so the view of the stage was immaterial. There was only one other person in the box, and he would rather spend the time talking to her than listening to Puccini. The champagne was Krug. God, how he loved boxes.

He made sure Madam was seated nearer the stage. At least he could look at her rather than at a collection of Europeans made up in white face paint in a vague and visually unsuccessful attempt to make them look like Japanese. He could hear the music without watching it. Usually the best way. In his experience, most opera singers he had come across could act almost as well as most actors could sing grand opera. The performance started and he did indeed spend most of the first twenty minutes of the performance looking at his companion. She really was extraordinarily beautiful. The dress caught the stage lights in a thousand tiny black mirrors in the embroidery and it shimmered as she breathed shallowly.

The interval arrived and they spent it chatting to sponsors and quaffing more Krug. Madam's arm remained firmly entwined in his throughout and he experienced the unaccustomed experience of receiving envious glances from the men who had no idea who he was and slightly arch glances from women who clearly felt they were somewhat eclipsed; as indeed they had been. It was half an hour where he hoped he said the right things to the right people but really wished he was somewhere – anywhere – else with Madam, of course. He had never had much time for this sort of thing. Cocktail parties and small talk were not a forté. Neither was his ability to disguise his feelings about it. Many times, in the past he had got home after one of these occasions proud of his success in hiding his terminal boredom with bright and amusing chatter to be bollocked by an ex-wife for misbehaving in one of a wide variety of ways.

After what was an eternity, they bid their adieus and Madam made an excuse of her father being not too well to explain missing the post-performance festivities. They were led back to the box by a flunky. As soon as the door closed and while they were still in the shadow at the back of the box, she reached up gave him a light kiss on the cheek. 'Well done. I thought you did very well, indeed.'

'Thank you, Madam.' he replied with exaggerated courtesy. 'Beautiful and patronising. Plus ça change...'

She smiled at him rather sharply and kicked him in the shin. The kick was gentler than the smile. They took their places and the second act started. Smith had only ever seen the three-act version, so he was not entirely sure where they were in the story. He really didn't care any very much anyway. As the performance started again, he found that listening to the music as a concert performance and shutting out the plot and the action made it quite a pleasant way to spend the time. He took to whiling away the time by wondering about his host. After a considerable time without any real female company it was a pleasure to be out and about and to be seen with Madam was no hardship at all. She was excellent company. He even believed her reason for inviting him much as he would like to think otherwise. However, what he had learned over the last few days gave him pause for thought.

Butterfly finally breathed her last, Pinkerton agonised, and the performance came to an end at about eleven thirty, and after many goodbyes and other formalities, they stepped out into the warm Marseilles night. The black Range Rover was parked directly outside. This time Jean-Marie got there first and was standing by the open door. Smith flashed him a smile in acknowledgement and was rewarded with a grin in return.

'Well,' she said. 'What did you think? Remember you have promised to be honest with me.'

'Did I? I don't seem to remember promising any such thing.'

'Well, perhaps you didn't. But you should have.' Her voice changed slightly as she continued, 'and I hope you will.'

'I still remain ambivalent about the opera. It is not really my sort of thing. As I'm bound to tell the truth, then I would say that I enjoyed the tunes but wasn't really concentrating too hard and really cannot remember much about it. I did, however, enjoy being with you a great deal. I would even go to Wagner opera if you invited me. If we get to know each other better, you will realise how much I dislike Wagner.'

'Will we get to know each other, better, Monsieur Smith?' she asked, lowering he voice to below the threshold at which Jean-Marie could hear clearly.

'I hope We'll, Madam DuGresson.'

'As do I, Monsieur Smith.'

They took the same route back as they came, along the

motorway north out of Marseilles towards Salon de Provence. It would take them back to Arles where they could drop Smith off before returning to the Mas. However, at Salon they were diverted off the motorway onto the old Roman road, between Salon and Arles. A harassed gendarme informed them that a Spanish driver had jacknifed his truck and blocked both lanes of the motorway a few miles ahead. They could, he informed them, get back on the motorway a few miles further up just before St Martin de Crau. Jean-Marie glowered at the unfortunate man as if the whole thing was his personal fault.

The old via Aurelia runs alongside the motorway for virtually all this distance and, although Jean-Marie was obviously annoyed at having his speed restricted, there would be very little loss of time. Smith was well used to this road. He often used it coming backwards and forwards to Marseilles airport to pick up people when they came to stay, and it gave him a perverse pleasure to avoid paying the tolls. The motorway was toll-free after Saint Martin to Arles. They slowed down for the roundabout where the road between Istres and Les Baux crosses.

It was a sound from his past that instantly became a horrifying part of the present. When he first heard it years ago, he had likened it to his dimly remembered grandmother ripping up cotton shirts to make them into cleaning cloths. The Range Rover bucked and swayed for a moment, then ploughed off the road stopping with a violent lurch as it lost a front corner into a shallow ditch. In the split second before the tearing started again, he knew exactly what was happening and what to do next. Some years ago, Her Majesties Government had spent a lot of money ensuring that he would. He leant over and grabbed Madam by the shoulders and pushed her violently down onto the floor behind the front seats and bent over her. The ripping noise started again. Glass fragments exploded above them. So much for bullet proof windows, he thought. Either those guys at Range Rover's special vehicles division were losing their touch or their attackers knew how to choose their ammunition.

He had followed her down onto the floor and put his hand none too gently across the back of her neck, his mouth next to her ear.

'Your survival depends on doing exactly what I say. Stay on the floor. Say nothing. Don't move. Don't look up. Do nothing at all until you hear my voice again.'

Smith slid across the rear seat, opened the far door and dived out of the car and rolled into the ditch. The bullets were coming from the side of the road. Perhaps these guys were not quite as clever as he feared. They had chosen the right bullets for the glass but not for the armoured bodywork. The dull thump of bullets entering but not penetrating the sides of the car was distinctive. He crawled round and opened the driver's door and, with shards of glass still exploding around his head, and pulled a bleeding Jean-Marie out and down into the ditch. The man was wounded, badly but not, Smith gauged, terminally - yet. He felt under the driver's jacket and offered a silent prayer of thanks. He pulled the gun out of the shoulder holster and ran at a crouch back away from the collision of headlights up the ditch about twenty yards. As he went, he felt the gun. Thank God. It was a Hecker and Koch P30. As he ran, he flipped the magazine out. By the weight it was full, a fact he confirmed by pushing down on the top round with his thumb. It didn't move. Simply looking at it, à la TV movie, only confirms that you have one. He knew he had a full fifteen. He estimated from the moment the car left the road he had no more than twenty seconds to solve this problem. He had already used about twelve of them.

The shooting had stopped. Their assailants had successfully targeted the driver and the Range Rover's tyres. That meant there were at least two of them and he had only heard two guns: familiar guns. Uzi SMGs. He prayed that they had the smallest magazines. They may make the gun easier to conceal but 20 rounds at a firing rate 600 round per minute didn't take too long to empty, especially in the hands of less experienced shooters. Had their attackers been professionals, Smith and his companion would be dead. They would assume success and they wouldn't not expect anyone to shoot back. Hopefully they might take a little time reloading.

Without hesitation he jumped out of the ditch and saw the two men less than ten metres away, standing in the full glare of headlights, walking towards the stricken Range Rover. Idiots. He felt contempt for them as he fired at the nearest man. Two shots at the forehead, aim adjusted slightly after the first, as fast as the gun would do it, just as he had done times before. Head shots kill people instantly, body shots don't. Yet again he saw instantaneously two small holes, one immediately below the other appear like a figure eight in the middle of the man's forehead an instant before the back of his head exploded into a crimson vapour cloud and disappeared into an oleander bush at the side of the road. 'Laurier rose', Smith thought grimly.

The second man had his Uzi halfway to the firing position when he realized that he still held the new full magazine in his left hand. He had less than half a second left to panic before his brain too was blown out into undergrowth.

Kill and move. That had been the mantra and that was what he did. The assailants had come in a car and there was no evidence that there had been only two of them. If there were just two, then they wanted more training. You always left someone to drive the car. He ran across the road and made his way quickly to a position in the dark behind the attackers' car, turning his dinner suit collar and lapels in to cover his worryingly white dress shirt. It was a big Jeep Cherokee, but nothing seemed to be moving inside it. If there had been only two of them then he had a little more time. Not too much. An ambush like this one would normally have a second team a mile or two further up the road. Hearing the shots and not seeing the Range Rover, the second team would probably make its way back to the scene of what they guessed would be a successful hit.

He checked the interior and both the wing mirrors from the back of the Jeep. He looked in the passenger side windows. Non-one. He hadn't been shot so presumably the third person was non-existent rather than just hiding in the ditch.

He opened the Jeep's rear door nearest the Range Rover and ran back across the road picking up one of the Uzis. It was one of the new so-called mini-Uzis with a rate of fire of 950 rounds per minute. 32 round magazines not 20. They'd been lucky. Probably firing the damn things with one hand like in the films, he thought. Even the best miniature machine pistol in the world is a dead loss used like that. He had inserted the new magazine and cocked the gun by the time he reached the ditched Range Rover.

'Martine, this is Peter. So far so good. However, it is not over. Don't move until I tell you. Are you injured at all?'

'Nothing apart from a rather bruised neck,' came the slightly aggrieved reply.

'Right, when I open the door, I want you to get out of the car and run like hell across to the Jeep, get into the back and lie down on the floor again. Do you understand?'

The voice was business-like: 'Yes. What about..?

'Leave Jean-Marie to me.' With that he wrenched open the door and pulled her like a sack of potatoes out of the car and dragged her across the thirty or so yards to the Jeep, bundled her in and slammed the door shut.

'Stay down,' he shouted as he ran back. He could have sworn that a sarcastic dog bark came from the back of the Jeep.

Jean-Marie was bleeding from a neck wound although it was not one of the carotid arteries. He would have been dead if that was the case. Lifting him out of the ditch, none too gently, Smith also saw that he had been hit just below the shoulder. He was conscious, just, and would probably last a little longer. Smith estimated that they were about half an hour from the Mas. He carried Jean Marie to the Jeep and dumped him across the back seats. He noticed that Madam had not moved. He took her hand.

'Right, we have at least one more problem to solve. I intend to drive us home. It will be very rough and very fast. Whoever is trying to kill us, if they have the remotest idea of their business, there'll be a second team coming this way in the next two of three minutes. They would have been the backup team further up the road. They will have heard to gunfire and as we haven't passed them, they will assume that the first team has been successful. I'm afraid we must stay here until they arrive, and you must stay exactly where you are. This Jeep isn't armoured but at least it is a metal box and they shouldn't be expecting to shoot at it as it is theirs. Hopefully I can kill them before they realise their mistake.'

The eyes that looked up at him were scared. The whole thing thus far had probably taken less than two minutes. He had been on automatic for all of it, but it must have felt like an eternity to her, lying face down in the dark. Her grip on his hand was like a vice. Taking some time that he could ill afford, he reached down and laid his other hand on her cheek and smiled gently at her.

'Courage, Martine. I'm afraid to admit that I have done this sort of thing before, and I used to be quite good at it. It was one of the things I left off my verbal CV to you a day or so ago. I'm, after all, still alive. Now, face down, please.'

The smile was returned. She let go his hand and turned away. Smith shut the door, took a quick detour around the back of the Jeep, and set about making some arrangements. He manhandled one corpse into the Jeep's driver's seat. The other, he propped halfway into the shattered side window of the Range Rover. It was a messy business and his dinner suit probably wouldn't recover. Both corpses had had spare magazines for the Uzis. He picked up the second gun and reloaded it. Swapping guns is faster than reloading. He killed the headlights on the Jeep. The Range Rover's has been shot away. He then ran about a hundred yards up the road and crouched in the same ditch as before.

It was less than a minute before he saw the headlights. The shot had to be accurate, so he unfolded the shoulder stock on the Uzi and waited. He had gambled that the second car would also be a Jeep and so it proved. His trip to the rear of the first Jeep had confirmed the location of the petrol tank and he had chosen that side of the road. The driver must have seen the pair of cars ahead at almost the same instant as they passed Smith going at about a hundred kilometres per hour. Taking careful aim and allowing deflection for a traversing shot, Smith loosed the entire magazine. In two seconds, thirty-two rounds hit the Jeep's petrol tank and one second later the it was a fireball. It disappeared off the road fifty yards later rolled like a Catherine wheel and ended up on all four wheels in the field blazing.

Smith added the second Uzi to his collection and hurried back to the cars. He ducked quickly into the tailgate of the Range Rover and extracted the first aid kit then into the back seats to retrieve Madam's small handbag. They would need her phone. He stepped away from the car and put a quick burst into its fuel tank as well. The road was lit like a film set. He tossed the first aid kit into the back and swung the machine around and accelerated as hard as he could up the road towards the Camargue, leaving two blazing wrecks and an unknown number of corpses in his wake. He hit a hundred and sixty kilometres an hour before a slightly exasperated voice from the back chirped up.

'Can I get up now?'

'Er, I would rather you didn't. There is still a possibility that something else might happen.'

She was obviously not prepared to let it go at that.

'And what route exactly do you intend to take back to Mas? Presumably the one on the map? The main roads? I'm not sure if that wouldn't occur to the people who are trying to kill us. I can navigate you back a slightly safer way. And in any case, Jean Marie is bleeding all over me. He needs some help.'

'All right. But you must be prepared to get down on the floor again if I tell you.'

He saw her beautiful but very bloodstained face appear in the rear-view mirror. She saw his concern.

'Please don't worry. I'm quite unharmed.' Smith's 'Thank God,' came out before he could stop it. He saw a sharp look from her in the mirror. 'His neck wound is not serious. However, the chest wound looks as if it might be at the top of his lung. All you can do is keep something pressed hard into the wound and hope he does not lose too much blood before we get him back.'

The rest of the journey was, for Smith at least, utterly hair raising. He drove very fast along roads narrow enough to touch both sides of the Jeep at once receiving a series of rally-style instructions from Madam that were issued much later than he would have liked but proved gratifyingly accurate.

'Please tell me when we are exactly five minutes away from the Mas, Madame.'

By now she knew better than to ask, so she just nodded and continued to concentrate on navigation from the back seat.

It was about fifteen minutes of very high speed and reckless driving later when Madame said: 'We are five minutes away at this speed.'

'Please call your father. Make sure it is him and once you have him on the phone hand it over to me. Don't talk to him. There will be time for that later.'

He could see that Madam was still having difficulty doing what she was asked without asking questions, but she nevertheless nodded and took her phone from her handbag.

A few second later she got through.

'Papa? Martine.'

Seeing Smith's hand reaching back over the seat, she placed the phone in it.

'Monsieur Aubanet? This is Peter Smith. Please listen and do what I ask. We have been attacked on the way back from Marseilles. Martine and I are uninjured. Jean-Marie has been shot in the neck and chest. He is alive but will need a doctor. We are five minutes away from you and are driving a black Jeep Cherokee. Please take some men with guns down to your front gate and open it immediately. I shall put the hazard lights on as we approach, and I'll not stop. Anyone trying to enter not in a Jeep with its hazard lights flashing must be stopped at any cost. Shut and guard the gates as soon as we come through and under no circumstances let anyone else in. Deploy as many reliable armed people as you can around the house for the rest of the night. You yourself must stay indoors. Don't come out into the courtyard even when we arrive. Monsieur, if you value your life and that of your daughter you will do exactly what I ask.'

Smith rang off without waiting for a reply and concentrated on the rest of their journey. The gates to the Mas were passed almost without slowing and within moments they pulled up in a cloud of dust and gravel. People came out, removed Jean-Marie and carried him into the house. Madam was also escorted inside. Smith sat quietly for a few moments before stiffly pulling himself out of the driving seat. The adrenaline was wearing off quickly and he felt shattered. He picked up both Uzis from the seat beside him - they had his fingerprints all over them - and wiped the steering wheel and gear knob clean. A very steely-eyed man in a Provençale shirt and jeans held the door open and, having waited for him to wipe the two door handles he had used, escorted him into the sitting room he had seen for the first time only a day or two before.

He collapsed into the nearest deep armchair oblivious to the fact that he was also covered in other people's blood. His escort asked in a manner that indicated he was obviously not used to any form of domestic service whether he wanted anything.

'Yes, thank you. I would like a very large whisky, no water or ice, a bottle of methylated spirits and some clean rags, please.'

The man left without any acknowledgement but within a few moments the same young lady who had served them lunch on his first visit returned with a tray bearing exactly what he had requested. It took him only a few moments to strip and clean his prints off the guns. He laid them and the cleaning equipment on a sideboard and then settled back into the chair and took a very large pull at the whisky. Knowing that explanations would be required soon, he went into recovery mode rather than sleep. He emptied the whisky in one further swig, laid his head back against the back of the chair and emptied his mind of absolutely everything other that trying to track the progress of the fiery liquid through his system. After five motionless minutes, he no longer felt any pain, the shivering had stopped, he was no longer exhausted. Most human feelings are constructs of the imagination and if that usually overactive faculty can be beaten into submission, then life can be forced to go on.

Five minutes later father and daughter can into the room. Smith rose. Monsieur Aubanet was in day clothes. Madam had obviously showered and changed into a floor length white satin robe. She was barefooted. Her hair was slicked back behind a band. She wore no makeup and looked both exhausted and ravishing.

'Monsieur, I'm sure you will agree that we must talk a little. Martine has told me what she remembers, and I think it is best if she goes to bed. I hope that's all right with you.'

'Yes, of course.'

Madam stepped forward and then stopped, uncertain as to what to do or say - or at least where to start. Smith crossed the distance between, took her hand gently and smiled gently directly into her eyes.

'Go to bed, Madam. Please. Now. We can talk later.'

She returned his smile. A tiny flash of defiance appeared in her eyes. She gave the tiniest bob of a curtsy and left. Smith returned to his seat and Monsieur Aubanet took the one opposite. New drinks appeared and the maid left, closing the door softly.

'Before anything else, Monsieur Smith, I would like to invite you to stay here stay here tonight. It's past one o'clock in the morning and it wouldn't be a good idea for you to travel home.'

'Ah, unfortunately I have my dog to think about, Monsieur.'

'I hope you don't mind but have taken the liberty of asking a friend in Arles - a very good and trustworthy friend - to collect him from your house and bring him here.' He looked at his watch. 'They should be here any minute. He'll be fed when he arrives.' It took him only an instant to dismiss the obvious practical question of collecting the dog from a locked house.

'Thank you. That's indeed a very good arrangement. I accept your kind invitation.'

'Next, Monsieur Smith, would you like to shower and change before we talk?'

'No. Thank you. I would prefer to brief you then go to bed myself.'

'Very well.'

Now that the formalities were over, Smith sensed that the old man didn't really know where to start with his questions, so he started himself. The whole story told quickly, without omissions, from leaving to opera to arriving back at the Mas. The old man just watched and listened.

Just as Smith finished his monologue the door opened and a joyful Arthur bounded in, greeted both men with equal enthusiasm and then went on a tour of the room before collapsing on the thickest rug to start digesting what was obviously very recently consumed meal.

'Thank you for your report, Monsieur. You can leave things with me now. Let me show you to your room.'

They walked out of the sitting room followed by a slightly annoyed dog, down a corridor and into a bedroom. The door to a lighted bathroom was open at the far end and sliding windows gave out onto the walled garden. Arthur's bed had been brought and his lead was hanging over the back of a chair. A selection of clothes and shoes had been laid out on the sideboard. Smith turned to his host. 'I would like to take the dog for a walk in the morning at about seven. I may want to sleep later but the dog wouldn't understand.'

'I quite understand, Monsieur. That will be perfectly all right. Breakfast will be at eight.'

The old man walked back towards the door but then turned back, laid a gentle hand of Smith's arm and looked up at him directly. The words came formally but hesitantly.

'You have daughters, I believe, Monsieur Smith. You will therefore understand the service that you have rendered to me this evening. You have my gratitude. You have saved the life of the only thing that matters to me in my life. I'm in your debt and always will remain so.'

Smith didn't know what to say. The attack could just as easily have been about him than about her. Finally, Aubanet turned, squared his shoulders, and walked out, closing the door behind him.

His phone had been vibrating silently off and on in his pocket for about half an hour. Four missed calls all without identification. One message. 'Call me. G.'

The phone hardly rang.

'It was not us, Monsieur. You must believe that. I'll find out and let you know, but it was not us.'

'OK. Thank you.'

The line went dead.

Smith finally stripped off his clothes, had a shower, got into bed and turned off the lights. He knew full well that he would be unable to sleep for some time. He lay on his side facing the uncurtained window. A light breeze shimmered the olive trees and bushes on the garden illuminated by a steely moonlight that filtered into his room.

So, a bit of his past that he had hoped dead and buried had really surfaced. Not for the first time, it had to be admitted, but never quite as seriously as this. It was worrying how easy it was to dredge up old skills. He had not shot a pistol in anger in ten years, but it still came as easily as it always had. His instructor had said he was a natural. He reached under his pillow to check that the gun was uncocked and the safety was off. He had now to begin the process of forgetting it all over again. God only knows if he could go through all that again. The professionals back in the UK had had enough trouble. Now he had to do it on his own and he was not looking forward to it.

Unsurprisingly he found it difficult to sleep. After a number of attempts he got up, pulled one of the bedroom chairs in front of the window and sat watching the moon move slowly across the clear sky. Arthur lifted an eyelid and watched the manoeuvre without moving anything else. The question was, of course, who were they after. Had he personally got sufficiently up the noses of some Marseilles mob that they had risked a considerable amount to kill him? He thought it unlikely. Gangsters rarely killed people unless there was a profit in it, and he had already assured them of his silence. If they had been after Madam, then equally they risked endangering a laissez faire policy that had existed between them and Les Frères for more than half a century and they wouldn't do that again unless there was a very good reason. There was, of course, a possibility that it was about Jean Marie but it seemed a lot of trouble to go to on account of a chauffeur bodyguard. Unless, of course, there was more to him than had met the eye to date. Perhaps the whole thing was a giant, violent, misunderstanding.

He got up and found his mobile phone and sent a short text message to Gentry. He wanted to be the one to tell him as soon as he could in the morning. Finally, he nodded off and slept fitfully until seemingly only minutes later dawn stared to break. He decided to get up and take a long shower. He shaved and found a set of clothes to suit. He found there was a faded pair of brown cords. A casual shirt and sweater and an unexpectedly well-fitting pair of Camargue boots. It was without surprise that he saw that they were the same pair that he had worn on his previous visit around the farm. Much to Arthur's delight, he opened the French doors onto the garden. It was now slightly past seven and the sun was already up and warming the land. There was no wind, so he decided to risk the walk without a coat. He fastened the dog's lead and then stopped when a thought struck him. He returned to the bed and retrieved the Heckler. He chambered a round, thumbed the safety, mentally remembering that he now had one ready to go and nine left in the magazine. Four rounds, two kills. His instructor would have been proud of him he thought grimly. He tucked the short gun into the back of his trousers, an action that made him change his mind about the jacket. Taking Arthur in hand he stepped out into the garden. It was as he remembered, and he made towards what looked like a garden door at the far end set into the high stone wall. It wasn't locked and he stepped through, stopped and looked around him.

He found himself immediately in the flat Camargue landscape. The last time he had this view, he was on the back of a horse and that little extra height played him false. From the horse he saw a landscape that extended to a far horizon that was interrupted periodically by clumps of trees or tall reed beds. The perspective was an open one, wide, desolate. Now on foot the view was utterly different; almost claustrophobic. The reeds that traditionally separated the fields towered, as did the trees and the occasional hedge. The view from the ground was much more limited.

Arthur had stood stock still, quivering slightly, scanning the view from an even lower perspective for something to chase and kill. The killing was hard - wired into his brain and no power on earth could stop his desire to chase anything that moved. His racing training merely polished something that was already there by thousands of years of breeding. How ironic, Smith thought, that humans were supposed to have a choice in the matter. Actually, of course, sometimes they didn't at all.

He set off down the path. Breakfast was at eight. It was now seven fifteen. Not knowing the farm, he decided to keep to the path and walk for twenty minutes then turn and walk back. Given what had happened last night, the call managed to sound at once completely correct and faintly ludicrous.

'Monsieur Smith.' He turned and was delighted to see Madam hurrying up the path towards him.

'May I join you and Arthur on your walk?'

'Of course, Madame. That would be an excellent idea. How

are you feeling.'

'I'm not exactly sure.'

They walked together up the path and she slipped her arm through his in the same way as she had after their meals together in the Roquette. He looked across at her. She looked fresh and very beautiful and very young. Her hair was swept back in a ponytail and she was dressed in her customary shirt, jeans and boots. A brown suede leather bolero jacket completed the ensemble. No makeup and just a black metal Camargue cross for jewellery.

She returned his gaze and spoke in a calm voice. 'There will be time later to talk later about what happened last night, but I wanted to say thank you for what you did. I don't know how you did it, but I owe you my life. I can never forget that. What I feel is actually much more than that, but that's all I wish to say now.'

Smith's embarrassment showed itself in a false bravado.

'Think nothing of it, Madam. It was, as they say, all in an evening's work. I'm afraid I like Madam Butterfly even less now.'

The rest of the walk passed all to quickly and in relative silence. Her arm remained in his and from time to time she leant her head against him for a few steps. Neither of them was shod adequately to venture far from the path, and before long they arrived at the garden door and she stopped him, drew his head down to her and kissed him lightly but lingeringly on the lips. Monsieur Aubanet was already seated at the breakfast table reading La Provence, the local morning paper. He turned toward them and rose as they came through the garden door. The narrow opening had required Madam to disengage her arm that had been threaded through Smith's for the duration of the walk. Although it was no more than thirty yards between door and table, Smith felt her retake his arm for a few steps before running the last few and embracing her father. For Smith, the handshake was firm and the glance full-faced and friendly.

'Good morning. Please sit, both of you.'

Arthur immediately gravitated to the end of the table that had proved to be such a fruitful source of titbits the last time he visited. His host was delighted and immediately tossed a large piece of jam-laden baguette to the expectant dog.

'How is Jean - Marie?' Smith asked.

'Thank you. It is good of you to ask. He is recovering well. The bullet in his shoulder was easy to get out and we filled him up with blood and antibiotics. He didn't need more medical treatment than we could give him here. He slept well and would like to see you if you have a moment. I believe he wants to thank you.'

'That's certainly not necessary, but I'd be delighted to see him.'

'Please eat your breakfast, you two. I've already had mine. I'll explain what has happened during the night. The Range Rover has been recovered and has been disposed of. The Jeep you borrowed, similarly has been destroyed. The two Uzis have been heavily burned and left at the scene. The Marseilles police arrived there about three hours ago well after we had extracted our car. We left all the bodies at the scene as well as the bullet casings. All but the ones you fired from the pistol will be traced to the Uzis. Although I understand you might want to keep it, might I suggest that you give me the Heckler? Although it is completely untraceable, if for any reason you have to use it again, then it might then be traced back to this incident if not to us personally. I'll furnish you with a replacement if you wish. What would be your preference?'

'A Glock 36,' replied Smith as he took the pistol from behind him, took out the clip, ejected the chambered round and passed it all across the breakfast table. Aubanet picked up the clip and weighed it in his hand.

'Eight?'

'Ten.'

'Four rounds, two kills. You have some unusual skills for a

retired art historian, Monsieur Smith. I understand why the little Glock's magazine of only six is not a difficulty for you. I'll have one to you within the hour.'

It occurred to Smith that the conversation over the breakfast table was utterly bizarre. He glanced across at Martine. She looked more like a fascinated student than a horrified widow. Monsieur Aubanet continued:

'We know who did this to you and the matter is to be addressed later today. In the meantime, I suggest you stay here at the Mas where you will be quite safe. After today it will be safe for you to return home and we can all hopefully return to our normal lives or as near normal as possible.'

'You are kind to offer, Monsieur. However apart from the fact that I would like to get home, if last night's events were about me, then you and I'll be happier and safer in an environment of my choosing. If you could find someone to drive me home, I would be grateful.'

Smith's tone was firm. For a reason he could not quite put his finger on, he wanted to leave the comfort of the farmhouse and get back to something simpler. He continued:

'However, I would like to see Jean Marie before I go.'

'As you wish. I'll arrange it.'

They continued their breakfast in virtual silence with Arthur receiving a succession of titbits from all three. When finally, it was over, Madam got up from the table.

'Let me show you where to find Jean-Marie.'

Smith let himself into the room that had doubled as a hospital room to see Jean-Marie heavily bandaged but sitting up in bed. The man had miraculous powers of recovery or Smith was not as good at fast diagnosis as he thought. Sitting next to the bed was a mountain of a man who rose as he came in.

'Please excuse me,' said Smith, 'I had expected Jean-Marie to be alone. I'll come back later.'

The man extended his hand. 'Please come in, Monsieur Smith. It is you I wish to see.'

Smith's hand was engulfed in a great paw, ridged with muscle and covered in calluses that clenched his with the subtlety of a car crusher.

'I'm Roger Chirou, Père Aubanet's cousin and Jean-Marie's father.'

Smith managed to extract his hand before permanent damage was done and decided that a slight exaggeration to the youth's father wouldn't be out of order. 'I'm delighted to meet you, Monsieur. You have a brave son.'

The older man's eyes glistened with pride. 'I'm here, Monsieur Smith to thank you for saving my son's life. For this I'm in your debt. If you have need of anything, I'm your man.'

After an embarrassed pause, the huge man left the room. Smith turned to find that Jean - Marie had fallen asleep so he made his way back to his room. The Glock was waiting on the bedside table. He loaded the little gun and attached one of the holsters to his belt behind him. A quick glance in the mirror confirmed that the jacket that had been provided was long enough. He walked out into the courtyard to see a new Range Rover parked up and a driver who could have been Jean Marie's twin brother. Dressed in jeans and a Camargue shirt, he was also wearing a denim jacket which, insofar as it was ever actually tailored, had now sprouted a very distinct bulge under the left armpit.

'Christ,' Smith thought, 'I hope to God he knows how to use it. I could be in more danger from the chauffer than the Mob'

The young man was holding Arthur on his lead and making something of a fuss of him.

'Bonjour, Monsieur. My name is Pierre and I'll be driving you into Arles.'

Smith extended his hand.

'Before we go,' the youth said, 'Le Patron would like to speak with you.'

With that he led the way into the house, Arthur trotting happily at the heels of this, yet another, new friend.

'Tart', thought Smith as he followed.

The door opened the door at their first knock, and he entered Monsieur Aubanet's study. Pierre and Arthur stayed behind outside. The study was dark ochre in colour. The shutters were almost closed and thus the room was dimly lit by desk and reading light. It was fully carpeted. In the gaps between the glass-fronted bookcases that lined the walls were a small but exquisite collection of pictures. Had he not known a little of the family history he would have thought they were fakes for he quickly counted three little van Goghs and two Gauguins. All glowed like jewels under their picture lights; all, to his certain knowledge, unpublished and unsuspected by the world outside.

Madame stood with her father by the fireplace. She had changed into a simple blue cotton summer dress, gathered at the waist with a thin gold belt. A scoop neckline just showed the swell of her breasts while the full skirt was cut just below the knee. Flat brown leather shoes and a white Provençale shawl completed the picture. Again, no jewellery save the diamond Camargue cross on its chain around her neck. Two well-worn, deep leather armchairs were placed either side of another great stone fireplace, with an equally battered sofa completing the square. His host motioned him in. There is always a dilemma when you have to choose a seat in someone else's house. Someone always has a favourite chair but is usually too polite to say so. Smith chose the less battered one. His host took the other with Madam perching in the arm.

'I wanted to have a little time with you go. Firstly, the matter of the attack last night will be attended to today. I have been talking to our, er, friends in Marseilles. What happened will not happen again. The people who tried to kill you were gangsters from one of the smaller crime families. They had been benefiting from Robert's fraudulent activities and they assumed that we had something to do with his death. Their attack on you was a stupid and immature attempt at some sort of badly thought out revenge. These idiots didn't understand the history of which they were part. We have been in this area for much longer than any Marseilles crime family and normally we leave each other alone. On this occasion we seem to have been put in the middle of what you young people call a turf war. In any case, the problem has been solved for us by the other, older families who consider the present status quo to be something to protect rather than see jeopardised in this way. This so-called family no longer exists. I have been asked to convey apologies - whatever that's worth.'

'Thank you monsieur.' Smith though grimly to himself. If the death sentence was not carried out immediately Girondou finished his recent lunch, then it had been now.

'We have their assurance that nothing like it will happen again. You can, I believe, feel completely safe at your home in Arles. However, I understand if you wish to keep the Glock for a while. You can return it to us at any time you wish. If you continue to escort my daughter, I'm not at all unhappy that you have it. Very obviously you know how to use it.'

'Good,' said the old man. 'One more thing finally. What happened last night obviously demonstrated that you have had, shall we say, an interesting life. I wanted to say to you that we trust you as I hope you will trust us. We don't wish to know anything about you that you don't wish to tell us. You must believe that. You have in England an expression that goes something along the lines of speaking as you find. If I understand the expression correctly, then it describes me and, I believe, my daughter. I'm only interested in what I see and know to be true. In reality nothing else matters. We both respect your privacy.'

'Thank you, Monsieur, I'm grateful for that.' The father took hold of his daughter's hand and continued.

'Last night you did me a great service, the greatest possible. I'm unable to imagine how I might repay you. Suffice it to say that I'm in your debt. This is the first time in my long life that I have ever had to say that to anyone.'

Smith felt the emotion in the old man's voice and decided to move things along.

'I was delighted to have been of service, Monsieur. I also enjoyed your daughter's company. However, I still have to finish my work for you, so if you would allow me, would like to get home.'

'Of course, of course. Martine, please see Monsieur Smith to the car.'

He stood and held his hand out. Smith took it and smiled into the old man's eyes. He turned and followed Madam out of the room back into the courtyard. Arthur was already installed in the Range Rover whose engine was idling softly to power the air conditioning. The mid-morning temperature was already in the thirties. He got into the passenger's seat and turned to Madam who was standing by the open door.

'A bientôt, Madam. Try and keep out of trouble.'
He offered his hand for a farewell handshake. Her eyes held his for a long moment. She took his hand and laid it gently to her cheek, then turned her head and kissed it gently.

'I'll try, Monsieur. Thank you - for everything. Come and see me again very soon. Please.'

With that she released his hand and slammed the door shut.

Sometime after the Range Rover had departed, father and daughter remained in the study, she perched on the arm of his chair.

He was holding her hand gently as he broached the original question.

'Well?'

'I don't know. I really don't know.'

'Your Mister Smith is not quite turning out as we expected.'

'No.'

The man sighed. 'I have a feeling that not for the first time, we are in his hands somewhat.'

She nodded slowly.

The trip back home had been uneventful and fast. Pierre turned out to be a competent driver, if slightly inexperienced, driver of the top-heavy Range Rover. Thus, the general jostle of the trip prevented Smith's mind drifting only anything other than a general consideration of the way the French drive. It seemed to him to be as if they have something to prove but there is often more than a smattering of indecision. Overtaking was often delayed well past the point where it would be easy, and risk-free but it didn't seem as this was the result of a desire for adventure. More, he felt, a general lack of concentration and a total belief in the idea that if you drive as fast as Alain Prost you will drive as well as he did. His concentration of matters of moment was also diminished by the unwelcome return of the memory of how uncomfortable it was riding in a car with a pistol stuck down the back of your pants.

As they crossed the motorway bridge over the Rhône, his phone vibrated silently in his pocket. It was Gentry who said nothing, just waited. It was the old habit when you telephone someone without knowing where they were and whether they were free to talk. Your respondent should find a way to tell you. Smith didn't doubt that he had heard about last night.

'Your place. Ten minutes.' he said.

He waited until they were driving up the Boulevard des Lices and had drawn level with the Hotel Julius César.

'Stop here, please, Pierre. I need to do some shopping.'

The centre of Arles was thronged with people, mostly tourists but locals too. It was hot. Very hot. It was that sort of day when anyone with any sense would head for the nearest air-conditioned restaurant or get home for a quite lunch and a siesta. What sometimes caught out the tourists was that noon was not the hottest yime. During the next four hours the temperature often rose, and Arles' guests often emerged from the cool bliss of lunch to find that their traditional love hate relationship with the sun was only intensified.

Smith led Arthur through the Place de la République and down to the maze of tiny streets and alleyways that are squashed in the small section of town bounded by the Rue de Quatre September, Rue de l'Hôtel de Ville, The Rue des Arènes and the Arena itself. Although there are a number of rather classy shops dotted around, there are also numerous passageways, dead ends and other byways. Access to Gentry's house was discouraged by a number of obstacles. Firstly, one had to go through a locked door less than two feet wide set into one end of a façade large house that fronted directly into the narrow street that formed a dark canyon between two continuous lines of four-story stone houses. The door had an electric bell push that was not connected to anything and a knocker in the usual French shape of a hand holding a ball. If an intrepid book collector got through, he entered an equally narrow covered passage lit by a single bulb. It was a low energy device that meant it was very cheap to run and almost useless to prevent the unwary tripping over a number of obstacles that lay along the sides of the passage. Once through a second door, the visitor finds himself in a tiny open courtyard approximately ten metres square, bounded on all sides by building walls more than fifteen metres high. In mid-summer when the sun was at its highest, sunlight touched the ground for less than ten minutes each day. There was a door in the middle of each wall. The observant visitor would notice that his chances of swift further progress to what after all was supposed to be a shop were small as

Gentry has thoughtfully provided a small park bench. On the floor next to the bench was a hand bell of the sort once ubiquitous in the United Kingdom's schools. Indeed, that's from where it came. Even when the temperature on the roof terrace, high up and out of sight was more than forty degrees, that on the bench seldom rose above twenty.

Only one of these doors opened to Gentry's showroom but once in successful visitor was transported into a miniature version of the manuscript room at the old British Museum Library before it moved to the Asda lookalike building in St Pancras. A large, permanently shuttered stone room with fireplace filled with the most beautiful collection of old, polished beech and mahogany shelving and a couple of glass topped showcases, edged, banded and cornered in brass, deep, worn dark red leather armchairs, thick oriental carpet and subdued, recessed lighting. A small but first-class collection of small eighteenth and nineteenth century English landscapes completed the room - that and almost certainly the most sophisticated and therefore invisible protection and alarm system in Arles.

Smith walked straight into the room confident that his arrival had been noted by miniature cameras at all three doors, the corridor and the courtyard. He hadn't heard each door lock electronically behind him only because they were kept very well-greased. Gentry's customers who, in any case, came only by appointment were actually his prisoners until he decided they could leave. In most cases this was empty handed, and very soon after they had arrived.

He sat in his usual chair. The shop doubled as Gentry's study and he found a freshly brewed cup of strong espresso on the low table at his elbow. His host sat opposite. Arthur after an effusive greeting hopped up on his familiar sofa and lay, watching them both steadily. He made no attempt to go to sleep.

'You all right?'

'Yes, thanks. Surprisingly well, really.'

'You really much get over this desire to relive you past. One of these days you won't.'

Smith ignored the very real warning.

'Any news?'

'Lots, I'm afraid. The 'official' word is that it was a minor Marseilles family trying to make a point to Girondou - your friend Seffradi.'

'Official?'
'Well, the word on the street, at least. Complete bollocks, of course, in spite of what anyone might tell you. Fact is, it's a bit of a mystery. How good were they?'

'Well equipped, badly trained.'

'As usual it would have been better the other way around. Why does everyone skimp on training?'

'Because you can't see what you're paying for,' said Smith in a sarcastic voice. Any guesses?'

'You know me, I don't guess. But if I did, I would look elsewhere. My gut tells me this is not gang related. Even members of Marseilles pond life would have been better prepared that your lot. It feels like a contract put out by someone unused to issuing them. They were probably screwed. However, this does mean that it was probably Madam they were after, not you. Can't see you being worth a contract these days.'

'Thanks for that. Not Girondou, then.'

'No definitely not Girondou. I would imagine that he would be quite put out if you suggested it.'

'He said it wasn't him. Nice to know there is one honest man in all this.'

Gentry got down to the practicalities.

'Now what about the gun. Do you want me to lose it?'

'Monsieur Aubanet has already done the necessary and replaced it. I accepted as I thought it would be good for him to know that I had one and didn't want to let him know that could get one for myself.'

'Let me see it.'

Gentry got up and moved to the table. Amongst other things, he was an excellent armourer. Smith passed the Glock across. Within ten seconds it was in pieces, lined up neatly and logically on the polished burr walnut surface. He cast an eye over them, looked through the barrel and at the firing pin, nodded and reassembled the pistol effortlessly.

'Brand new, never been fired, no numbers, .45 hollow points. Needs a little oil and firing-in. You say that Aubanet had this 'in stock' as the say?'

'Yes, interesting is it not? It puts this doddery old farmer into a slightly different light.'

'I don't think either of us ever thought he was that. Do you want me to do the trigger pressures?'

'No thanks. If I need to, I'll find out on the job. I'm not going to any target shooting.'

'Give me the holster.'

Gentry vanished to make the adjustments that would ensure that the gun stayed where it was supposed to and came to hand when that was required, leaving Smith to savour again the great magic of this room. It felt, and probably was, the safest place in Arles but more than that, it had a comfort and a dignity and Smith had hoped would also attend his retirement. Gentry had achieved it, but it looked as if Smith never would. He began to feel very, very tired and rather depressed. He leant back and emptied his head of as much as he could. After a while, Gentry returned and as he was handing back the gun and holster, Smith could see that something had happened.

'I just got a message that might change a few things, Peter. About half an hour ago Chief Superintendent Blanchard was found dead in the Arena, in the same place that you and Robert were found.'

'Christ. I wasn't expecting that,' exclaimed a startled Smith. 'What's the story? Another suicide?'

'Hardly. He was found naked. His balls had been cut off while he was still alive and stuffed into his mouth. It seems he was held until he choked to death and left to bleed out. Kind of tricky to do that to yourself.'

They sat silently. It was not the horror. That would consume most people. But they had both seen this sort of thing before and they knew this was not just another killing. There was something too symbolic about it. It was a message but from and to whom and about what was difficult to say at this point. An idea began to come to Smith and it was he who spoke first.

'I think I had better get back and finish poking around in the data that I had downloaded from Robert's archive. I have a feeling at least some answers are in there.'

Gentry nodded and added: 'You might get a story ready for whoever investigates this - if anyone bother to, that's. I suspect that it will bypass the locals and you might get a visit from some bigwigs from Paris or Brussels. Suzanne even. Police departments tend to get rather savage when someone kills one of their own.'

'Do we know when they think Blanchard was killed?'

'I got the impression it was this morning rather than last night. But I'll find out and let you know.'

Smith got out his mobile, put it on speaker so Gentry could hear it and called Marseilles. As usual Girondou answered at first ring and started without preamble.

'Not us this time either. Blanchard was useful to us.'

'Ok,' Smith saw little reason to disbelieve him at this point.

The man continued: 'What the hell is going on up there in Arles?'

'Not sure, yet.'

'Let me know when you are, would you? Strikes me that you are more likely to find out than any other of the fucking idiots who are blundering around in this matter. All this attention is bad for business. I'll make it worth your while.'

He continued after a small pause.

'Glad you survived yesterday night's adventure, by the way, although from what I hear they didn't have much of a chance. We really must have a chat when all this is over.'

Smith rang off without further comment.

'Shit,' he thought, 'Another employer.'

Gentry looked over his half glasses.
'You seem to be getting rather pally with the South of France's Mr Big. Entirely wise?'

'Probably not. But at this stage it is a matter of keeping one's enemies closer again. I would much rather have Girondou looking after for me than coming after me.'

Gentry sighed. 'You are probably right.'

Smith was always reluctant to leave Gentry's room and today it was a particular wrench. However, he left and turned eastwards up the hill towards the Place de la Major and home. Given the potential unpleasantness of the task, Smith found himself in no great hurry to sit at his computer. Having picked up bread on the way home, he and Arthur sat in the shade of the garden and had a leisurely lunch together with more than his usual single glass of wine. However about two o'clock, driven inside more by the heat than a sense of duty he went up to his study, took the USB memory stick out of his safe and set to work.

Firstly, he went to DuGresson's financial records. In addition to his monthly retainer, he had been paid a flat sum of thirty thousand euros for each individual transaction in the Euroscam and all these payments were mirrored by deposits in the first of Roberts Swiss accounts. However, the second account had more irregular deposits. A quick comparison of the sums of money stolen from all the EC contracts with the amounts passed on to Girondou showed that there was a discrepancy that amounted, give or take, to about eight million euros, the balance of the second account. It looked as if, not content with his 'salary', he was also skimming. That would immediately provide someone like Girondou with a motive for murder if he was found out.

However there seemed to be no evidence that he'd been rumbled but in spite of the fact that Girondou stuck him as being something of a pragmatist, his need for DuGresson wouldn't extend to showing a blind eye if he had. Girondou was not a man who had got where he was by being soft. And Blanchard was DuGresson's man.

That left the bit he had been dreading. He had no idea whether Blanchard had been part of DuGresson's paedophiliac activities but given that the two had a close business relationship, he had, at least to check. Robert DuGresson had been as orderly in his arrangement of his pornography as he had been about his accounts. Files of pictures, video clips and records of payments were all arranged by date and location. He started with the last overseas holiday made by DuGresson to Thailand. Judging by the folder names it had been a regular destination. The task of wading through image after disgusting image was made a little easier because he was only looking at the faces of adults, but it was the most marginal of improvements. He felt sick. Fortunately, confirmation of his fears was not long in coming. Blanchard was indeed present as an irregular participant in the scenes but a participant, nevertheless. The pieces of the picture suddenly came together. Having found what he needed, Smith closed the files with relief, returned the memory stick to his safe, went downstairs and poured himself a very stiff drink. The solution to the puzzle was at least clear.

It was time for the moment he had not been looking forward to. He even found himself hoping that she wouldn't answer her phone. She did, of course. Without referring to the previous night's events, he purposely went straight in.

'Good afternoon, Madam. I'm sorry to bother you but I think that it is time for me to present my marketing report. It's finished and I think that there is very little to be gained by further work. I wonder if you and your father might be free some time tomorrow?'

There was a palpable gap while Madam adjusted to the reality.

'Yes, of course. Perhaps lunch tomorrow? About one?'

Smith made it plain that, for once, he didn't wish to mix business with pleasure.

'Thank you, Madam, but I would prefer a little later. May I suggest around four?'

She was clearly startled. This sounded a very different Smith than the once she had seen less than twenty-four hours before.

'Er, yes. Of course. Four o'clock would be fine.'

He rang off without pleasantries and as he put the phone down as was somewhat startled when it immediately rang back at him. His first reaction was to think it was Madam changing her mind but it was too quick even for that.

'Monsieur Smith, are you free for supper this evening? I

would like to talk with you.'

To say he was surprised wouldn't really cover it. The widow Blanchard was certainly resilient.

'You are most kind, Madam, but I wouldn't wish to impose too much on you at this time.'

She interrupted him crossly.

'Oh, don't worry about that. Seven o'clock?' The phone went dead without her waiting for a reply.

'Now there's a thing,' thought Smith.

He wasn't entirely happy. He didn't like being taken by surprise. What the hell did she want so soon after what was, more or less, the ritual slaughter of her supposedly beloved husband. These seems only one possible explanation. A couple of hours later he rang the doorbell on the apartment on the Boulevard Haussmann. He was greeted with a broad smile and no real sign of grief.

'Do come in, Monsieur Smith.'

To be fair, Madam Blanchard was wearing black. But that was about as far as it went. From the other night Smith remembered an attractive, petit lady with dark hair. Very precise, elegant, slightly reserved, almost bird like. The widow remained all those things but her widow's weeds were by Chanel. A straight black skirt cut a couple of inches or so above the knee and a well-tailored jacket both with the lightest of pinstripe. Cream silk blouse open enough to offer a touch of white lace underwear and a hint of cleavage. This was not a case of buttons being left undone. There weren't any until mid-bosom. Fully and expertly made up and coiffured. The woman had not spent the day in tears. The picture was completed as she turned away and led him through into a bright, sunny sitting room. Dark seamed stockings and black patent stiletto court shoes with enough height to be the sort that made men of Smith's vintage happy to walk a few yards behind.

She gestured to one of the high-backed armchairs that were arranged either side of the floor to ceiling windows that opened onto a small but beautiful garden full of dappled shade and colourful bushes.

'Please sit. Drink?'

Without waiting for a reply, she poured two glasses of champagne - Kristal, he noted - set one on the spindly little table beside Smith's chair and the other next to her. Then using that elegant but slightly dated hitch of her skirt around her hips to stop it creasing, she sat and faced him. She crossed her legs in that way that men find impossible, legs crossed, resting against each other and canted down to the floor at an angle. The manoeuvre as well as length of the skirt as well meant that a good few centimetres of very well-turned thigh above the knee were visible. Smith found himself being slightly diverted but didn't feel the need to conceal his admiring gaze. It was only when he saw her slight smile that her realised that was her intent. Again, not the sort of behaviour, he thought, for a grieving widow.

'Madam, I should say first that I'm sorry for your loss. It was a dreadful business.'

'Thank you, Monsieur, you are kind. However, having been in the police for nearly twenty years, I'm probably less affected by this sort of thing than many people would be.'

Smith had a sudden thought that being married to this handsome woman might not have been the unalloyed joy that it might seem at first glance. Then he remembered that any woman who achieved commissioner rank in a Europe-wide police force well before the age of forty has to have more than the usual personal qualities to be found in career policemen; much more.

'However, it was kind of you to accept my invitation. Now tell me, how are your enquiries going?'

Smith allowed a frown to cross his face.

'I'm just doing some work for the Aubanet businesses, Madam. Your late husband may have thought otherwise but those are my instructions.'

'My husband was probably right, Monsieur. But what you are instructed to do and what you do can easily be very different things.'

'Suddenly, Madam, my visit to offer my sympathies and take supper seems to be turning into a police interview.'

She was smilingly unrepentant. 'Yes, it does feel that way, doesn't it?'

The steel in the woman was breath-taking and Smith didn't find it unattractive. He again got a glimpse of why she had risen to her present job. Before he could reply, she got up and took his glass over to the sideboard for a refill. Madam turned away to refill her own glass and regain her seat. Smith didn't need a tape measure to see that the skirt had slipped even higher. Madam wore stockings not tights. Under other circumstances he would have enjoyed the experience. Even had he not known the truth about Blanchard, he might have felt sorry for him. However, this was a woman whose professional competence was disconcerting to even him and he had been interrogated by some of the best. She continued:

'I'm afraid I don't cook and therefore my offer of supper is slightly disingenuous. I can, however, offer you bread and cheese and a wine that might please you.'

He replied with exaggerated courtesy: 'Madam, I'm honoured to be your guest.'

She snorted and downed her full glass in a single gulp.

'That's ridiculous.'

She got up and moved across to a small kitchen table, motioning him to follow. The scrubbed wooden surface was reminiscent of a farm table. It was set for two. A simple plate and knife and a new wine glass flanked by a starched linen napkin. A wooden plate in the middle bearing a large selection of cheese, a large basket of sliced baguette and a plain decanter three quarters full of red wine. She motioned him into a seat.

'I'm told that Provence does not do cheese well.'

Smith stiffened at the recent memory.

She continued. 'I don't agree. Perhaps you might give me your opinion later?'

Her glance was very steady as she waited for his reply. God, thought Smith, she is good. Very good indeed.'

'Madam, I'll be happy to give you my thoughts on the cheese after I have tasted it and insofar as you are really interested.'

She looked across the table archly.

'Oh, I'm interested, believe me. In a number of things. But for the present, I'll take your opinion of this.'

She poured a large measure of the red into his glass without ceremony. He lifted the glass and smelt it. He found the unmistakable aroma of a fine claret, a Bordeaux of some distinction. He knew, of course. He had spent a lifetime engrossed in the wines of the Médoc. The question was how much he should reveal. He decided to go play the game for broke.

'Château Haut-Brion 1990. Could be a very badly kept '89.'

She did him the courtesy of looking as impressed as she felt.

'Good Lord,' she mused, 'Perhaps it is true what they say about Englishmen and their famous claret. Yet again, Monsieur Smith, you surprise. It is one of my late husband's collection.'

Smith raised his glass.

'To the future, Madam.'

For an instant the mask slipped, and more vulnerable almost hunted look flew across her face only to disappear instantly. She looked him straight but unsmilingly in the eye.

'Yes, indeed, Monsieur, the future. It might be interesting for both of us, I feel.'

Again, almost half the glass was drained in a single swallow. There was scant respect for a great Bordeaux wine. Perhaps, he thought, it was to do with where it had come from. He drank somewhat more methodically. They each helped themselves to bread and cheese and started to eat. Smith decided to get a little more of a foothold into proceedings.

'Much as I might enjoy sitting here with an attractive woman, dressed like a slightly risqué version of a fashion plate, the fact that it is happening within few hours after death of her husband leaves me a little confused.'

He just avoided referring to the method of Blanchard's death that actually made his confusion even more acute. However, he remembered just in time that he probably shouldn't admit to knowing the details.

Her smile was thin but completely relaxed.

'Come now, Monsieur, irrespective of my husband's death, I still need to know what you have found out about the activities and the death of Robert DuGesson. You have had an adventurous time over the last few days. You must have learned something that I need for my investigation.'

Smith persisted with a line that, by now, they both knew was rubbish. However, until his meeting tomorrow, he had little option. He forced a little exasperation into his tone.

'Madam, you continue to assume that I'm doing your job for you. It was the same mistaken assumption made by your unfortunate late husband as well. I have no interest in DuGresson's death other than a mild annoyance at having been caught up in it in the first place. And before you ask, my work for Madam DuGresson is, as they say, strictly business - her business.'

The double entendre was clearly not lost on her.

Smith began to get a bit fed up. Going on meaningless fishing trips seem to be a speciality of both the Blanchards. He had been in some pretty odd situations in his life in some pretty odd places, but he could not recollect meeting too many people quite like the woman who now faced him over the bread and cheese. He reminded himself of the fact that this was not the first time that someone had said that it was difficult to find good cheese in Provence. He purposely got a little angry whilst knowing that it would probably have little effect on this woman.

'Madam. I came here primarily to offer my condolences on the death of your husband, an event by which you seem to be remarkably unmoved. You take the opportunity to interrogate me knowing full well that you have absolutely no authority to do so. I'm as uninterested in talking to you about DuGresson's death as I was to your late husband. The correct procedure I would guess would be either for you to instruct the local police to interview me or to get a warrant that enables you to do it yourself in France.'

'So, if you will forgive me, I'll take my leave of you. I thank you for the supper and again I offer you my sympathies on your loss. Now I have a dog to walk and some sleep to catch up on.'

With that he rose and turned for the door. Suddenly he just wanted to get out into the fresh air. Once committed to an exit, he didn't particularly wish to indulge in any further pleasantries. His host rose after him and caught him up at the front door. She put a hand on his arms. Even now she was not prepared to give up.

'Monsieur Smith, we'll talk again. Possibly officially.'

'I doubt that. Madam.'

'We'll see, I think there is much more you can tell me.'

Smith took her hand from his arm with an exaggerated gentleness that he wasn't feeling and looked down at her.

'Then, Madam Blanchard - Assistant Commissioner Blanchard - I suggest you ask your cousin.'

The slightly angry look on her beautifully made-up face was replaced by a look of astonishment.

'My cousin?'

'Yes, your cousin.'

With that, he spun on his heel and walked away.

10. Dénouement

Smith took his time driving out to the Mas des Saintes. He was purposely late. He had also left Arthur at home. After the customary shared baguette, paté and camembert the dog had shown little inclination to move from the shaded terrace. In any case Smith wanted to avoid the possible informality that the dog's presence would lend to proceedings. The day had developed past its usual hot midday and by the later afternoon it was a windless 30 degrees. Even with both windows and the roof open the passing air hardly cooled the interior of the VW Polo. He drove in through the open gate to the mas with a frown. After recent events he had at least expected it to be closed.

As usual he was met by Martine although the welcome of considerably less warm that one previous occasion. She looked pale. As before she led him through the house into the garden where her father stood beside the table. Smith sat and laid his briefcase beside the chair having removed his marketing report which he laid on the table. An envelope containing his invoice was ostentatiously placed on top. All three of them ignored it. He started:

'I'd like to talk this through as much as I can. If you have questions, I would be grateful if you could, as they say in all the best conferences, keep them to the end when I shall be delighted to try to answer them.'

They both nodded their assent. He was pleased that they both looked slightly apprehensive.

'Just over a week ago, Madame Aubanet, you came to me and asked me what I remembered about that morning when Robert was killed. Subsequently, you both asked me to make enquiries about Robert's death and to see if it might have an effect on your business. You didn't ask me outright to see if I could find out who did it, but that seemed implicit. We constructed a subterfuge of a marketing plan to cover my asking questions around the place. Subsequently a Euro policeman who had concocted a suicide story to justify keeping the local police out of the murder turns out to be investigating Robert for embezzlement of European funds, although he said he wasn't getting very far. He asked me to pass anything that I might learn on to him. In fact, I learned more from him than he had from me, which wouldn't be hard as I didn't actually tell him anything.'

He looked directly at Monsieur Aubanet. 'Two nights ago, after the adventure at the Marseilles Opera you said two things that put me in a difficult position. Firstly, you said that you didn't want to know anything about me that I didn't want to tell you.'

The old man nodded slowly.

'Secondly you said that you trusted me, and you wanted me to trust you. In a way I found these two mutually exclusive. However, in order to understand not just what I have discovered but also how I have managed to find out these things, you need to know a little at least of my past, a past that I had fully intended to stay dead and buried when I came here to live.'

'After spending some few years teaching art history, I embarked on a career in business. After a few years working for a couple of companies doing export sales throughout the world, I started to work on short term projects for businesses that went beyond simple consultancy to create and put into practice sales and marketing strategies for companies who didn't have the expertise in-house to do it for themselves. I chose computing as my preferred field as it was obviously going to be a major area for the future. I put myself through some very intensive training with some of the major companies in the computing business.'

'The venture was a success and I was seldom without work. Increasingly my work took me to places that were shall we say less stable than others. I was obviously very mobile and found it relatively easy to go anywhere as I usually had the sponsorship of a major company or institution in each particular country.'

'To cut a long story short, I was recruited by an old university friend who worked, shall we say, for a branch of the British Government. I'll not tell you what I did for them. However, as you now know, I had to learn certain skills in order to do the work. You saw some of those the other night. I also learned some computer skills that, shall we say, are not exactly orthodox. All right, enough of me. The two issues are Robert's criminal activities and the second concerns a series of related deaths, starting with Robert's.'

Aubanet interjected: 'related?'

Smith was running this conversation and he didn't bother answering.

'Firstly, as you very well knew, Robert was involved in the embezzlement. He moved the money around for a widespread group of people around Europe. He was very good at it. He was also quite good at hiding what he was doing. He put all his information in a vault on the internet.'

He reached down beside the table and put a laptop case on the coffee table in front of them.

'This contains Robert's laptop and iPhone. Although it took some considerable time to decode and check, they actually didn't contain anything of great value, with one exception. Robert was slightly more sophisticated in his attempts to hide his information but there were still, shall we say, enough traces left for me to find the locations and access codes to his internet archive. It took some time to find it. The internet archive contained encrypted records of everything, contacts, bank details, dates, contracts, everything. I took the liberty of downloading and decoding all of it.'

'I copied the entire archive. Then I emptied the archive, made sure it was completely clear and, for good measure, put a piece of spy ware that will tell me if anyone tries to access the vault.'

"Firstly, there are details of the fraud; Robert's contacts, methods, account numbers for the transfers of all the funds and all the transaction details. Locally there were payments to a couple of Marseille crime syndicates.'

He smiled thinly. 'I gather the number has recently been reduced by one. This information is certainly enough to wrap the whole thing up if sent to the right place. It might solve the problem for a month or two before someone else figures out another way to part the European Union from its money. Personally, I don't really care much either way. It also contains details of Blanchard's connection. He is on Robert's list of employees. But I think you already knew that.'

'I also uncovered details of Robert's personal accounts. He was either paid or embezzled some fourteen million Euros. I have access sole access to these funds at present, but I'll come back to this in a moment.'

'I have completely wiped the laptop and the iPhone. I can guarantee there is nothing left on them. I have placed copies of the information in safe keeping abroad and I have also put copies of it in an internet archive. Believe me you will waste your time if you try to find them. However, their remaining secret depends on my continued good health.'

'You originally said that you wanted me to see if Robert's death would harm the business. It won't. However, what you really hired me to do was to see if I could find out who killed him. Well I have.'

Smith felt his guests stiffen imperceptibly. Both looked at him very steadily. He took a deep breath. This was the tricky bit.

'The records contain proof that both Robert and Blanchard were involved in paedophilia. I have no idea when this started.'
The faces of both Aubanets remained completely still. here was the proof if ever Smith felt he needed any. He continued.

'Robert may have been one all his life in one form or another. The records start about five years ago and mainly deal with activities while on holiday and business visits overseas, eastern Europe, Far East and so on. However, it also shows that about six months ago they started their disgusting activities here in Arles. There are records, details of where Mademoiselle Brique procured the children, passwords to internet sites and so on. Lists of other paedophiles both internationally and locally. All these are on the memory stick in this briefcase. I believe this should be used. These people, at least, we can stop. This brings us to the nub of the matter. Robert was skimming from the embezzled funds as well so he may well have been killed by Girondou, but I doubt it. It was too easy and profitable a little scam and Robert was too important a part of it. Girondou is first and foremost a businessman and would probably have indulge in a little, shall we say, retraining rather that batter him to death. That would make sense, a least. However, all this is a red herring. Because I believe somehow that you found out about Robert, Mademoiselle Brique and Blanchard. This was a family disgrace well beyond mere criminality. In many of the places I have visited the preservation of family honour is paramount. For a Provençale catholic family whose service to the community goes back hundreds of years, Robert's sexual degradation must have been unbearable. My guess is that you killed Robert. Your family or your friends killed him and Mademoiselle Brique and Chief Inspector Blanchard. I don't know who, in particular, actually did it. Monsieur Mistraux or someone like him would be top of my list if I was making one. But I'm not nor am I interested in doing so. Blanchard may even have been killed by his wife. She strikes me as being perfectly capable of it.'

He was gratified to see the look of horror on her face, although he was unable to be certain which particular revelation caused it. Neither of them moved for a long time. Obviously, his guess was accurate. Tears fell silently down Martine's face. Monsieur Aubanet was the first to speak.

'And what do you intend to do with this knowledge, Peter?'

Smith smiled inwardly. Provence seemed suddenly full of people asking this question. His reply was same as before.

'Absolutely nothing. Let me make myself completely understood. As you have pointed out once or twice before, I'm also a father. Sexual crimes against children appal and disgust me. I have worked in many parts of the world where honour killing is regarded as morally justifiable. I don't presume to judge. I believe that what you did was justified, even possibly right, although the law might say differently. I'm beginning to learn a little a little about the way you have lived here over the years. You are good people and whoever did it or who ordered it, it would have great courage.'

'Do you think there is there any evidence of all this, Peter?' Monsieur Aubanet asked quietly.

'That was what you actually hire me to find out, wasn't it? There was never any question that Robert's death would harm your business as you originally said. You wanted to find out if there was any chance that the death would be laid at your door. Well, I'm pretty sure that it can't. The presence of Blanchard has done a good job of deterring any local investigation and Madam Blanchard, wearing her Brussels hat, is well placed to divert any further interest. I presume that she has already washed the blood off her Aubanet one.'

Both father and daughter stiffened. Obviously, Madam Blanchard had not told them that he knew. After a while Emil Aubanet let out a long sigh.

'You have, of course, got it absolutely ...'

Smith held up his hand and interrupted.

'No, Monsieur. Neither of us needs an admission. I'm not the police. At some stage you might understand me better, but for now, for me at least, all this is now past and, in my experience, the only way to make it stay there is firstly to stop talking about it. If you do that, then after a while you will stop thinking about it, too. Once you stop thinking about it every day, in time you might only remember it more occasionally. Once the whole thing has become a memory then you can learn to live with that memory. It will take time, possibly a long time, but the memory will recede and take its place with all the others, good and bad.'

'Monsieur Smith. Yet again my daughter and I have cause to be grateful to you, for your understanding as much as anything else.'

They sat for a moment in silence. Smith continued.

'Now, I have had some ideas about the use of Robert's money. While the right thing might be to give it back to the EC, I find little or no reason to do that in that. In any case, Girondou or the many others like him would only find a way of stealing it again. There are, I'm sure, many groups of people, including some official charities, in this region that would benefit greatly from a small increase in their funds. I would prefer to see the money used as a little extra regional aid here in the Camargue. In particular, as it is my intention to make very good use of Robert's immaculate records of his dealings with his paedophile acquaintances to do them all considerable and terminal damage, it would be nice to use some of the money to ensure that this particular deviancy is removed from here. Perhaps you might like to help to find a way sensitively to use this considerable sum of money.'

Martine Aubanet remained very still as she nodded slowly.

'Yes, Monsieur Smith. I think that would be a very good thing to do with the money. I would be delighted to help you do this.'

The look in her face was one of complete honesty with more than a tinge of relief. It was as if she saw a way of exorcising a few recent devils. The look on her father's face was a good deal less happy. Smith decided to let that pass for the moment. She continued, her composure returning all the time. She recovered fast.

'Perhaps we could talk about the future a little, Peter. I have had enough of the past for one day. Would you join me in a ride over the farm?'

He felt a slight pang of sympathy for the father. The future she wanted to talk about didn't seem to include him very much, and he knew it. He seemed to have somehow got smaller as he sat listening. For the first time, Smith thought he detected a little unsteadiness in the old man as he got to his feet. He looked old. He extended his hand to Smith and once it had been taken, held it firmly.

'I thank you for your report, Peter. This has been a dreadful business. We are a strong community and life will go on. But increasingly it will not be up to me to guide the future. I leave that to my daughter.'

Smith noted that he still talked only of Martine. The old man continued, looking at his daughter with the sort of gentleness that fathers often use with their daughters.

'My daughter and I owe you her life. I hope that you will continue to give her wise council. I have a feeling that she is more as likely to listen to you than to me now.'

He let go Smith's hand.

"You and your dog will always welcome guests in my house, Peter. Now if you will forgive me, I would like to sleep a while.'

'Thank you, Monsieur.' Smith replied.

- - - - - - - - -

They left the garden and rode off over the farm, making a very leisurely tour. Madam's interests were less taurocentric than those of her father. The wildlife for which the Camargue is famous was obviously a passion and their morning was filled with sightings of herons, cormorants, ducks of all sorts, harriers, hawks and even a spotted eagle, let alone coypu, water rats, voles and other assorted river bank life. The sun had started its slow slide towards the horizon and the temperature began to wane slightly with it. They approached one of those gardian's *cabane* that are dotted around the Camargue. It was single storied rectangular building, semi-circular at one end with a high-pitched thatched roof and white painted walls. This one, however showed signs of renovation. It was significantly bigger that the usual version and had more and larger windows. A covered veranda had been constructed along one side and there were stables and outbuildings scattered around. The cottage was surrounded by pine trees. They tied and unsaddled the horses under a field shelter and made sure they had water.

Madame led Smith into the shade of the veranda and installed him in one of two reclining chairs arranged to look out over a small étang that was covered with thousands of flamingos. She disappeared inside through a pair of long windows and returned with a pair of glasses and a cold bottle of Crémant.

'Welcome, Peter. Everything you have seen so far, the farm, the businesses, are owned jointly by my father and myself. This house, however had always been mine. My grandfather gave it to me when I was born. I come here a lot to think to work or to read. It has always been my escape. Other than staff, only three people have been here with me since my mother died fifteen years ago. Robert came here once just after we were married and hated it. He stayed about an hour. The other has been my father who comes here from time to time as my guest and only on my invitation. You are now the third.'

The cold Crémant was delicious. The view stunning. As they sat looking out over the shimmering water, there was a deep tranquillity about this place. The water was almost completely covered with flamingos. Little lizards scuttled from one piece of shade to another. But Smith felt slightly uncomfortable. By coming here, he seemed to be stepping deeper into her life and he was really not sure that was where he wanted to be. Whatever her attractions, and there were numerous, there was a darker side to her. Things did seem to have moved rather quickly over the last couple of days. She addressed him without taking her eyes from the *étang*.

'I meant what I said earlier. This is not just because of what you for me did last Saturday night. That will never be forgotten but it has passed. We are here because I wanted to show you my house. I thought that you would like it, and, unlike Robert, you would understand what it means to me. I would like to share it with you. That's all.'

She took Smith's hand, lifted the hand to his lips and kissed it gently. She tightened her grip and pulled them both to their feet.

'Let me show you around. I'm afraid there is not much to see. Come inside.'

Like most of these Gardian cottages, it consisted primarily of one large room with a beamed roof rising up into the high thatched eaves. However, this one had been brought very well up to date. It was deliciously cool thanks to air conditioning. The windows were covered by half-closed shutters. The walls had a scattering of bookcases, paintings and shelves with ornaments. Rugs were distributed over the flag stone floor. At one end was a huge stone fireplace flanked by two, old-fashioned square armchairs, one overlooked by a reading lamp was well used, the other looked almost new. In the middle of the room was a dining table, chair at each end. At the other end was a large wooden bed and some bedroom furniture. It was a beautiful, civilised room and he said so.

She smiled with pleasure. 'I have always felt at peace here.'

Looking round he suddenly got the impression of a very solitary life. One or two things started to become clearer. He wanted to get back out into the afternoon heat under the veranda. It felt more honest to him. Once they were seated again, she turned to him.

'We seem to have reached the end of whatever all this was about.'

Smith looked at her steadily.

'Madam, you know what all this has been about. You always have. I have many failings - or at least I have usually been surrounded by people who say I have - but being stupid has never been one of them.'

Their recent conversation caught up to them in a hurry and they fell silent. It remained that way as they made their way back to the Mas. Suddenly Smith just wanted to get home.

They had played chess together for years. For most of the time it was just one of their irregular meetings where they sat in silence, giving all their concentration to the game. Occasionally it had been when debriefing. They both found it a better method that a plain interview room.

They were both good players; excellent, in fact, very well matched, but quite different. They played like their personalities. Gentry was restrained, classical. He was a long-term strategist. His attacks were methodical, expertly conceived and always error-free. They had been playing for more than twenty years and Smith couldn't remember Gentry ever actually making a mistake. In defence he could be almost impregnable. Smith, on the other hand, was more adventurous. The classical openings and defences were for him only starting points. He was by no means rash. His game could be equally restrained but would occasionally play off the book. Gentry never did.

Smith usually made his move into unorthodoxy towards the end of the middle game relying on his wits for a successful conclusion rather than on any pre-conceived strategy. It was this unpredictability after a long period of restraint that made him a success. However, his errors were more frequent. He therefore won more games than his friend, but he also lost more as well. Gentry's victories were inevitable. Smiths never were. Draws were frequent and the only real difference between the two players was that Gentry tended to take more pleasure in them than Smith. However, he knew that it was Smith's occasional unorthodoxy that not only made him a dangerous opponent but also ensured that their regular games didn't become boring or formulaic. Since Smith's retirement to Arles their games had become more regular, almost weekly, and they were a profound pleasure to them both.

The first few exchanges were conducted in silence. Gentry played white and started with Ruy Lopez. He used the traditional opening regularly. It suited his style and he was invariably successful when he used it. He chose it this time because he knew that they would be talking during the game and his familiarity with the opening and its many defences would allow him to split his concentration. He also assumed that Smith, realising also that his attention would be divided, would become unorthodox sooner. Neither of them ever admitted it but they both had valued these "debriefing" games slightly less than the others.

Gentry's comfort was short lived. Smith responded with the unfashionable, and for him highly uncharacteristic, Steinitz defence and when he declined to use the usual deferred variant that offers Black better chances, slight alarm bells began to sound in Gentry's head. Smith was not a man to put himself at a disadvantage on purpose. Either he had some new plan, or he had decided to improvise even in defence. That was often when Smith was his best and given that they were about to start talking, Gentry had a sinking feeling that he was going to lose this one. He took a sip of his whisky.

'Well. Who dunnit, as they say?'

'In truth, God knows. Could be any of them or all. Probably was.'

The conversation started to develop as it always had on these occasions. Gentry leading, Smith responding. Contemplative periods over the chessboard punctuated the conversation. They both had no difficulty maintaining continuity in either play or conversation.

'I suppose it's less important that you know, than that they think you know and, more importantly, can prove it.'

'Yes. There are, of course, more than one 'it', as it were.'

As Smith knew he would, Gentry frowned slightly at the inelegance before taking on the conversation.

'Well let me sum up. We seem to have three suspicious deaths, one attack on you, one on you and Madam of a slightly more serious nature. You have met the godfather of Marseilles crime, one of the leaders of the Camargue and its secret society, one, or possibly two, bent senior European policemen, one now dead in a somewhat alarming manner, uncovered evidence of an international financial conspiracy and major paedophile ring. You have been courting in your own detached, but to me obvious, way an attractive, rich widow who is, as yet, unaware that she is the first woman you have let anywhere near your life in ten years. Finally, but not insignificantly, you have sole access, for a day or two only, I suspect, before the good bankers of Berne twig that Robert is dead, to two accounts containing a total of twenty-two million completely untraceable euros. Nothing washes money like a good death. You've had an eventful few days, my friend.'

They were just entering the middle game and Smith was peculiarly quiescent. He had accepted a position of slight inferiority without a struggle. He was down on piece count, although not as much, Gentry noted, as he should be given their respective strategies. The game continued in silence for a while. He still could not quite work out what Smith was up to. Usually by now Gentry had a good idea of where the game would go, but his opponent was playing a very uncharacteristic game. He was beginning to realise what Smith, of course, had known throughout their working relationship, that uncertainty could a powerful weapon especially against someone for whom being uncertain was an admission of defeat. Life was seldom about certainty and making use of that fact was often the secret of success. Smith knew enough to be technically solid even when he was making it up as he went along and that had been his secret. It was also why he was still alive while others weren't.

Smith made his move. More consolidation thought Gentry. He was used to reacting to his friend's aggression and was getting close to frustration. He was not a natural aggressor even when playing White and he felt his usual serene view of the campaign getting unfocussed. What made it worse, Smith seemed quite happy to talk.

'The important thing is that Monsieur Aubanet and his daughter think I know what they were up to. Not in terms of who did what to whom. I think, give or take, we all know that. They asked me to find out who killed Robert. Actually, they wanted me to find out whether there was any way they could be linked to any of this.'

'And can they?'

'No. Not really.'

'Why not?'

Smith continued without lifting his gaze from the board. 'Well primarily, I think, because there is no-one really trying to investigate the whole thing. We have the deaths of two people who were involved in embezzling European funds. This, on many levels, is little more than the great European institutional sport. For most of us the money is lost, or at least written off, before it gets into the EC coffers. I personally knew a Euro MP in Norfolk who boasted about the fact that he just went each day into the European Parliament, clocked in so he would get his attendance allowance, and then left without taking his seat. Life for him was lunch paid for by his constituents.'

He took a good pull from his Islay Mist, leant over the board and made another non-committal move. It brought Gentry forward in his seat and his sense of impending doom deepened. Smith continued.

'These two these idiots were greedy and started to go into business for themselves. But the amount they stole from the thieves was relatively small in relation to the overall amounts that were drained from Brussels's coffers. No one would investigate that even if it provided a good motive for murder. The widow Blanchard will keep a lid on Europol's ambitions, I think.'

'Finally, of course, there is the paedophilia. But given that the local plod seems to have been kept at a distance from this whole thing by person or persons unknown, who is going to follow that particular line of enquiry? Any of these wouldn't stay alive within a week of entering a French prison. What has happened just saved a lot of money and paperwork.'

Smith broke from what he was amused to see had become a monologue and made another move. Gentry's frustration was palpable, and he was quietly enjoying the rare, very rare, experience of having his opponent at a slight disadvantage. What Gentry didn't know was that Smith had spent almost six months looking at the responses to the Ruy Lopez opening. The opening gambit that bears sixteenth century cleric's name had become one of the great opening strategies and has been more studied than almost any other. Smith had picked the most unpopular and potentially supine of the traditional defensive responses to work up into an unlikely attack. It was unlikely because it took patience and self-restraint, not Smith's most obvious characteristics. However, it was working. He continued as if the debrief had become part of the game, as, for him, of course, it had.

'There is corruption and criminality in high places. Immorality and bestiality in lower ones. The former matters very little to me, the latter much more so.'

'Yes, to me too,' Gentry agreed.

'I can't honestly say that I give a damn who actually did the killings. What matters to me is that the right people are dead.'

Gentry found himself in an extraordinary position. A good number of pieces up but equally sure that he was going to lose. With a sense of impending doom, he castled into an even more defensive position. Defensive but not necessarily defensible. That, he knew, was his great friend's strength. Smith had often survived because his opponents had confused these two very different things. A truly agile force would always have the advantage over a static mind, irrespective of strength.

'The money?'

'Ah, the money.'

Smith made another well-thought-out but ultimately neutral move. He was enjoying an unaccustomed feeling of superiority. It was not often that his opponent looked a bit ragged on the board; quite the contrary. He felt a rare frisson of pleasure of being the architect of his opponent's discomfort while being utterly blameless. Gentry was about to self-destruct, and he had yet to lift a hand. If it went on like this, he needn't actually run the risk of carrying out his extremely hazardous final assault.

'Ah the money, yes. Well.' He peered over the board at Gentry's latest move. Almost a mistake. Not a silly one. Not even, under usual circumstances, a particularly significant one. But these were not usual circumstances. More a sin of omission rather than commission. A failure to think under pressure. Gentry had always sat planning and organising in the shadows; calm in a world that was cool, logical irrespective of whatever may have been swirling around the world outside. He always made the right decisions because he had the time. With Smith it has always been the opposite. He made another inconsequential move ramping up the tension in this cerebral game of chicken.

'The money. Hum. Well, passing it on to Girondou would go against the grain. I think. However, I have no great desire to return it to the EC where it will only be stolen again. The far from grieving widow certainly doesn't need it and wouldn't accept it even if offered. I know you or I don't want it or rather wouldn't take it.'

Smith decided that enough was enough. Although he was still down in pieces, he felt that his opponent was sufficiently demoralised for his offensive to stand a chance. Tactically Gentry's position was sound but there were a couple of rather extended and inelegant exchanges on offer that would leave him depressed if not really weakened. Smith initiated the first of these. After four more moves each he had gained a pawn. More successful than he anticipated. The second sequence saw him gain a further knight and a pawn. Back to all square. But the main damage had been done to Gentry who simple detested this sort of what he called Neanderthal chess. Smith continued as if nothing had happened.

"I wonder if we might not try to do some good with these funds. Firstly, I want terminally to damage those who were part of DuGresson's paedophilia circle. You and I also know plenty of small charities that need money. I'm pretty sure that there are some good local ones here that would appreciate a bit of a hand from you. Finding some children's charities, especially some that work with victims of paedophilia, would be a good place to start would be a good place to start. Madam Aubanet would probably also be someone who might help.'

A ghost of a smile crossed Gentry's face.

'I think that could be rather a good idea. You will need to shift the money pretty quickly. It will vanish for good once the gnomes realize Robert is dead.'

He looked down at the now relatively emptier board. Things were by no means hopeless, but his heart had gone out of it. He looked across at Smith in that way that all chess players do when they decide to offer a draw. Having no great desire to see his friend suffer any more, Smith accepted. It was a gesture that they both understood.

Having shaken hands they reset the pieces, got up from the chess table and sat around the fireplace. Gentry refilled their glasses.

'How did the family react?'

'As you might imagine. Calmly but they were a little worried, I think.'

'Well, at least you can reclaim your life. I hope your fee was big enough to make all this worthwhile.'

Smith laughed.

'Probably not but it'll help.'

Gentry took another long draw on his whiskey.

'It does, however, mean that you can shake the Aubanet family out of your hair. I have had a feeling all long that there is more there that one might like to find. You are best out of it.'

'Ah.' murmured Smith.

'What do you mean, Ah?'

'Well..'

'Well what?'

'I've invited Martine DuGresson to lunch next week.'

Gentry managed to look resigned and appalled at the same time.

'Oh Christ,' he sighed as he reached again for the bottle.

Printed in Poland
by Amazon Fulfillment
Poland Sp. z o.o., Wrocław